20

# SELECTED TRANSLATIONS OF TWENTIETH CENTURY AMERICAN POETRY

# 二十世纪美国诗歌选译

王 文 编译

西安交通大学出版社
XI'AN JIAOTONG UNIVERSITY PRESS
国家一级出版社
全国百佳图书出版单位

**图书在版编目(CIP)数据**

二十世纪美国诗歌选译：汉、英 / 王文编译. —西安：西安交通大学出版社，2022.6

ISBN 978-7-5693-2656-7

Ⅰ.①二… Ⅱ.①王… Ⅲ.①诗集-美国-现代-汉、英 Ⅳ.①I712. 25

中国版本图书馆 CIP 数据核字(2022)第 109926 号

二十世纪美国诗歌选译
ERSHI SHIJI MEIGUO SHIGE XUANYI

**编　　译** 王　文
**责任编辑** 焦　铭
**责任校对** 庞钧颖

**出版发行** 西安交通大学出版社
（西安市兴庆南路 1 号　邮政编码 710048）
**网　　址** http：//www. xjtupress. com
**电　　话** (029)82668803　82667874(市场营销中心)
(029)82668315(总编办)
**传　　真** (029)82668280
**印　　刷** 西安五星印刷有限公司

**开　　本** 787mm×1092mm 1/16　**印张** 21.375　**字数** 508 千字
**版次印次** 2022 年 6 月第 1 版　2023 年 3 月第 1 次印刷
**书　　号** ISBN 978-7-5693-2656-7
**定　　价** 98.00 元

如发现印装质量问题，请与本社市场营销中心联系。
订购热线：(029)82665248　(029)82667874
投稿热线：(029)82665371　(029)82668531

# 前　言

美国文学是世界文学的重要组成部分。作为文学的一种特殊形式，诗歌在美国文学的发展过程中自然而然地起着举足轻重的作用。早在美国的殖民时期（1607—1753），新英格兰就有安妮·布拉德斯特里特、菲利普·弗伦诺等作家用诗歌赞美生活、歌颂自然、抒发情感。

早期的美国诗歌虽然少有如英国维多利亚时期的罗伯特·勃朗宁、马修·阿诺德，浪漫主义时期的威廉·华兹华斯、约翰·济慈，以及杰弗里·乔叟、威廉·莎士比亚、约翰·弥尔顿等一般举世瞩目的伟大诗人，但在19世纪中期出现了以艾米丽·狄金森和瓦尔特·惠特曼为代表的创新诗人。在诗歌创作实践中，他们积极倡导自主自立，努力冲破欧洲的羁绊，带领美国诗歌走向独立发展的道路。

进入20世纪，随着美国社会经济的日益繁荣，特别是随着科学技术、商业兴盛、城市化的深入给人们生活带来巨大的变化，美国诗歌也得到了长足发展，诗人辈出、流派纷呈。意象派、象征派、传统派、新批评、垮掉派、黑山诗派、哈莱姆文艺复兴、自白派、语言诗派、旧金山诗派、纽约诗派等诗歌流派，形成欣欣向荣的蓬勃景象；随之出现了一批又一批闻名遐迩的代表诗人，如艾兹拉·庞德、T. S. 艾略特、希尔达·杜利特尔、艾米·洛威尔、罗伯特·弗罗斯特、华莱士·斯蒂文森、威廉·卡洛斯·威廉姆斯、E. E. 卡明斯、玛丽安·摩尔、兰斯顿·休斯、查尔斯·奥尔森、罗伯特·克利里、埃德温·阿林顿·罗宾逊、卡尔·桑德堡、克劳德·麦凯、艾伦·金斯伯格、杰克·斯比塞、肯尼斯·雷克斯罗斯、加里·斯奈德、罗伯特·洛威尔、西尔维尔·普拉斯、安妮·塞克斯顿、约翰·阿什贝利、肯尼斯·考克等。

为了帮助中文读者更好地理解美国诗歌，系统掌握美国文学的精华，国内已先后出版发行了多个中文译本的美国诗歌选集，每个译本都有各自的特点。

《二十世纪美国诗歌选译》选取了美国文学史上20世纪初到20世纪七八十年代的主要诗歌作品，涉及27位诗人和近300首诗歌，基本涵盖了该世纪的主要诗歌流派。所选诗人及其作品有些为大家熟知，有些相对陌生，但均为美国诗歌史上的重要作家和其代表作品。

译者在翻译过程中尽量围绕各个诗人所属流派的特征以及每位诗人的风格特点，在参阅大量相关资料以及前人翻译的基础上，按译者本人的理解对原诗进行翻译。为了便于读者理解，对每位诗人的生平、代表作品和风格特征做了简单介绍，对诗中的一些重点词语加以注解，并且附上了英文原诗。

文学翻译是个艰苦的过程，诗歌翻译更是一个巨大挑战。其中错误在所难免，请各位同行批评指正。

# 目　录


**黑山诗派** …………………………………………………………………… ( 1 )

查尔斯・奥尔森(Charles Olson, 1910—1970) ………………………… ( 2 )

罗伯特・克利里(Robert Cryly, 1926—2005) ………………………… ( 21 )

**意象诗派** …………………………………………………………………… ( 32 )

艾米・洛威尔(Amy Lowell, 1874—1925) ………………………… ( 33 )

希尔达・杜利特尔(Hilda Doolittle, 1886—1961) ………………………… ( 42 )

威廉・卡洛斯・威廉姆斯(William Carlos Williams, 1883—1963) ………… ( 53 )

**传统诗派** …………………………………………………………………… ( 62 )

埃德温・阿林顿・罗宾逊(Edwin Arlington Robinson, 1869—1935) ………… ( 63 )

罗伯特・弗罗斯特(Robert Frost, 1874—1963) ………………………… ( 75 )

**芝加哥诗派** …………………………………………………………………… ( 94 )

卡尔・桑德堡(Carl Sandburg, 1878—1967) ………………………… ( 95 )

埃德加 ・ 李・马斯特斯(Edgar Lee Masters, 1868—1950) ………… ( 98 )

维切尔・林赛(Vachel Lindsay, 1879—1931) ………………………… ( 103 )

**哈莱姆文艺复兴** …………………………………………………………… ( 112 )

克劳德・麦凯(Claude McKay, 1889—1948) ………………………… ( 113 )

琼・图默(Jean Toomer, 1894—1967) ………………………… ( 121 )

康蒂・卡伦(Countee Cullen, 1903—1946) ………………………… ( 129 )

兰斯顿・休斯(Lanston Hughs, 1902—1967) ………………………… ( 140 )

马娅・安杰卢(Maya Angelou, 1928—2014) ………………………… ( 151 )

丽塔・达夫(Rita Dove, 1952—) ………………………… ( 168 )

**垮掉派** …………………………………………………………………… ( 180 )

艾伦・金斯伯格(Allen Ginsburg, 1926—1997) ………………………… ( 181 )

格雷戈里・柯索(Gregary Corso, 1930—2001) ………………………… ( 189 )

加里・斯奈德(Gary Snyder, 1930—) ………………………… ( 199 )

**旧金山文艺复兴** ……………………………………………………………… ( 211 )
杰克・斯比塞(Jack Spicer，1925—1965) …………………………………… ( 212 )
肯尼斯・雷克斯罗斯(Kenneth Rexroth，1905—1982) …………………… ( 222 )

**自白派** ……………………………………………………………………… ( 236 )
罗伯特・洛威尔(Robert Lowell，1917—1977) ……………………………… ( 237 )
西尔维亚・普拉斯(Sylvia Plath，1932—1963) …………………………… ( 255 )
安妮・塞克斯顿(Anne Sexton，1928—1972) ……………………………… ( 271 )

**纽约诗派** …………………………………………………………………… ( 289 )
弗兰克・奥哈拉(Frank O'Hara，1926—1966) ……………………………… ( 290 )
约翰・阿什贝利(John Ashbery，1927—2017) ……………………………… ( 307 )
肯尼斯・考克(Kennith Koch，1925—2002) ………………………………… ( 320 )

# 黑山诗派

黑山诗派也称“投射派”。1950 年，黑山诗派代表人物查尔斯·奥尔森发表了《投射派》，这篇语言犀利的论文被看作是黑山诗派的宣言书。该文章首先认真回顾了 20 世纪三四十年代的美国诗坛，认为当时的诗风受艾略特的新批评理论影响，形式单一、封闭，毫无生气。《投射派》提出优秀的诗应当是开放的，因为“ 一首诗是从诗人那里得到的能量转换而来……靠着诗本身和其他方式又给予读者。好吧，那么诗本身必须在任何一点上都是由高度的能量构成，而且又在任何点上是能量的发泄。”[1]也就是说诗是“能量的结构”和“能量的放射”，形式只是内容的延伸。于是诗人写作时必须摆脱对传统的依靠，抛弃旧的形式、句法和格律，以便使诗歌获得“放射性、振动性和透视性”。要做到这一点，在他看来，诗歌首先要冲出印刷这一机械形式，冲破韵律节拍的局限，顺应呼吸的“音乐片语”节奏，或者说 “开放形式”的诗要求诗人从自己的呼吸即瞬间的自然节奏中获得属于自己的形式。奥尔森说：“现在，在 1950 年，诗歌如果要向前走，如果要有根本的用处，我认为，必须抓住呼吸的某些规律和可能性，并将它们融入诗中：那是写诗的、也是听诗的人的呼吸。”[2]黑山诗派的代表人物有查尔斯·奥尔森(Charles Olson)、罗伯特·克里利 (Robert Creeley) 、罗伯特·邓肯 (Robert Duncan) 等。

① 丹尼尔·霍夫曼：《美国当代文学》(下)，《世界文学》编辑部译，中国文联出版公司，1985，第 766 页。

② 同上。

# 查尔斯·奥尔森
## (Charles Olson，1910—1970)

查尔斯·奥尔森 1910 年生于马萨诸塞州的伍斯特镇(Worcester)。中学毕业后，奥尔森离开家乡，来到位于康涅狄格州米德尔敦(Middletown，Conneticut)的卫斯理大学(Wesleyan University)学习文学，先后获得学士和硕士学位。1936 年奥尔森开始在哈佛大学攻读美国文化博士学位的课程，1947 年完成博士论文《叫我以实玛利》(*Call Me Ishmael*)，但遗憾的是由于他的论文书写方法奇特、论点大胆前卫而未能获得博士学位。1951 年奥尔森接替画家约瑟夫·亚伯斯(Josef Albers，1888—1976)出任北卡罗来纳州"黑山学院"院长，直至 1956 年，其间招徕了一大批旨在改革创新的诗人和艺术家，使"黑山学院"成了战后闻名遐迩的全美艺术界"反学院派"的重要基地。

在诗歌创作中，奥尔森倡导所谓的"投射或开放诗"，也称"田野写作"。他认为诗歌的构成不应围绕诗行、诗节或诗歌的形式，而要依照感知的自由流动。他主张诗歌的韵律遵循诗人创作时呼吸的节奏，而非其他程式化的格式。因此，他号召诗人借助键盘写诗，因为键盘能够记录下"精确的呼吸、停顿，甚至音节的悬停、词的各部分的叠加。"①

奥尔森的主要诗集有《在冰冷的地狱，在灌木丛里》(*In Cold Hell，in Thicket*，1953)、《距离》(*The Distances*，1960)、《早晨的考古学家》(*Archaeologist of Morning*，1971)和《马克西姆斯诗篇》(*The Maximus Poems*，1975)等。

### New England March

Atlantic
river, sea
roar
with the mood tide

The moor,
frantic
rots with flood

---

① 丹尼尔·霍夫曼:《当代美国文学(下)》,《世界文学》编辑部译，中国文联出版公司，1985，第 756 页。

Over all the gulls
white
hungry
gray

## 新英格兰的三月

大西洋
江河，大海
咆哮
随着情绪涨落

沼泽，
狂乱
在洪水中腐烂

空中成群的海鸥
白色
饥饿
灰色

## Sing，Mister，Sing

Hills are grey elephants
the sun is a prince
the plain is an ocean
Bigman's pants

        Pound the earth，pound the earth
        I dance，I dance

The prince is astride
the grey hills glide

the ocean's a tide
Bigmans hide

Round the earth, round the earth
I ride, I ride

Ride and prance
brag and dance
round the world, round the world
Bigmans chance

## 唱吧，先生，唱吧

山丘是灰色大象
太阳是王子
平原是海洋
大佬的裤子

撞击大地，撞击大地
我手舞足蹈，我手舞足蹈

王子骑着
灰色山丘掠过
海洋是潮流
大佬隐藏

环绕地球，环绕地球
我骑马奔驰，我骑马奔驰

骑马飞跃
炫耀欢腾
周游世界，周游世界
大佬在冒险

## The Songs of Maximus: Song 1

Coloured pictures
of all things to eat: dirty
postcards
And words, words, words
all over everything
No eyes or ears left
to do their own doings (all
invaded, appropriated, outraged, all senses
including the mind, that worker on what is
And that other sense
made to give even the most wretched, or any of us, wretched,
that consolation) greased
lulled
even the street-cars
song

## 马克西姆斯之歌之一

所有食物的
彩色图片：污秽的
明信片
还有单词、单词、单词
全都在每一件东西之上
没有一只眼睛或耳朵可以
做自己的事(全部
被干扰、被盗用、被激怒，所有感官
包括大脑、那个什么都做的劳工
以及迫使给予最可怜的、
或我们其中任何一位、可怜的、以安慰的
那另一感官)涂上润滑油
使其安静
甚至街车
歌曲

## Maximus, to Himself

**1**

I have had to learn the simplest things
last. Which made for difficulties.
Even at sea I was slow, to get the hand out, or to cross a wet deck.
The sea was not, finally, my trade.
But even my trade, at it, I stood estranged
from that which was more familiar. Was delayed,
and not content with the man's argument
that such postponement
is now the nature of
obedience.
    that we are all late
    in a slow time.
    that we grow up many
    And the single
    is not easily
    known

It could be, though the sharpness (the achiote)
I note in others,
makes more sense
than my own distances. The agilities

    they show daily
    who do the world's
    business
    And who do nature's
    as I have no sense
    I have done either

I have made diologues.

have discussed ancient texts,
have thrown what light I could, offered
what pleasures
doceat ① allows

        but the known
this, I have had to be given,
a life, love, and from one man
the world.
        Tokens.
        But sitting here
        I look out as a wind
        and water man, testing
        And missing
        some proof

I know the quarters
of the weather, where it comes from,
where it goes. But the stem of me,
this I took from their welcome,
or their rejection, of me

        And my arrogance
        was neither diminished
        nor increased,
        by the communication

**2**

It is undone business
I speak of, this morning,
with the sea
stretching out
from my feet

① doceat：拉丁语，原意为教授、博士。

## 马克西姆斯致自己

一

后来我只好学些最简单的
东西。这惹上了麻烦。
即使在海上我的行动也很慢，无论是伸手拿东西还是穿过潮湿的甲板。
大海——绝对——不是我的行业。
然而即使我的行业，在海上，面对习以为常的东西
我也会束手无策。拖延，
而且不赞成他人的观点
认为这种延迟
眼下是顺从的
天性。
　　在缓慢的时光里
　　大家都迟缓。
　　我们长大后基本都一样
　　而与众不同者
　　不易
　　为人知

或许如此，虽然在别人身上看到的
鲜亮的色彩(胭脂树[①])，
与我自己的差距比起来
更有意义。

　　他们每日展露出
　　哪些人能做商业的

---

① 胭脂树：(achiote，学名 Bixa orellana)，属于胭脂树科、胭脂树属的多年生植物，是热带地区最有名的染料植物；多年生落叶小乔木或灌木，树皮呈灰白色，有白斑，叶具长柄，互生，心形，先端锐尖，近于全缘，两面平滑。圆锥花序顶生，密布褐色短毛；花瓣5片，粉红色，萼形小，不整齐二裂，基部具腺体5个。其果实为扁三角形(鸡心形)，其红色外种皮是良好的胭脂材料。亚马逊河流域与西印度群岛的原住民取胭脂树的种子，拌合唾液，再用手掌搓揉，涂抹皮肤，作为身体的装饰，看起来就像涂上胭脂一般，因此得名。

事务
哪些人能做自然的事务
而我愚钝
两者都没做

我编过对话，
讨论过古文，
解释过力所能及的问题，曾给予
学究们许可的
快乐

但是已知的
这个，我不得不付出，
生命、爱心，从一个人那里得到
世界。
标记。
而我坐在这里
小心翼翼地犹如风水师，检验
和回忆
某个证据

我略懂天气，
它为何这般，
会怎样变化。然而我的支柱，
来自于我的感受，他们是喜欢，
还是讨厌，至于我

我的傲慢
既没有减弱
也没有增强，
经过交流

二
这是未竟的事务
我说起，今天早晨，

大海
在我的脚下
延伸

## Celestial Evening, October 1967

Advanced out toward the external from
the time I did actually lose space control,
here on the fort and kept turning left
like my star-nosed mole batted
on the head, not being able to
get home 50 yards as I was
from it. There is a vast

internal life, a sea or organism
full of sounds & memoried
objects swimming or sunk
in the great fall of it as,
...

... it all
comes in as also outward leads
us after itself as though then
the horn of the nearest moon was
truth. I bend my ear, as,
if I were Amoghasiddi and,
here on this plain where
like my mole I have
been knocked flat, attend
to turn & turn within
the steady stream & collect which
within me ends as in her hall and I

here all, the new moon new in all
the ancient sky

My impression is we did—
That is, death and myself, regard each other. And
There wasn't anything more than that, only that he had appeared,
And we did recognize each other—or I did, him, and he seemed
To have no question about my presence there, even though I was uncomfortable.

## 1967年10月夜晚的星空

向着外部行进
从我实际失去控制空间的时候起，
就在贸易站继续左转
如同头部遭受撞击的星鼻鼹鼠，
家近在咫尺却回不去。

内在生命庞大无比，似海洋，似有机体
充满声音以及勾起回忆的
物体在它那美妙的秋季
漂荡或沉没，
……

……它一览无余地
出现同样带领我们向外就像
离我们最近的月亮上的号角般
真实。我洗耳恭听，如同，
阿摩加西德①或者，
就在这平原上
如同鼹鼠
被打翻在地，想在
涓涓溪流中转身
或者在她的窝里捡些
身上的残片

---

① 阿摩加西德：五大智慧佛陀之一。

我就在这里，新月
在古时的空中
刚刚出现

我的感觉是我们的确——
就是说，死亡和我本人，相互注视。
也就如此，只是他来了，
我们相互看见了——或者说，我看到了他，他似乎
对我的出现一点都不奇怪，虽然我不大舒服。

## Variations Done for Gerald van de Wiele

**Ⅰ Le Bonheur**

Dogwood flakes
what is green

the petals
from the apple
blow on the road

mourning doves
mark the sway
of the afternoon, bees
dig the plum blossoms

the morning
stands up straight, the night
is blue from the full of the April moon

iris and lilac, birds
birds, yellow flowers
white flowers, the diesel
does not let up dragging
the plow

as the whippoorwill,
the night's tractor, grinds
his song

and no other birds but us
are as busy (O saisons, O chateaux!)
Délires①!

What soul
is without fault?

Nobody studies
happiness

Every time the cock crows
I salute him

I have no longer any excuse
for envy. My life

has been given its orders: the seasons
seize

the soul and the body, and make mock
of any dispersed effort. The hour of death

is the only trespass

**Ⅱ The Charge**

Dogwood flakes
the green

---

① Delires：法语，妄想症。

the petals from the apple-trees
fall for the feet to walk on

the birds are so many they are
loud, in the afternoon

they distract, as so many bees do
suddenly all over the place

With spring one knows today to see
that in the morning each thing

is separate but by noon
they have melted into each other

and by night only crazy things
like the full moon and the whippoor will

and us, are busy. We are busy
if we can get by that whiskered bird,

that nightjar, and get across, the moon
is our conversation, she will say

what soul
isn't in default?

can you afford not to make
the magical study

which happiness is? do you hear
the cock when he crows? do you know the charge,

that you shall have no envy, that your life
has its orders, that the seasons

seize you too, that no body and soul are one
if they are not wrought

in this retort? that otherwise efforts
are efforts? And that the hour of your flight

will be the hour of your death?

**Ⅲ Spring**

The dogwood
lights up the day.

The April moon
flakes the night.

Birds, suddenly,
are a multitude

The flowers are ravined
by bees, the fruit blossoms

are thrown to the ground, the wind
the rain forces everything. Noise—

even the night is drummed
by whippoorwills, and we get

as busy, we plow, we move,
we break out, we love. The secret

which got lost neither hides
nor reveals itself, it shows forth

tokens. And we rush

to catch up. The body

whips the soul. In its great desire
it demands the elixir

In the roar of spring,
transmutations. Envy

drags herself off. The fault of the body and the soul
—that they are not one—

the matutinal cock clangs
and singleness: we salute you

season of no bungling

## 变奏曲——为杰拉尔德·范德维尔[①]而作

**一、幸福**
山茱萸脱下
绿色

苹果树上的
花瓣
在路上吹来吹去

哀鸠[②]
下午时分随处可见，
蜜蜂在盛开的梅花里
采蜜

---

① 杰拉尔德·范德维尔："黑山学院"学生(1954—1956)，著名画家。
② 哀鸠：产于北美的一种鸟。

清晨
晴空万里，
仲春满月的夜空一片湛蓝

鸢尾和丁香，鸟儿
鸟儿，黄的花
白的花，柴油机
依然牵引着
耕犁

夜鹰，
夜间牵引机，
刺耳地鸣叫

除了我们，没有别的鸟
在忙碌(啊，庄园，啊，城堡!)
狂热!

什么样的灵魂
没有过错?

没有人探讨
幸福

每当公鸡喔喔叫
我向他致敬

我再没有
嫉妒的借口，

我的人生
已经有所调整:

一年四季
紧紧抓住

灵魂和肉体，
鄙视其他努力。死亡时刻

是唯一的罪过

**二、谴责**
山茱萸脱下
绿色

苹果树上的花瓣
落在地上让脚踩着走

成群结队的鸟儿在喧叫，
下午

鸟儿散去，
蜜蜂瞬间铺天盖地地飞了过来

春天到了，
人们如今明白

早晨各自为营的事物，
中午就会融化在一起

而到了晚上只有狂热的东西，
比如满月和夜鹰

还有我们，才会忙忙碌碌。
我们忙于能否抓住那只长胡子的鸟

那只夜鹰，并且说清楚，
月亮成了我们的交际对象，她会说

什么样的灵魂

没有违约?

你真的不去做
那种幸福的神奇研究吗?

你听到公鸡的叫声吗?
你知道那个谴责吗?

不会有人嫉妒你，
你的人生根本没有改变，

四季也将抓住你，
在这一谴责中，

如果没有特意训练
肉体和灵魂怎能合而为一?

其他的努力也是努力?
你一旦逃避

就是你的死期?

**三、春天**
山茱萸
点亮这一天。

四月的明月
离开了夜空。

鸟儿，顷刻间，
密密麻麻

花丛中
蜜蜂飞舞，

果树花吹落在了地上，
风雨导致一切。噪音——

甚至夜晚也被夜鹰
沉闷的叫声所惊扰，

我们一如既往地忙碌，
耕种、走动、摆脱、相爱。

失去的秘密
既不遮掩也不流露，

只透露迹象。
我们匆忙追赶。

肉体鞭挞灵魂。
抱着美好的愿望

它诉求灵丹妙药
在春天的怒吼中，蜕变。

嫉妒将自己拽入歧途。
肉体和灵魂的过失
——它们不是一体——

黎明的公鸡高亢鸣叫
聚精会神：我们向你致敬

不算蹩脚的季节

# 罗伯特·克利里
# (Robert Cryly，1926—2005)

罗伯特·克利里 1926 年生于马萨诸塞州的阿灵顿。1943 年他进入哈佛大学学习，正值第二次世界大战之际，随后被派往缅甸和印度服役。战争结束后，他返回哈佛大学继续学业，但没有毕业就离开了学校。他曾经开过救护车，当过养鸡场工人，出版过报纸和书籍。20 世纪五十年代初他结识奥尔森，受其邀请于 1954 年前往黑山学院任教，创建并主编《黑山评论》。1955 年获新墨西哥大学文学硕士学位。20 世纪六十年代黑山学院关闭后，克利里离开北卡罗来纳州，前往水牛城的纽约州立大学任教。

克里利的诗歌写作深受威廉姆·卡洛斯·威廉姆斯、查尔斯·奥尔森、罗伯特·邓肯等诗人的影响。他主张诗歌的用词应该“利用反馈的技巧回归最原始的情形，也就是说，措辞的重新布局，使词汇回归一种存在的最客观状态，从而让词汇‘说’而不是某人通过它们来说。”①在诗歌创作实践中，克里利追求对潜意识或者内心体验的直接表达。他的大部分诗歌短小精悍，力求真实地再现情感的脉动。

克里利的主要诗集有：《为了爱：1950—1960 诗选》(*For Love*：*Poems* 1950—1960)(1962)、《词》(*Words*)(1967)、《你好》(*Hello*)(1976)、《后来》(*Later*)(1979)、《罗伯特·克里李诗选 1945—1975》(*The Collected Poems of Robert Creeley*，1945—1975)(1982)、《生与死》(*Life and Death*)(1998)等。

## Colors

Colors of stars,
all you people. Cars,
lights, wet streets.

## 色彩

星星的色彩，
你们这些人。汽车，
灯光，潮湿的街道。

---

① J. D. McClatchy，*The Vintage Book of Contemporary American Poetry*，(New York：Random House，1990) P. 231.

## I Know a Man

As I said to my
friend, because I am
always talking, —John, I

said, which was not his
name, the darkness
surrounds us, what

can we do against
it, or else, shall we &
why not, buy a goddamn big car,

drive, he said, for
christ's sake, look
out where you are going.

## 我认识一个人

正如我给朋友
说过，因为我总爱
唠叨，——约翰，我

说，他不叫这个
名字，黑暗笼罩着
我们，我们

该咋办，要么，我们
干吗不买一辆该死的大轿车，

开开，他说，千
万，注意
你要到哪里去。

## For Friendship

For friendship
make a chain that holds,
to be bound to
others, two by two,

a walk, a garland,
handed by hands
that cannot move
unless they hold.

## 为了友谊

为了友谊
做一条连在一起的链子，
同他人绑在
一起，一对一对，

步行，花环，
由僵硬的
手传递
除非它们捧着。

## Again

One more day gone,
done, found in
the form of days.

It began, it
ended—was
forward, backward,

slow, fast, a
sun shone, clouds,
high in the aire I was

for a while with others,
then came down
on the gound again.

No moon. A room in
a hotel—to begin
again.

## 再次

又一天过去了,
结束,发现
以一天一天的形式。

开始,结束
向前,向后,

缓慢,快速,
太阳出来,云彩,
高挂空中我

一会儿与他人在一起,
然后下来再次
来到地上。

没有月亮。
酒店的房间——重新
开始。

## Myself

What, younger, felt

was possible, now knows
is not—but still
not changed enough—

Walked by the sea,
unchanged in memory—
evening, as clouds
on the far-off rim

of water float,
pictures of time,
smoke, faintness—
still the dream.

I want, if older,
still to know
why, human, men
and women are

so torn, so lost,
why hopes cannot
find better world
than this.

Shelley is dead and gone,
Who said,
'Taught them not this—
to know themselves;

their might could not repress
the mutiny within,
And for the morn
of truth they feigned,

deep night

Caught them ere evening... ’

## 我自己

年轻时觉得
可能之事，如今发现
难以做到——但变化
仍然不够大——

漫步海边，
往事依旧——
傍晚，云彩
在远处的

水面浮动
时间的印记，
烟雾，朦朦胧胧——
依然梦幻。

即使年龄再大点，我仍然
想知道
为何，人们，
男女

如此煎熬，如此失落，
为何找到
比这好的生活
的希望会落空。

雪莱作古而去，
他曾经说过，
“别告诉他们这点——
要认识自己；

他们不会抵制

内心的叛逆，
为了虚构的
真理的黎明，

深夜
傍晚之前缠绕着他们……"

## The Languange

Locate I
love you some—
where in

teeth and
eyes, bite
it but

take care not
to hurt, you
want so

much so
little. Words
say everything.

"I
love you"
again,

then what
is emptiness
for. To

fill, fill.
I heard words

and words full

of holes
aching. Speech
is a mouth.

## 语言

将“我爱你”
在牙齿与
眼睛

的某个部位
定格，咬住
它但

当心别
伤着，你
想要的太多

太少。词语
说明一切。

“我
爱你”
再次，

那么
空洞是
为了什么。

填充，填充。
我听过词语
以及到处是
漏洞的词语

隐隐作痛。言语
是张嘴。

## Goodbye

Now I recognize
it was always me
like a camera
set to expose

itself to a picture
or a pipe
through which the water
might run

or a chicken
dead for dinner
or a plan
inside the head

of a dead man.
Nothing so wrong
when one considered
how it all began.

It was Zukofsky's
"Born very young into a world
already very old... "
The century was well along

when I came in
and now that it's ending,
I realize it won't
be long.

But couldn't it have all been
a little nicer,
as my mother'd say. Did it
have to kill everything in sight,

did right always have to be so wrong?
I know this body is impatient.
I know I constitute only a meager voice and mind.
Yet I loved, I love.

I want no sentimentality.
I want no more than home.

## 告别

如今我意识到
我经常如同一架
调好焦距
拍照的

照相机
或者一根
流水的
管子

或者一只端上
餐桌的鸡
或者一个
死人大脑里的

计划。
如果想想
最初的情形
也就没什么大错。

如朱可夫斯基[①]所言
“年纪轻轻来到了
已经老态龙钟的世界……”
世纪辉煌时

我来了
如今本世纪就要结束，
我发现它即将
终结。

然而如同家母常说
难道一切不会再好一点，
一定要把眼前的
全部都毁灭，

必须等到出现重大错误之后才会改正吗?
我知道这副肉体不省心。
我明白我的声音和想法微不足道。
但是我爱过，我依然爱。

我不想多愁善感。
我只想有个家。

---

① 朱可夫斯基：(Louis Zukofsky，1904—1978)，美国客观派诗人。

# 意象诗派

意象诗派是20世纪初英美文学史上一个重要的文学流派，被认为是“现代诗歌的起点”（T. S. 艾略特），英美现代诗歌和后现代诗歌的发展与其有着千丝万缕的联系。意象诗派的起源地在英国伦敦。发起人是一群以美国人为主的青年诗人，但其最初领导人是英国批评家、诗人托马斯·厄内斯特·休姆。休姆认为维多利亚时代诗歌中的浪漫主义代表着“邪恶的人道主义”的没落，三百年来这种人道主义一直统治着西方文化思想，要清除它就得有一种新诗出现。这种新诗必须简洁、有力，避免一切虚假的感情并对宇宙问题不做说教式的评论。①

意象派诗人接受中国、日本、希腊、希伯来诗歌以及普罗旺斯民谣的影响，从以绘画为主的现代艺术中寻求灵感，在诗歌创作中坚决抵制“象征主义的专制”（威廉·卡洛斯·威廉姆斯），积极倡导以简洁、清晰、具体为主要特征的客观、直接的作诗方法。其主要代表人物包括美国诗人艾兹拉·庞德、希尔达·杜利特尔、艾米·罗威尔、约翰·古德·弗莱切和英国诗人理查德·阿尔丁顿、弗兰克·斯图亚特·弗林特、托马斯·厄内斯特·休姆、福特·马多克斯·惠弗、戴维·赫伯特·劳伦斯等。

① 威勒德·索普：《二十世纪美国文学》，濮阳翔、李秀成译，北京师范大学出版社，1984，第39页。

# 艾米·洛威尔
# （Amy Lowell，1874—1925）

艾米·洛威尔 1874 年出生于美国马萨诸塞州布鲁克林的一个名门世家。祖父是大诗人詹姆斯·拉塞尔·洛威尔的堂弟。哥哥帕西瓦尔·洛威尔是美国著名天文学家；姐姐劳伦斯·洛威尔曾任哈佛大学校长。这样的家庭背景使艾米·洛威尔形成了恣意妄为的性格。

1913 年，正当意象派诗歌运动如火如荼地在英国风靡之时，艾米·洛威尔只身来到伦敦，迫不及待地加入意象派诗人的行列，求教于庞德的门下。但没过多久她便与庞德发生激烈争执，愤然离开、另起炉灶，自封“意象派先驱”。她撰写文章，四处演讲，资助其他意象派诗人，出乎意料地推动了意象派诗歌运动的纵深发展。

在总结意象诗派的创作宗旨和方法时，洛威尔将意象诗派早期的“三原则”扩展为“六原则”：一是语言要通俗准确，不用模棱两可、无关紧要的修饰语；二是创作新节奏，并不一定用自由体，但自由体最能表现诗人的个性；三是题材完全自由；四是要有意象，但不能空泛；五是表达要具体、明晰，切忌含糊不清；六是简练、浓缩。

在诗歌写作实践中，洛威尔也是一位大胆的创新者，敢于冲破理论的限制。她一生先后出版了 11 部诗集，共计 600 多首诗。每一首诗都是她个人强烈情感的真实流露。她说：“我敢说只有诗人才能体会到写诗的痛苦。每根神经、每块肌肉绷得紧紧的，几乎要断了。写出来之前不能中断，否则会更加痛苦。最后诗终于从大脑杀出一条道来，奔泻而出。”洛威尔热情奔放地投入诗歌创作改革的大潮之中，坚持不懈、不知疲倦地推动诗歌的理论创新，被艾略特誉为“精力旺盛的女诗歌推销员”。

洛威尔的诗集主要有《彩色玻璃大厦》（*A Dome of Many Colored-Glass*，1912）、《剑刃与罂粟籽》（*Sword Blades and Poppy Seeds*，1914）、《男人、女人和鬼魂》（*Men, Women and Ghosts*，1916）、《浮世绘》（*Picture of the Floating World*，1919）、《东风》（*East Wind*，1926）、《艾米·洛威尔诗歌作品全集》（*The Complete Poetic Works of Amy Lowell*，1955）等。

## Decade

When you came, you were like red wine and honey,
And the taste of you burnt my mouth with sweetness.
Now you are like morning bread,
Smooth and pleasant.

I hardly taste you at all for I know your savour,
But I am completely nourished.

## 十年

你来时如红酒和蜂蜜，
尝一口甘之如饴。
如今你和早晨的面包一般，
品起来爽口宜人。

熟知你的美味几乎没再品尝，
但我得到了充足的滋养。

## Crowned

You came to me bearing bright roses,
　Red like the wine of your heart;
You twisted them into a garland
　To set me aside from the mart.
Red roses to crown me your lover,
　And I walked aureole and apart.

Enslaved and encircled, I bore it,
　Proud token of my gift to you.
The petals waned paler, and shriveled,
　And dropped; and the thorns started through.
Bitter thorns to proclaim me our lover,
　A diadem woven with rue.

## 加冕

你手捧鲜艳的玫瑰向我走来，
玫瑰鲜红如同你心中的美酒；
你将它们绕成一个花环

　　让我超群绝伦。
你用红玫瑰加冕我，你的心上人，
　　我身披光环离去。

戴着它，我将不再自由，唯你是从，
　成为你引以为荣的礼品。
花瓣凋零，枯萎，
　残落；荆棘开始从中穿过。
痛苦的荆棘告诉我　我们是恋人，
　一个懊悔织成的王冠。

## The Taxi

When I go away from you
The world beats dead
Like a slackened drum.
I call out for you against the jutted stars
And shout into the ridges of the wind.
Streets coming fast,
One after the other,
Wedge you away from me,
And the lamps of the city prick my eyes
So that I can no longer see your face.
Why should I leave you,
To wound myself upon the sharp edges of the night?

## 出租车

当我离你而去
地球停止了律动
如同松弛的鼓。
对着明亮的星星我呼叫
朝着阵阵狂风我大喊。
街道飞驰而来，
一条接着一条，

把你从我身边驱离。
城市的灯光刺伤了我的眼睛
再也无法看清你的面容。
我为什么要离开,
用夜的利刃戳伤自己?

## The Little Garden

A little garden on a bleak hillside
　　Where deep the heavy, dazzling mountain snow
　　Lies far into the spring. The sun's pale glow
Is scarcely able to melt patches wide
About the single rose bush. All denied
　　Of nature's tender ministries. But no, —
　　For wonder-working faith has made it blow
With flowers many hued and starry-eyed.
　　Here sleeps the sun long, idle summer hours;
Here butterflies and the bees fare far to rove
　　Amid the crumpled leaves of poppy flowers;
Here four o'clock, to the passionate night above
　　Fling whiffs of perfume, like pale incense showers.
A little garden, loved with a great love!

## 小小公园

荒凉的山坡上有一个小小公园
　　山的深处覆盖着厚厚的耀眼白雪
　　来年晚春才慢慢融化。太阳苍白的光芒
无法融化掉玫瑰花丛
四周大片积雪。这里没有
　大自然的精心呵护。不,不对,——
　创造奇迹的信念让这里
花海浮动、色彩缤纷,令人叹奇。
　太阳在这里长眠,度过它懒洋洋的夏季时光;
蝴蝶和蜜蜂在这里飞舞

在褶皱的罂粟花叶中觅食；
这是四点钟，充满激情的夜空
漂浮着阵阵芳香，犹如淡淡的熏香扑面而来。
小小公园，令我心旷神怡之地！

## Dreams

I do not care to talk to you although
Your speech evokes a thousand sympathies,
And all my being's silent harmonies
Wake trembling into music. When you go
It is as if some sudden, dreadful blow
Had severed all the strings with savage ease.
No, do not talk; but let us rather seize
This intimate gift of silence which we know.
Others may guess your thoughts from what you say,
As storms are guessed from clouds where darkness broods.
To me the very essence of the day
Reveals its inner purpose and its moods;
As poplars feel the rain and then straightway
Reverse their leaves and shimmer through the woods.

## 梦想

不想对你说
虽然你的言语唤起了千万个同情，
我生命中沉默的和声全部苏醒，
颤抖着汇入乐曲。你的离去
犹如突如其来的沉重打击
折断了所有琴弦，带来恐怖的安逸。
不，别说话；让我们紧紧抓住
熟悉的沉默这一亲密礼物。
别人会从你的话中猜到你的想法，
就像从乌云孕育的黑暗中预测风暴。
在我看来，今天的关键是

暴露了它的内在目的和情绪;
就像杨树感觉到了雨
马上翻转叶子，透过林子熠熠发光。

## Happiness

Happiness, to some, elation;
Is, to others, mere stagnation.
Days of passive somnolence,
At its wildest, indolence.
Hours of empty quietness,
No delight, and no distress.
Happiness to me is wine,
Effervescent, superfine.
Full of tang and fiery pleasure,
Far too hot to leave me leisure
For a single thought beyond it.
Drunk! Forgetful! This the bond: it
Means to give one's soul to gain
Life's quintessence. Even pain
Pricks to livelier living, then
Wakes the nerves to laugh again,
Rapture's self is three parts sorrow.
Although we must die to-morrow,
Losing every thought but this;
Torn, triumphant, drowned in bliss.
Happiness: We rarely feel it.
I would buy it, beg it, steal it,
Pay in coins of dripping blood
For this one transcendent good.

## 快乐

快乐，对有些人来说，是兴高采烈;
而在其他人眼里仅仅是停滞不前。

疯狂至极、懒惰、
消极、萎靡不振的日子。
几个小时空荡荡的宁静，
没有欢乐，没有痛苦。
快乐之于我是杯美酒，
沸腾、精美、
甘醇、充满火热的愉悦，
如此令人心醉神迷，
让我无暇顾及其他。
大醉！健忘！于是这样约定：
竭尽全力获取生命的精华。
甚至生活中的痛苦因刺激而成欢乐，
从而唤醒神经再次欢笑，
狂喜的背后是三分的悲痛。
虽然我们将来都要死去，
除此之外其余想法都要抛弃；
撕心裂肺、洋洋得意、幸福陶醉。
快乐：我们很少感觉得到它。
我想购买它、乞求它、窃取它，
用血淋淋的钱币
换取这至高无上的好东西。

## The Weather-Cock Points South

I put your leaves aside,
One by one:
The stiff, broad outer leaves;
The smaller ones,
Pleasant to touch, veined with purple;
The glazed inner leaves.
One by one
I parted you from your leaves,
Until you stood up like a white flower
Swaying slightly in the evening wind.

White flower,
Flower of wax, of jade, of unstreaked agate;
Flower with surfaces of ice,
With shadows faintly crimson.
Where in all the garden is there such a flower?
The stars crowd through the lilac leaves
To look at you.
The low moon brightens you with silver.

The bud is more than the calyx.
There is nothing to equal a white bud,
Of no color, of all,
Burnished by moonlight,
Thrust upon by a softly-swinging wind.

## 风信鸡指向南方

我拨开你的叶子,
一片一片:
坚硬、宽大的外叶片;
窄小的叶片,
触感惬意,带有紫色的叶脉;
光滑的内叶片。
一片一片
把你从叶子中一层一层剥离,
最后犹如一朵白花矗立
在晚风中轻轻摇曳。

白花,
蜡之花、玉之花、完美无缺的玛瑙之花;
表面结冰的花,
影子暗红的花。
花园之中哪有这样的花?
星星争相透过丁香树叶
一睹你的芳容。
月亮低垂给你披上银色盛装。

花蕾胜于花萼。
白色花蕾无与伦比，
无色、完整，
在月光下熠熠生辉，
一阵轻轻摆动的风猛然穿入。

## Anticipation

I have been temperate always,
But I like to be very drunk
With your coming.
There have been times
I feared to walk down the street
Lest I should reel with the wine of you,
And jerk against my neighbours
As they go by.
I am parched now, and my tongue is horrible in my mouth,
But my brain is noisy
With the clash and gurgle of my filling wine-cups.

## 盼望

我向来节制有度，
然而你的到来
令我难以把持。
曾经多次
我不敢在街上行走
唯恐因你这杯酒而踉跄，
遇到邻居
一头猛撞过去。
我现在口干舌燥，
满脑子全是
酒杯的叮当声和倒酒的哗啦声。

# 希尔达·杜利特尔
## (Hilda Doolittle，1886—1961)

杜利特尔于1886年生于宾夕法尼亚州的伯利恒市。在她8岁时，全家搬迁到了费城。其母亲喜欢音乐和绘画，热衷于摩拉维亚教的宗教活动，父亲是天文学家和数学家，曾任宾夕法尼亚大学弗罗天文台主任。15岁时，杜利特尔结识了当时在宾夕法尼亚大学读书的庞德，并与他相爱，但因家人反对，不久便与之分手。庞德随后离开美国去了伦敦，杜利特尔则进入布赖英学院读书，她对诗歌产生了浓厚兴趣，开始翻译拉丁文诗，并且开始诗歌创作。由于难以忍受学习上的压力，两年后杜利特尔退学回家。1911年在伦敦旅行时，杜利特尔与庞德再次相见。庞德介绍杜利特尔认识了伦敦文学界名流，帮助她修改诗作，并将她的作品推荐给美国新诗运动的核心期刊《诗刊》。杜利特尔的作品成功发表，作者署名为"意象主义者H. D. "。

1913年杜利特尔与英国诗人、小说家兼批评家理查德·奥尔丁顿结婚。婚后不久奥尔丁顿有了婚外情，他们两人的婚姻也随即告终。与此同时，杜利特尔同庞德的友谊也出现了裂痕。接连不断的打击对杜利特尔的精神造成极大伤害，她不久便患上了精神分裂症，时常产生幻觉，整日精神恍惚。

1933年杜利特尔先后去往伦敦和维也纳，接受西格蒙德·弗洛伊德的心理分析治疗，并且开始研习弗洛伊德的精神分析理论。后来她将学习成果编写成一本散文体著作，取名《献给弗洛伊德》。第二次世界大战爆发后，杜利特尔重新回到了英国。

从1913年在《诗刊》杂志初次露面到1961年去世，杜利特尔创作了大量的诗歌作品，主要收集在以下诗集中：《海的花园》(*Sea Garden*，1916)、《赫利尔多拉及其他诗》(*Heliodora and Other Poems*，1924)、《给青铜器的红玫瑰》(*Red Rose for Bronze*，1931)、《墙没倒塌》(*The Walls Do Not Fall*，1944)、《海伦在埃及》(*Helen in Egypt*)(1961)以及她死后出版的《神秘的定义》(*Hermetic Definition*，1972)和《三部曲》(*Trilogy*，1973)等。杜利特尔的诗歌一般具有以下特征。一是意象贯穿作品始终，意象处理精准，语调平直，这与她早年和庞德的交往不无关系。二是她对古希腊文化情有独钟，诗中充满希腊神话的隐喻。通过意象手法，她常把希腊神话同现实世界及个人生活紧密地结合在一起，将古典神话现代化；三是因个人极不寻常的生活经历，以及庞德和弗洛伊德等20世纪早期一些著名人物的影响，她后期的作品个性化特色明显。

### Epitaph

So you may say,

"I died of living,
having lived one hour";

so they may say,
"she died soliciting
illicit fervor";

so you may say,
"Greek flower; Greek ecstacy
reclaims for ever

one who died
following
intricate songs' lost measure."

## 祭文

于是你就会说,
"我死于生计,
活得很短暂";

于是他们会说,
"她因醉心于
非法的狂热而死";

于是你会说,
"希腊之花;希腊迷幻
一直在熏陶

那个为遵守
复杂诗歌已失方法
而献身的人。"

## The Moon in Your Hands

If you take the moon in your hands

and turn it round
(heavy, slightly tarnished platter)
you're there;

if you pull dry see-weed from the sand
and turn it round
and wonder at the underside's bright amber,
your eyes

look out as they did here,
(you don't remember)
when my soul turned round,

perceiving the other-side of everything,
mullein-leaf, dogwood-leaf, moth wing
and dandelion-seed under the ground.

## 月亮在你手中

如果你把月亮捧在手中
转动一下
(沉重、有点暗淡的圆盘)
你就会明白;

如果你从沙里拔出干枯的海草
转动一下
发现底部闪亮的琥珀而惊叹不已,
你的眼睛

照例留意,
(你忘了)
当我的心已做调整,

察觉到所有东西的另一面,
毛蕊花叶、山茱萸叶、蛾翅

还有地下的蒲公英籽。

## At Baia

I should have thought
in a dream you would have brought
some lovely, perilous thing,
orchids piled in a great sheath,
as who would say (in a dream),
"I send you this,
who left the blue veins
of your throat unkissed."

Why was it that your hands
(that never took mine),
your hands that I could see
drift over the orchid-heads
so carefully,
your hands, so fragile, sure to lift
so gently, the fragile flower-stuff—
ah, ah, how was it

You never sent (in a dream)
the very form, the very scent,
not heavy, not sensuous,
but perilous—perilous—
of orchids, piled in a great sheath,
and folded underneath on a bright scroll,
some word:

"Flower sent to flower;
for white hands, the lesser white,
less lovely of flower-leaf,"

or

"Lover to lover, no kiss,
no touch, but forever and ever this."

## 在拜亚[①]

我在梦里应该想到
你会带来
某种可爱而危险的东西,
堆在大叶鞘里的兰花,
好像你在说(在梦里),
"我没有吻你
脖子上的青筋,
送你这个。"

为什么你的手
(从来没有握过我的手),
我能看见你的手
小心翼翼地
滑过兰花的花头,
你的手,那样的脆弱,一定能
轻轻地提起脆弱的花儿——
啊,啊,为什么

你从未送(在梦中)
那种样子,那种气味,
小巧,庄重,
但十分危险——十分危险——
兰花,堆在一个大叶鞘里,
下面卷起一个光亮的条幅,
上面写着几个字:
"送给花的花;
给手白净的,不那么白净的,

① 拜亚:古罗马旅游胜地。

花叶不那么可爱的，”

或者

“情人给情人，没有亲吻，
没有抚摸，永远如此。”

## Never More Will the Wind

Never more will the wind
cherish you again,
never more will the rain.

Never more
shall we find you bright
in the snow and wind.

The snow is melted,
the snow is gone,
and you are flown:

Like a bird out of our hand,
like a light out of our heart,
you are gone.

## 风不再

风不再
珍惜你，
雨不再。

风雪中
我们不再会看到
你的光亮。

雪融化了，
雪消失了，
而你飞走了：

宛如飞出手掌的鸟儿，
宛如心中泯灭的灯光，
你走了。

## Sheltered Garden

I have had enough.
I gasp for breath.

Every way ends, every road,
every foot-path leads at last
to the hill-crest—
then you retrace your steps,
or find the same slope on the other side,
precipitate.

I have had enough—
border-pinks, clove-pinks, wax-lilies,
herbs, sweet-cress.

O for some sharp swish of a branch—
there is no scent of resin
in this place,
no taste of bark, of coarse weeds,
aromatic, astringent—
only border on border of scented pinks.

Have you seen fruit under cover
that wanted light—
pears wadded in cloth,
protected from the frost,

melons, almost ripe,
smothered in straw?

Why not let the pears cling
to the empty branch?
All your coaxing will only make
a bitter fruit—
let them cling, ripen of themselves,
test their own worth,
nipped, shrivelled by the frost,
to fall at last but fair
with a russet coat.

Or the melon—
let it bleach yellow
in the winter light,
even tart to the taste—
it is better to taste of frost—
the exquisite frost—
than of wadding and of dead grass.

For this beauty,
beauty without strength,
chokes out life.
I want wind to break,
scatter these pink-stalks,
snap off their spiced heads,
fling them about with dead leaves—
spread the paths with twigs,
limbs broken off,
trail great pine branches,
hurled from some far wood
right across the melon-patch,
break pear and quince—
leave half-trees, torn, twisted

but showing the fight was valiant.

O to blot out this garden
to forget, to find a new beauty
in some terrible
wind-tortured place.

## 带棚子的花园

我已经受够了。
我喘不过气来。

每条道都到了尽头，每条路，
每条小径最终通向
山顶——
然后你回到原来的路径，
或者发现与另一边一样的斜坡路，
不期而遇。

我已经受够了——
路边的粉红花、康乃馨、蜡百合、
香草、甜水芹。

啊，一些树枝发出的响亮的沙沙声——
在这里
没有树脂的芬芳，
没有树皮的幽香，没有劣等杂草的清香，
没有芳香、没有酸涩——
只有一片片气味浓郁的粉红色。

叶子下面需要阳光的水果——
为防霜冻，
梨子用布包裹着，
快熟了的西瓜
用稻草捂得严严实实，

你可曾见过?

为什么不让梨挂在
光秃秃的枝条上?
你费尽心机地侍弄只能收获
一个苦果——
让它们挂着，自己成熟，
检验它们自己的价值，
因霜冻冻死、枯瘪，
最终掉落，但因裹着
黄褐色的外壳而亮丽。

或者西瓜——
让它在冬日的阳光下
变得淡黄，
即使味道变酸——
霜的味道——
奇妙无穷的霜——
要比棉布和枯草的味道好。

说到这个美，
柔弱的美，
快要窒息而死。
但愿风能打破这窒息，
驱散这些粉色的茎秆，
吹落它们香气扑鼻的花朵，
与枯叶一起随风飘荡——
路上撒满小树枝，
折断的枝条，
远处大松树的树枝
被风刮过西瓜地，
落在了小径上，
砸烂了梨子和柑橘——
树木被折断、撕裂、东倒西歪，
表明搏斗是何等的壮烈。

啊，遮蔽这个花园，
忘掉它，
到风肆虐的地方
寻找新的美。

# 威廉·卡洛斯·威廉姆斯
# (William Carlos Williams，1883—1963)

威廉·卡洛斯·威廉姆斯 1883 年生于新泽西州的拉瑟福德镇(Rutherford，New Jersey)。早年随母亲和哥哥到欧洲生活。1902 年考入宾夕法尼亚大学医学院，取得医学学位后，先后去了纽约的法国医院和儿童医院实习，随后又去了德国莱比锡大学(Leipzig)进修儿科医学。进修结束后他回到家乡行医，直至退休。

在宾夕法尼亚期间，威廉姆斯结识了艾兹拉·庞德和希尔达·杜利特尔，与他们的交往激发了他对诗歌创作的兴趣。然而，对他的诗风起决定性影响的是油画家查尔斯·德姆斯(Charles Demuth)。在德姆斯及其他画家朋友的影响下，威廉姆斯开始学习油画，他的油画作品充分展现出他卓越的绘画天赋，油画的影响也在他的诗歌作品中随处可见。在诗歌创作中，他极力反对以艾略特为代表的维多利亚诗风，坚持诗歌写作应贴近现实、贴近生活，并力求用美国本土语言写作。他的主要作品是长篇叙事诗《佩特森》(1963 年全部发表)。它以新泽西州一座小城的历史和社会生活为背景，反映了美国的文化和现代社会人们的精神风貌，堪称当代美国哲理诗的代表作品之一。

## The Great Figure

Among the rain
and lights
I saw the figure 5
in gold
on a red
firetruck
moving
tense
unheeded
to gong clangs
siren howls
and wheel rumbling
through the dark city.

## 巨大的数字

雨中
灯光里
我看见一个金色的
数字 5
在一辆红色的
消防车上
没人理会
急速
驶向锣鼓声大作
警声尖叫的地方
车轮轰鸣
穿过黑暗的城市。

## The Nightingales

My shoes as I lean
unlacing them
stand out upon
flat worsted flowers
under my feet.
Nimbly the shadows
of my fingers play
unlacing
over shoes and flowers.

## 夜莺

我身体前倾
解鞋带
脚下踩着
扁平的精纺毛料花。
鞋和花上

映照出
手指敏捷地
解带的影子。

## The Young Housewife

At ten A. M. the young housewife
moves about in neglige behind
the wooden walls of her husband's house.
I pass solitary in my car.

Then again she comes to the curb
to call the ice-man, fish man, and stands
shy, uncorseted, tucking in
stray ends of hair, and I compare her
to a fallen leaf.

The noiseless wheels of my car
rush with a cracking sound over
dried leaves as I bow and pass smiling.

## 年轻主妇

早晨 10 点年轻主妇
身穿轻薄晨衣在丈夫屋里
木墙后面来回走动。
我独自驱车走过。

随后她又来到路边
召唤卖冰人、渔夫，面带
羞涩，衣着松散，理着
蓬松的乱发，恰似
一片落叶。

我欠身微笑着驶过

悄无声息的车轮碾压着
干枯的叶子噼里啪啦作响。

## This Is Just to Say

I have eaten
the plums
that were in
the icebox

and which
you were probable
saving
for breakfast

Forgive me
they were delicious
so sweet
and so cold

## 便条

我吃了
放在
冰箱里的
梅子

你或许
留作
早餐
用

对不起
它们鲜美
甘甜
冰凉

## Poem

As the cat
climbed over
the top of

the jamcloset
first the right
forefoot

carefully
then the hind
stepped down

into the pit of
the empty
flowerpot

## 诗

当猫
爬过
壁橱

顶部
先是右
脚

小心翼翼
然后后腿
踩下

深深踏进
空花盆里

## To a Poor Old Woman

munching a plum on
the street a paper bag
of them in her hand

They taste good to her
They taste good
to her. They taste
good to her

You can see it by
the way she gives herself
to the one half
sucked out in her hand

Comforted
a solace of ripe plums
seeming to fill the air
They taste good to her

## 致可怜的老妪

在大街上她手里拿着
满满一纸袋子梅子
嘴里嚼着一颗

她喜欢梅子
她喜欢
梅子。她喜欢
梅子

这可以在她
手握吮吸了

一半的梅子的
专注神态中看出

安逸
成熟梅子的慰藉
似乎弥漫了天空
她喜欢梅子

## Proletarian Portrait

A big young bareheaded woman
in an apron

Her hair slicked back standing
on the street

One stockinged foot toeing
the sidewalk

Her shoes in her hand. Looking
intently into it

She pulls out the paper insole
to find the nail

That has been hurting her

## 无产者画像

一位年轻妇女，身躯庞大，系着围裙
没戴帽子

她的头发整齐地后梳
在街上站着

穿着长筒袜一只脚脚尖
踩着人行道

她的手里拿着鞋。全神贯注地
瞅着鞋内

她抽出纸垫
发现了那颗

扎脚的钉子

## Danse Russe

If when my wife is sleeping
and the baby and Kathleen
are sleeping
and the sun is a flame-white disc
in silken mists
above shining trees, —
if I in my north room
dance naked, grotesquely
before my mirror
waving my shirt round my head
and singing softly to myself:
"I am lonely, lonely,
I was born lonely,
I am best so!"
If I admire my arms, my face,
my shoulders, flanks, buttocks
against the yellow drawn shades, —

Who shall say I am not
the happy genius of my household?

## 俄罗斯舞曲

如果当妻子入睡
婴儿和凯瑟琳
入眠
太阳犹如燃烧的白色圆盘
悬挂在明亮的树顶，——
如纱的薄雾之中
如果我在北边房子的
镜子前
荒诞不经地赤身跳舞
头顶挥舞着衬衫
低声自唱：
“我孤独，孤独，
命里注定孤独，
如此甚好！”
在闭合的黄色百叶窗下
我欣赏我的双臂、容貌、
肩膀、侧部、臀部，——

谁说我不是
这所房子的快乐精灵？

# 传统诗派

20 世纪的美国诗歌，特别是 20 世纪中后期的诗歌绝大多数都摒弃了 19 世纪及其以前的传统形式和思想。然而依然有一些甘于寂寞、独守传统的诗人。他们借助人们熟悉的手法、形式和词汇书写经久不衰的主题，似乎要向世人证明传统形式在当下诗坛不仅魅力依旧，而且能够很好地提升诗歌的美蕴。这些诗人大都来自于文化底蕴较为深厚的美国东部或南部，有的在大学任教，包括约翰·霍兰德(John Hollander)、理查德·霍华德(Richard Howard)、詹姆斯·梅里尔(James Merrill)、威特· 宾纳(Witter Bynner)、埃莉诺·怀利(Elinor Wylie)等，其中最著名的有埃德温·阿林顿·罗宾逊(Edwin Arlington Robinson)、罗伯特·弗罗斯特(Robert Frost)罗伯特·洛威尔(Robert Lowell)。

# 埃德温·阿林顿·罗宾逊
# (Edwin Arlington Robinson，1869—1935)

埃德温·阿林顿·罗宾逊出生在缅因州的海德泰德(Head Tide)。出生后不久，他就随全家移居到了加丁纳(Gardiner)，在那里度过了27个春秋。加丁纳小镇不仅哺育了他幼小的生命，而且滋养了他年轻的心灵，成为他认识世界、观察人生的第一个窗口。镇上那些穷困潦倒、命运凄惨的普通居民后来成了他作品中的人物，出现在化名为"蒂尔伯里镇"的小镇中。

虽然出生在殷实之家，但在成长过程中，罗宾逊从未感受到家庭的温暖和幸福，也未感到自己是家庭里的一分子。家里三个男孩中他排行老三，很少得到父母的理解和帮助。他年幼时患上了严重的耳疾，时刻会伤及大脑，因此深感痛苦。他早年喜欢上了一位姑娘，但却被跟随父亲经商的大哥捷足先登。后来大哥生意破产，身患重病而亡，他再次向那位姑娘求爱，但遭到拒绝。二哥在家乡行医，由于不堪忍受工作的艰辛而酗酒吸毒，不久便命归黄泉。虽然罗宾逊上了哈佛大学，但两年后因母亲去世、父亲身体欠佳以及家道中落而辍学。生活中接二连三的打击对罗宾逊的心灵造成重大影响。

虽然家道中落、生活拮据，但罗宾逊一生笔耕不辍，撰写出版了多部诗集，塑造了一系列令人难以忘怀的失意者形象。罗宾逊的作品注重人物内心世界的探索，特别擅于描写内心世界与现实世界的矛盾。其诗歌富于哲理，饱含机智和讽刺，情调阴郁，格律工整，用字贴切，立意清新。主要诗集有《激流与昨夜》(*The Torrent and the Night Before*，1896)、《夜之子》(*The Children of the Night*，1897)、《克雷格船长》(*Captain Craig*)、《河下游的城镇》(*The Town Down the River*，1910)、《墨林》(*Merlin*，1927)、《朗斯洛》(*Lancelot*，1920)和《崔斯特瑞姆》(*Tristram*，1927)等。

## An Old Story

Strange that I did not know him then,
　That friend of mine!
I did not even show him then
　One friendly sign;

But cursed him for the ways he had
　To make me see

My envy of the praise he had
　For praising me.

I would have rid the earth of him
　Once, in my pride!...
I never knew the worth of him
　Until he died.

## 陈年往事

那位友人，
　我那时不认识他，难以置信!
甚至从没有
　向他表示过一点好意;

然而他却赞扬我
　让我意识到
自己对赞美的渴望
　他真可恶。

我曾经想要他从地球消失，
　多么傲慢! ……
他死后我才认识到了
　他对我的好处。

## Eros Turannos

She fears him, and will always ask
　What fated her to choose him;
She meets in his engaging mask
　All reasons to refuse him;
But what she meets and what she fears
Are less than are the downward years,
Drawn slowly to the foamless weirs
　Of age, were she to lose him.

Between a blurred sagacity
  That once had power to sound him,
And Love, that will not let him be
  The Judas that she found him,
Her pride assuages her almost,
As if it were alone the cost. —
He sees that he will not be lost,
  And waits and looks around him.

A sense of ocean and old trees
  Envelops and allures him;
Tradition, touching all he sees,
  Beguiles and reassures him;
And all her doubts of what he says
Are dimmed with what she knows of days—
Till even prejudice delays
  And fades, and she secures him.

The falling leaf inaugurates
  The reign of her confusion:
The pounding wave reverberates
  The dirge of her illusion:
And home, where passion lived and died,
Becomes a place where she can hide,
While all the town and harbor side
  Vibrate with her seclusion.

We tell you, tapping on our brows,
  The story as it should be, —
As if the story of a house
  Were told, or ever could be;
We'll have no kindly veil between
Her visions and those we have seen, —
As if we guessed what hers have been,

Or what they are or would be.

Meanwhile we do no harm; for they
That with a god have striven,
Not hearing much of what we say,
Take what the god has given;
Though like waves breaking it may be
Or like a changed familiar tree,
Or like a stairway to the sea
Where down the blind are driven.

## 爱罗斯·特兰诺斯①

她惧怕他，而且总在想
为什么一定选他；
被他的假情假意迷惑
完全有理由离弃；
然而逝水芳华，
岁月渐归平淡，
所遇所惧已微不足道，
怎能劳燕分飞。

朦朦胧胧的精明
让她曾对他做过试探；
爱慕，让她感觉
他不会成为犹大②，
洋洋得意削弱了她的戒备，
似乎仅此而已——
他决心做到清醒、冷静，
耐心、斟酌。

① 爱罗斯·特兰诺斯：希腊语“爱情，国王”，古希腊悲剧诗人索福克勒斯的悲剧《俄狄浦斯王》的标题。

② 犹大：背叛基督的门徒。

发现海洋和老树
　环绕着他，向他发出诱惑；
传统，触及到眼前一切，
　欺骗但消弭了他的顾忌；
比起往日的遭遇
她对他信誓旦旦的质疑已没有意义——
后来甚至成见搁置
　渐失，让他更加肆无忌惮。

飘零的树叶开启了
　困惑的统治：
汹涌的波浪回荡着
　虚幻的挽歌：
家，情感依存但已消失的地方，
成了她的藏身之处，
而整个小镇和港湾
　为她的隐逸而发颤。

我们手拍脑瓜，把故事
　原原本本讲给你听，——
好像讲的是一间
　屋子，或许可能是；
在她的期望和我们亲眼所见之间
大家从不委婉地遮掩，——
犹如猜想她的期望总是这样，
　或者就是可能这样。

然而我们并无恶意；因为
　在神的引导下他们
怀疑我们的故事，
　笃信神的旨意；
即使它如同破碎的浪花，
或者一颗葱郁不在的老树，
或者一架双目失明者被驱赶上的
　通向大海的阶梯。

## George Crabbe

Give him the darkest inch your shelf allows,
Hide him in lonely garrets, if you will,
But his hard, human pulse is throbbing still
With the sure strength that fearless truth endows.
In spite of all fine science disavows,
Of his plain excellence and stubborn skill
There yet remains what fashion cannot kill,
Though years have thinned the laurel from his brows.
Whether or not we read him, we can feel
From time to time the vigor of his name
Against us like a finger for the shame
And emptiness of what our souls reveal
In books that are as altars where we kneel
To consecrate the flicker, not the flame.

## 乔治·克拉布①

将他置于书架最不起眼的地方，
将他置于无人问津的阁楼，假如你乐意，
而他那坚强、人性的脉搏依然跳动
以不偏不倚的真理所赐予的自信力量。
即使华而不实的人文学科都不认可，
他那朴素无华、不可理喻的技巧
岁月可以消磨他头顶的桂冠，
但时尚无法扼杀他的功绩。
不管我们能否读懂他，
时常感受到他赫赫英名的活力
如手指般指着我们
书中臣服于摇曳的火光，
而非火焰

① 乔治·克拉布：(George Crabbe，1754—1832)英国诗人，其作品内容以现实主义手法叙述普通劳动人民生活为主。

思想所流露出的愚昧
和弊端。

## Mr. Flood's Party

Old Eben Flood, climbing alone one night
Over the hill between the town below
And the forsaken upland hermitage
That held as much as he should ever know
On earth again of home, paused warily.
The road was his with not a native near;
And Eben, having leisure, said aloud,
For no man else in Tilbury Town to hear:

"Well, Mr. Flood, we have the harvest moon
Again, and we may not have many more;
The bird is on the wing, the poet says,
And you and I have said it here before.
Drink to the bird." He raised up to the light
The jug that he had gone so far to fill,
And answered huskily: "Well, Mr. Flood,
Since you propose it, I believe I will."

Alone, as if enduring to the end
A valiant armor of scarred hopes outworn,
He stood there in the middle of the road
Like Roland's ghost winding a silent horn.
Below him, in the town among the trees,
Where friends of other days had honored him,
A phantom salutation of the dead
Rang thinly till old Eben's eyes were dim.

Then, as a mother lays her sleeping child
Down tenderly, fearing it may awake,
He set the jug down slowly at his feet

With trembling care, knowing that most things break;
And only when assured that on firm earth
It stood, as the uncertain lives of men
Assuredly did not, he paced away,
And with his hand extended paused again:

"Well, Mr. Flood, we have not met like this
In a long time; and many a change has come
To both of us, I fear, since last it was
We had a drop together. Welcome home!"
Convivially returning with himself,
Again he raised the jug up to the light;
And with an acquiescent quaver said:
"Well, Mr. Flood, if you insist, I might."

"Only a very little, Mr. Flood—
For auld lang syne. No more, sir; that will do."
So, for the time, apparently it did,
And Eben evidently thought so too;
For soon amid the silver loneliness
Of night he lifted up his voice and sang,
Secure, with only two moons listening,
Until the whole harmonious landscape rang—

"For auld lang syne." The weary throat gave out,
The last word wavered; and the song being done,
He raised again the jug regretfully
And shook his head, and was again alone.
There was not much that was ahead of him,
And there was nothing in the town below—
Where strangers would have shut the many doors
That many friends had opened long ago.

## 弗拉德先生的聚会

一天晚上，老依本·弗拉德独自爬上

山巅，下面一边是小镇
一边是位于高处的荒废修道院
修道院是他在世间
最熟悉之地，小心翼翼地止住了脚步。
路上行人稀少；
因蒂尔伯里镇没有一人会听，
于是依本悠闲自得地大声说：

“弗拉德先生，今日又是获月①，
我们这样的日子或许已经不多；
鸟儿飞翔，诗人说，
你我以前曾在此地说过。
为鸟儿干杯。”对着明月
他举起已经斟满的酒杯，
用沙哑的声音回应说：“好吧，弗拉德先生，
既然你这样说，那就喝吧。”

孑然一身，似乎要坚持到底，
一幅破烂不堪、希望俱损的勇者铠甲，
他站立在山路的中央
如同罗兰②吹着无声号角的鬼魂。
脚下，树木环绕的镇上，
往日待他为上宾的朋友，
死者一声幽灵般的致意轻轻传来，

---

① 获月：秋分前后的满月。

② 罗兰(Roland)：在意大利语中称为奥兰多(Orlando)，法国传说中的英雄。在中世纪早期，宫廷吟游诗人传唱他英勇的骑士行为。他们认为罗兰伯爵(Count Roland)是查理曼大帝(742—814 年)的侄子。传说中，罗兰是一个游侠，或者是查理曼大帝仪仗队中的一员。罗兰拥有力量、风度以及勇气。罗兰在与一位巨人的决斗中取得了一把神奇宝剑——圣剑迪朗达尔(Durandel)以及一个象牙号角，即罗兰的号角，这支号角发出的声音可以传出 20 英里(32 千米)。只有罗兰才能挥动迪朗达尔圣剑并吹响象牙号角。根据传说，公元 778 年，为掩护查理曼大帝从西班牙北部撤退，罗兰率领 2 万人担任后卫。查理曼大帝曾在西班牙与撒拉逊人奋战。叛徒冈隆(Ganelon)泄露了罗兰的位置——比利牛斯山脉(Pyrenees)的隆塞斯瓦利艾斯(Roncesvalles)隘道。于是罗兰被 40 万撒拉逊人伏击。虽然查理曼大帝就在附近，但是罗兰太骄傲而不愿吹响自己的号角求助，一直战斗到最后，只有 50 名骑士幸免于难。在这条浴血的隘道中，罗兰拼尽最后的力量吹响号角，但是查理曼大帝以为罗兰不过是在猎鹿而已。为了拯救他的骑士们，罗兰一直吹，直到他脖子上的血管爆裂为止。他踉跄着走到悬崖边，将自己的神剑扔到奔腾的溪流中，最后因伤势过重而死去。

泪水模糊了老依本的双眼。

接着，如同母亲轻轻地放下
熟睡的孩童，唯恐将他弄醒，
双手颤颤巍巍、小心翼翼地把酒杯放在
脚下，他知道大部分东西容易破碎；
确信杯子直立在坚硬的
地上——人类变幻莫测的生命
肯定做不到——他才慢慢走开，
手伸了出去又停了下来：

“唉，弗拉德先生，我们好久没有
这样相聚了；自从上次我们小酌之后，
我想，我们两人都有了
不少变化。欢迎回家！”
他欢快地自己回来，
再次对着月光举杯；
声音颤抖着默许说：
“好吧，弗拉德先生，既然你想，那我再来一杯。”

“就一小杯，弗拉德先生——
为了往日的美好时光。不能再喝了，先生；好了。”
是的，眼下，的确不能再喝了，
依本显然也这样想；
随后在孤寂的银色夜晚
他放声高歌，
毫无顾忌，只有两个月亮在听，
歌声在祥和的景色中回荡——

“为了往日的美好时光。”疲倦的嗓音越来越小，
最后一个歌词颤悠而出；歌唱完了，
他遗憾地重新端起酒杯
摇了摇头，又是独自一人。
他的时日屈指可数，
山下的小镇也无多少眷恋——

那里众多友人昔日敞开的大门
多半会被陌生人关上。

## The Mill

The miller's wife had waited long,
  The tea was cold, the fire was dead;
And there might yet be nothing wrong
  In how he went and what he said:
"There are no millers any more,"
  Was all that she had heard him say;
And he had lingered at the door
  So long that it seemed yesterday.

Sick with fear that had no form
  She knew that she was there at last;
And in the mill there was a warm
  And mealy fragrance of the past.
What else there was would only seem
  To say again what he had meant;
And what was hanging from a beam
  Would not have heeded where she went.

And if she thought it followed her,
  She may have reasoned in the dark
That one way of the few there were
  Would hide her and would leave no mark:
Black water, smooth above the weir
  Like starry velvet in the night,
Though ruffled once, would soon appear
  The same as ever to the sight.

## 磨坊

磨坊主的妻子等了很久,

　茶已凉，火已灭；
他昨天离开时的神态和说的话
　好像都很正常：
“再也没有磨坊主了，”
　她只听到他说了这一句；
随后好像在门口
　徘徊了许久。

心生无法言说的恐惧
　她不知不觉最终到了那里；
磨坊里弥漫着
　往日的温暖和粉香。
除此之外，唯一再次想说的
　就是他为什么要这样；
挂在横梁上的东西
　不会在意她去哪里。

假如她觉得它跟着她，
　她或许会在黑暗中推断
为数不多的一种办法
　是将她藏起不留任何痕迹：
黑色的水，在堰上平展光滑
　就像夜间闪闪发亮的天鹅绒，
虽然曾经满腔怨恨，但像往日一样
　很快就会出现在众人面前。

# 罗伯特·弗罗斯特
## (Robert Frost，1874—1963)

罗伯特·弗罗斯特于 1874 年生于旧金山的一个牧师家庭。他幼年丧父，家境贫寒，后随母亲到马萨诸塞州劳伦斯镇的祖父家。1895 年弗罗斯特结婚，其后两年，与妻子帮助母亲管理一所私立学校。1897 年弗罗斯特进入哈佛大学学习，但因肺病中途辍学。祖父为他在新罕布什尔买了一个农场。1900 年弗罗斯特举家迁往自己的农场，但因经营不善农场不久便倒闭。

弗罗斯特从 16 岁开始诗歌创作，20 岁时发表第一首诗歌《我的蝴蝶》(*My Butterfly*，1894)；诗歌发表后反响平淡。

1912 年，弗罗斯特离开美国去了英国伦敦，开始了他的艺术流浪生活。这也是他诗歌创作的转折点。在伦敦期间，弗罗斯特结识了埃兹拉·庞德、T. S. 艾略特、T. E. 休姆等诗人。在他们的鼎力帮助下，伦敦大卫·华纳公司答应出版他的诗集。1913 年，第一本诗集《一个男孩的愿望》(*A Boy's Will*)出版，虽然并没有引起评论界的广泛关注，但却得到了庞德的高度评价；1914 年第二本诗集《波士顿以北》(*North of Boston*)出版后，在英国产生轰动。英国评论界的热情赞扬引起大洋彼岸出版界的重视，三家出版公司争相向他发来约稿函。1915 年弗罗斯特一家返回美国新罕布什尔农场。当时他的两本诗集已在纽约出版，并受到美国读者的热烈欢迎。

弗罗斯特一生笔耕不辍，共出版了十多部诗集。除上面提到的两部外，著名的诗集还有《西去的溪流》(*West-Running Brook*，1928)、《有一片牧场》(*A Further Range*，1936)、《见证树》(*A Witness Tree*，1942)、《理智的假面具》(*Masque of Reason*，1945)、《做国王》(*Be King*，1951)、《林间空地》(*In the Clearing*，1962)等。

弗罗斯特的诗歌清新流畅、朴素自然；他的诗“始于欢乐，终于智慧”，受到普通读者的喜爱。他一生中曾四次荣获普利策文学奖，被哈佛大学等多所高等学校聘为“住校诗人”；美国参议院曾经两次向他表示祝贺，这在美国诗坛极为罕见；艾森豪威尔总统和肯尼迪总统先后向他表达敬意。在总统就职仪式上，肯尼迪邀请他朗诵诗歌，后来又请他出任美国驻苏联的友好大使。可以毫不夸张地说，弗罗斯特堪称二十世纪美国诗坛独领风骚的明星诗人。然而就诗歌本身说来，弗罗斯特的伟大贡献不只是这些荣誉，而是他在继承英语诗歌传统的基础上，创造性地利用日常题材，用简练的语言以描写新英格兰的自然风光或风俗人情，不知不觉地进入哲理的境界，最后达到警句似的结论，给人以不可言喻的欢乐的阅读体验。

## Reluctance

Out through the fields and the woods
　　And over the walls I have wended;
I have climbed the hills of view
　　And looked at the world, and descended;
I have come by the highway home,
　　And lo, it is ended.

The leaves are all dead on the ground,
　　Save those that the oak is keeping
To ravel them one by one
　　And let them go scraping and creeping
Out over the crusted snow,
　　When others are sleeping.

And the dead leaves lie huddled and still,
　　No longer blown hither and thither;
The last lone aster is gone;
　　The flowers of the witch hazel wither;
The heart is still aching to seek,
　　But the feet question 'Whither?'

Ah, when to the heart of man
　　Was it ever less than a treason
To go with the drift of things,
　　To yield with a grace to reason,
And bow and accept the end
　　Of a love or a season?

## 不乐意

越过田野，穿过树林
　　跨过围墙；

登上风景如画的山丘
　　俯视尘世，顺道而下；
沿着公路回家，
　　哎，结束了。

地上的叶子均已枯死，
　　四周沉寂
只有橡树叶子
　　一片片交织在一起
在冰封的雪地上
　　嘎吱、嘎吱地爬行。

枯叶蜷缩在一起，一动不动，
　　再不会被风吹得四处乱跑；
最后一株紫菀业已枯萎；
　　神奇的榛树花已经凋零；
心依旧在苦苦地追寻，
　　而脚却问“凋零?”

啊，随物而去，
　　体面地面对现实，
低头接受一种爱
　　或一个季节的结局
还有什么比背叛人心
　　更令人痛苦?

## Storm Fear

When the wind works against us in the dark,
And pelts with snow
The lowest chamber window on the east,
And whispers with a sort of stifled bark,
The beast,
‘Come out! Come out!’—
It costs no inward struggle not to go,

Ah, no!
I count our strength,
Two and a child,
Those of us not asleep subdued to mark
How the cold creeps as the fire dies at length, —
How drifts are piled,
Dooryard and road ungraded,
Till even the comforting barn grows far away
And my heart owns a doubt
Whether 'tis in us to arise with day
And save ourselves unaided.

## 暴风带来的恐惧

黑暗中暴风迎面而来，
裹挟着雪撞击
底层房间的东窗，
发出沉闷的吼声，
这只野兽，
“出来！出来！”——
显而易见不能出去，
啊，不！
看看我们的实力，
两个大人，一个小孩，
无法入睡，默默瞧着
炉火燃尽，寒气袭来，——
漂浮物在门口
和劣等路上堆积，
最后甚至给人慰藉的谷仓
也离我们远去
于是心里在想
明日我们是否还会有人醒来
不用帮助救救我们自己。

## Dust of Snow

The way a crow
Shook down on me
The dust of snow
From a hemlock tree
Has given my heart
A change of mood
And saved some part
Of a day I had rued.

## 雪尘

铁杉树上
一只乌鸦
把雪尘抖落
在我身上
引起我
情绪的变化
一天的懊恼
随抛之心外。

## Neither out Far Nor in Deep

The people along the sand
All turn and look one way.
They turn their back on the land.
They look at the sea all day.

As long as it takes to pass
A ship keeps raising its hull;
The wetter ground like glass
Reflects a standing gull.

The land may vary more;
But wherever the truth may be—
The water comes ashore,
And the people look at the sea.

They cannot look out far.
They cannot look in deep.
But when was that ever a bar
To any watch they keep?

## 不远也不深

站在沙边的人
集体转身目光一致。
他们背向陆地。
整日面朝大海。

来往船舶
荡起行进的船体;
如镜湿地
倒映站立的海鸥。

陆地纵有千态万状;
而真相会在哪里——
海水冲到岸上,
人们却眺望大海。

他们瞧不远。
他们望不深。
但是那个限制他们持续
眺望的障碍始于何时?

## For Once, Then, Something

Others taunt me with having knelt at well-curbs

Always wrong to the light, so never seeing
Deeper down in the well than where the water
Gives me back in a shining surface picture
Me myself in the summer heaven, godlike,
Looking out of a wreath of fern and cloud puffs.
Once, when trying with chin against a well-curb,
I discerned, as I thought, beyond the picture,
Through the picture, a something white, uncertain,
Something more of the depths—and then I lost it.
Water came to rebuke the too clear water.
One drop fell from a fern, and lo, a ripple
Shook whatever it was lay there at bottom,
Blurred it, blotted it out. What was that whiteness?
Truth? A pebble of quartz? For once, then, something.

## 曾经、然后、某物

旁人讥笑我跪在井沿
总是背向光，所以永远看不到
井的深处，只有闪亮的水面
出现一张我自己的倒影
夏日的天空，圣神庄严，
从蕨草和云朵的花环里探出头。
曾经，试着用下巴抵着井沿，
我看到(我以为)，透过倒影、
在倒影的更深处有种白色、模糊的东西，
——接着消失了。
蕨草上掉下一水滴，看哪，横卧在井底的
那个不知何物的东西因涟漪而晃动、
模糊、遮蔽。那白色是什么?
真相? 石英石? 曾经、然后、某物。

## Come In

As I came to the edge of the woods,

Thrush music—hark!
Now if it was dusk outside,
Inside it was dark.

Too dark in the woods for a bird
By sleight of wing
To better its perch for the night,
Though it still could sing.

The last of the light of the sun
That had died in the west
Still lived for one song more
In a thrush's breast.

Far in the pillared dark
Thrush music went—
Almost like a call to come in
To the dark and lament.

But no, I was out for stars:
I would not come in.
I meant not even if asked,
And I hadn't been.

## 进来

我来到林边，
画眉在叫——听！
林外薄暮，
林内昏暗。

树林漆黑鸟儿
虽有灵巧的翅膀
也难以栖身在理想的过夜之木，
但它依旧鸣叫。

太阳的余晖
已在西边的天空消失
还在等待画眉
胸中的再次鸣叫。

远方柱状的黑处
传来画眉的叫声——
犹如进入黑暗
和哀叹的呼唤。

但不，我出来是观赏群星：
我是说即使请我，
我也不进去。
但没人请过。

## Away

Now I out walking
The world desert,
And my shoe and my stocking
Do me no hurt.

I leave behind
Good friends in town,
Let them get well-wined
And go lie down.

Don't think I leave
For the outer dark
Like Adam and Eve
Put out of the Park.

Forget the myth.
There is no one I

Am put out with
Or put out by.

Unless I'm wrong
I but obey
The urge of a song:
I'm—bound—away!

And I may return
If dissatisfied
With what I learn
From having died.

## 离开

我外出步行
世界的沙漠，
脚上的鞋和袜子
舒适称心。

我将好友
留在镇上
让他们吃饱喝足
安然入睡。

不要以为我前往
那外界的黑暗
好像亚当和夏娃
被逐出伊甸园。

别提那虚构的故事。
它们毫无例外令我
无法忍受
或者让我漠然处之。

除非我错了
否则只顺从
一首歌里的规劝之词：
我——注定——要离开！

但死后
我如果感觉
不爽快
或许我会回来。

## Home Burial

He saw her from the bottom of the stairs
Before she saw him. She was starting down,
Looking back over her shoulder at some fear.
She took a doubtful step and then undid it
To raise herself and look again. He spoke
Advancing toward her: 'What is it you see
From up there always—for I want to know.'
She turned and sank upon her skirts at that,
And her face changed from terrified to dull.
He said to gain time: 'What is it you see,'
Mounting until she cowered under him.
'I will find out now—you must tell me, dear.'
She, in her place, refused him any help
With the least stiffening of her neck and silence.
She let him look, sure that he wouldn't see,
Blind creature; and awhile he didn't see.
But at last he murmured, 'Oh,' and again, 'Oh.'

'What is it—what?' she said.

'Just that I see.'

'You don't,' she challenged. 'Tell me what it is.'

'The wonder is I didn't see at once.
I never noticed it from here before.
I must be wonted to it—that's the reason.
The little graveyard where my people are!
So small the window frames the whole of it.
Not so much larger than a bedroom, is it?
There are three stones of slate and one of marble,
Broad-shouldered little slabs there in the sunlight
On the sidehill. We haven't to mind those.
But I understand: it is not the stones,
But the child's mound—'

'Don't, don't, don't, don't,' she cried.

She withdrew shrinking from beneath his arm
That rested on the banister, and slid downstairs,
And turned on him with such a daunting look;
He said twice over before he knew himself:
'Can't a man speak of his own child he's lost?'

'Not you! Oh, where's my hat? Oh, I don't need it!
I must get out of here. I must get air.
I don't know rightly whether any man can.'

'Amy! Don't go to someone else this time.
Listen to me. I won't come down the stairs.'
He sat and fixed his chin between his fists.
'There's something I should like to ask you, dear.'

'You don't know how to ask it.'

'Help me, then.'

Her fingers moved the latch for all reply.

'My words are nearly always an offense.
I don't know how to speak of anything
So as to please you. But I might be taught
I should suppose. I can't say I see how.
A man must partly give up being a man
With women-folk. We could have some arrangement
By which I'd bind myself to keep hands off
Anything special you're a-mind to name.
Though I don't like such things 'twixt those that love.
Two that don't love can't live together without them.
But two that do can't live together with them.'
She moved the latch a little. 'Don't—don't go.
Don't carry it to someone else this time.
Tell me about it if it's something human.
Let me into your grief. I'm not so much
Unlike other folks as your standing there
Apart would make me out. Give me my chance.
I do think, though, you overdo it a little.
What was it brought you up to think it the thing
To take your mother-loss of a first child
So inconsolably—in the face of love.
You'd think his memory might be satisfied—'

'There you go sneering now!'

'I'm not, I'm not!
You make me angry. I'll come down to you.
God, what a woman! And it's come to this,
A man can't speak of his own child that's dead.'

'You can't because you don't know how to speak.
If you had any feelings, you that dug
With your own hand—how could you? —his little grave;
I saw you from that very window there,

Making the gravel leap and leap in air,
Leap up, like that, like that, and land so lightly
And roll back down the mound beside the hole.
I thought, who is that man? I didn't know you.
And I crept down the stairs and up the stairs
To look again, and still your spade kept lifting.
Then you came in. I heard your rumbling voice
Out in the kitchen, and I don't know why,
But I went near to see with my own eyes.
You could sit there with the stains on your shoes
Of the fresh earth from your own baby's grave
And talk about your everyday concerns.
You had stood the spade up against the wall
Outside there in the entry, for I saw it.'

'I shall laugh the worst laugh I ever laughed.
I'm cursed. God, if I don't believe I'm cursed.'

'I can repeat the very words you were saying:
Three foggy mornings and one rainy day
Will rot the best birch fence a man can build.
Think of it, talk like that at such a time!
What had how long it takes a birch to rot
To do with what was in the darkened parlor?
You couldn't care! The nearest friends can go
With anyone to death, comes so far short
They might as well not try to go at all.
No, from the time when one is sick to death,
One is alone, and he dies more alone.
Friends make pretense of following to the grave,
But before one is in it, their minds are turned
And making the best of their way back to life
And living people, and things they understand.
But the world's evil. I won't have grief so
If I can change it. Oh, I won't, I won't!'

'There, you have said it all and you feel better.
You won't go now. You're crying. Close the door.
The heart's gone out of it: why keep it up.
Amy! There's someone coming down the road!'

'You—oh, you think the talk is all. I must go—
Somewhere out of this house. How can I make you—'

'If—you—do!' She was opening the door wider.
'Where do you mean to go? First tell me that.
I'll follow and bring you back by force. I will! —'

## 家葬

他在楼梯下望着她
她看见了，向楼下走去，
心怀恐惧不时回头瞅瞅。
迟疑地迈开腿接着又收了回去
身体站直又看了看。
他举步上前说："你一直待在上边
究竟看到了什么？——给我说说。"
闻罢此言她转过身去裙子铺地一屁股坐了下去，
表情由恐惧转为呆滞。
他催促到："你到底看到了什么？"
他身体前倾趴伏在她缩成一团的身体之上。
"我就想知道——请告诉我，亲爱的。"
她卷曲在那儿一声没吭，
只伸了伸脖子。
让他去找，他绝对不会看见，
视而不见的家伙；他马上明白了。
于是喃喃自语地说，"天啊，""天啊。"

"是什么——什么？"她问。

“就是我看到的那个。”

“不对，”她故意说。“说说是什么。”

“奇怪的是我没马上明白。
第一次站在这里看。
我肯定熟视无睹——这就是问题所在。
埋葬亲人的小墓地！
窗框太小了看不清整个墓地！
比一间卧室大不了多少，对吧?
阳光下的山坡上，
摆放着三块石片、一块大理石，
和宽厚的小石板。我们没必要为那些而苦恼。
但我知道：不是那些石头，
而是小孩的坟头——”

“不，不，不，不，”她大声喊。

她向后退了两步，身体在他搁在楼梯扶手的
胳膊下缩了缩，然后快步走下楼梯，
神情愠怒地看着他；
他冷不丁连说两遍：
“难道就不能提起自己失去的孩子吗?”

“你不能！——啊，我的帽子呢? 见鬼，不要了！
我得出去。呼吸一下新鲜空气。——
我不知道是否有人会说。”
“艾米！眼下别离我而去。
听我说。我不会下去。”
他坐着，双手托着下巴。
“想问你件事，亲爱的。”

“你不知道怎样开口。”
“那你教教我吧。”

她一声不吭，只用手指拨了拨门闩。

“我的话好像总让你讨厌。
不知道怎样说才能
让你开心。但你可以教教我，
我想。不能说我知道怎样。
在女人面前男人必须放下点
尊严。我们可以有个约定
这样我就不会去碰
你不想提到的任何特殊事情。
虽然我并不喜欢爱人之间这样行事。
不爱的人缺了这些无法生活在一起。
相爱的人有了这些却无法相守。”
她轻轻地拨动了下门闩。“别——别走。
眼下别让外人看出来。
如果人的天性如此就告诉我。
让我分担你的痛苦。你站在那里
离我远远的，好像我就是个外人。
给我机会。
虽然在我看来你的确有点过分。
到底是什么让你想起它，那件
令你这位失去第一个孩子的母亲
如此惆怅的事——在爱面前。
你认为只有这样才是对他的思念——”

“你在嘲笑我！”
“没有，没有！
你令我生气。我下去。
天啊，女人啦！咋会这样，
不许男人说他自己死去的小孩。”

“就是不许，因为你根本不懂怎样说。
如果你也有感情，你能
亲手给他挖墓；怎么能？
我从那个窗口看见你在挖，

铲起砂土，抛向空中，
扬起来，就那样，就那样，土轻轻地落下
顺着坑边的土堆滚回来。
我想，那是谁呀？没想到是你。
我走下楼梯，又爬了上去
再次看了看，你还在挥舞铁锹。
后来你回来了。你站在厨房外

喃喃细语，我不明白，
走过去亲眼看了看。
你竟然坐在那儿，鞋上粘着泥土
那是你自己孩子坟头的新土，
说你的家常琐事。
你把铁锹竖着靠在墙上
就在门外，我看见了。"

"我想笑，笑出一辈子最苦的笑。
我该死！天啊，我真该死。"

"我记得你说过的那些话：
三个多雾的清晨再加一个雨天
就能让一个人搭起的最结实的桦木栅栏腐烂。
想一想，在这个时候怎能那样说！
桦树多长时间腐烂与
昏暗的客厅里的东西又有何干？
你不会在意！亲密无间的朋友能
和任何人一块去死，但到目前为止都不会再有，
他们甚至从来没想过要那样。
没错，从病得快要死的时候起，
他就孤单，死的时候更孤单。
朋友们假惺惺地把他送到墓地，
可他尚未入土，他们的心思就变了，
想着赶快回归生活，
回到活人中间，干他们熟悉的事情。
世事险恶。我们无能为力，

只能伤心。是的，伤心，伤心！”

“好啦，你说完了吧，感受好点吧。
别走了。你正在哭。把门关上。
已经忘了：咋还去想？
艾米！路上有人过来了！”

“你——哎，你以为说说就完了。我一定得走——
离开这所房子。怎么才能让你——”

“你走试试！”她把门敞开。
“你要到哪儿去？告诉我。
我会过去把你拽回来，说到做到！——”

# 芝加哥诗派

1921年1月，哈里特·门罗(Harriet Monroe，1861—1936年)在芝加哥创办了旨在推动诗歌创新的《诗刊》。该杂志的创刊犹如三月的春风立刻给沉寂多年的美国诗坛带来了活力。以芝加哥为中心，反对传统的诗歌写作技巧、题材、目的的“新”诗运动瞬间在美国全境兴起。与统治东部海岸的主流文坛不同，这些“新”诗人以戏剧性的现实主义手法，主张以平民化的语言反映平民百姓的日常生活中的真情实感，其代表人物有卡尔·桑德堡、埃德加·李·马斯特斯和维切尔·林赛。

# 卡尔·桑德堡
## (Carl Sandburg，1878—1967)

卡尔·桑德堡 1887 年出生于伊利诺伊州的盖尔斯堡(Galesburg)一个瑞典移民家庭。因家境贫寒，幼年的桑德堡并没有接受过正规的学校教育。为了减轻家里的负担，他常年四处漂泊，以打工为生，先后为别人擦过皮鞋、当过铁路工人和农场工人。1898 年美西战争爆发后，他随美国伊利诺斯第 6 步兵团奔赴战场。

战争结束以后，桑德堡进入家乡伦巴学院(Lombard College)学习。1902 年，桑德堡离开了伦巴学院，又开始了四处漂泊、以打工求生的生活。1907 年，他流落到密尔沃基(Milwaukee)，靠给几家报纸撰写广告和报道为生，并在那里结婚生子。1912 年，桑德堡去了芝加哥，在《芝加哥日报》做记者，工作之余开始撰写诗歌。

1914，桑德堡将撰写完的诗歌整理之后邮寄给《诗刊》(*Poetry*)的主编哈里特·门罗，总共九首，包括《芝加哥》。身为诗人的门罗仔细读了桑德堡寄来的诗后立刻被诗中所展露出的才华震惊。她感觉到桑德堡不久就会成为普通民众喜爱的惠特曼式的民主诗人。他那粗犷的风格和惠特曼式的呐喊将会给死气沉沉、温文尔雅的传统诗坛带来生气。

20 世纪 20 至 30 年代，桑德堡利用《芝加哥日报》记者的身份，在采访过程中，接触了各个阶层的普通民众，了解熟悉他们的日常生活，并到全国各地开展演讲、朗诵自己最新创作的诗歌作品。这一时期，桑德堡先后出版了几本诗集，包括赞美农场生活的《剥玉米的人》(*Cornhuskers*，1918)、歌颂工人的《烟与钢》(*Smoke and Steel*，1920)和在大萧条时期激励民众的《人民，是的》(*The People*，*Yes*，1936)等。同时，桑德堡开始撰写亚伯拉汗·林肯的传记。传记分为上下两个部分：《亚伯拉罕·林肯：草原年代》(*Abraham Lincoln：The Prairie Years*，1926)和《亚伯拉罕·林肯：战争年代》(*Abraham Lincoln：The War Years*，1939)。传记出版后获得巨大成功，不仅为他赢得了“林肯专家”的美誉，而且还荣获了 1940 年的普利策历史奖。

第二次世界大战结束后，桑德堡全家搬迁到了北卡罗来纳州福莱特洛克市附近的一个农场。1950 年，桑德堡的《诗歌全集》(*Complete Poems*)出版，并获得当年的普利策诗歌奖。1963 年，他的最后一部诗集《蜜与盐》(*Honey and Salt*)出版。桑德堡于 1967 年 7 月去世。

桑德堡的诗歌继承了 19 世纪美国著名诗人沃尔特·惠特曼的诗风。出生于普通劳动大众家庭，桑德堡对生活在社会底层人民的生活谙熟于心，了解他们的忧愁和欢乐。他的诗歌主题自始至终贴近普通民众，特别是芝加哥地区民众的思想情感和生活愿望；诗歌形式自由多变，语言通俗直白，“为朴素的人民写朴素的诗”是他诗歌创作永远追求的目标。

## The Plowboy

After the last red sunset glimmer,
Black on the line of a low hill rise,
Formed into moving shadows, I saw
A plowboy and two horses lined against the gray,
Plowing in the dusk the last furrow.
The turf had a gleam of brown,
And smell of soil was in the air,
And, cool and moist, a haze of April.

I shall remember you long,
Plowboy and horses against the sky in shadow.
I shall remember you and the picture
You made for me,
Turning the turf in the dusk
And haze of an April gloaming.

## 耕童

夕阳散发出最后一抹余晖，
低矮的山岭上升起黑色的夜幕，
黄昏里移动着耕童
和两匹马的影子，
翻起最后的犁沟。
草皮泛起褐色的光，
空气中弥漫着泥土的气息，
还有，四月清凉、潮湿的薄雾。

我将永远不会忘记你，
夜幕下的耕童和马匹的影子。
记住你和你呈现给
我的画面，
日落时分翻动草皮
还有四月的夕暮薄雾。

## Noon Hour

She sits in the dust at the walls
        And makes cigars,
Bending at the bench
With fingers wage-anxious,
Changing her sweat for the day's pay.

Now the noon hour has come,
And she leans with her bare arms
On the window-sill over the river,
Leans and feels at her throat
Cool-moving things out of the free open ways:

At her throat and eyes and nostrils
The touch and the blowing cool
Of great free ways beyond the walls.

## 午间休息

坐在布满灰尘的墙根
她俯身在凳子上
        做烟卷，
为了生计手指
辛勤地赚取每日的酬劳。

午间休息时间到了，
她裸露的双臂倚靠在
河边屋子的窗台，
喉咙感觉到自由宽阔的
水道飘过来的凉爽物：

墙外自由宽阔的水道
吹来的凉爽触动到
她的喉咙、眼睛和鼻孔。

# 埃德加 · 李 · 马斯特斯
# (Edgar Lee Masters，1868—1950)

埃德加·李·马斯特斯 1868 年出生于堪萨斯州的加内特市(Garnett，Kansas)。1880 年全家迁到了祖父位于伊利诺伊州刘易斯镇的农场。在那里马斯特斯读完了中学，随后进入一所专科学校学习，但一年之后便离开学校，去了他父亲的律师事务所学习法律。在父亲的精心指导下，经过不懈努力他终于成了芝加哥的著名律师。1898 年马斯特斯结婚，但婚后生活并不愉快。

身为律师，马斯特斯却特别钟情于文学创作。早在中学时期，他就开始诗歌创作。1915 年，他已出版了四本诗集，还有七部剧本和一本随笔，但没有一本引起文学界的广泛关注。后来，通过阅读希腊诗歌，马斯特斯受到启发，希腊诗集中的简短隽语和墓志铭式的诗文，使他获得了灵感，灵感也来自伊利诺伊州小城居民未能充分享受人生而产生的沉痛感；此外他还从别人——特别是桑德堡写自由诗的经验中，获得灵感。[①]此后马斯特斯的诗歌创作发生了脱胎换骨的变化。他仿照古希腊悼亡诗的形式，以他在律师工作中接触的各种人士、各种隐私为主要内容，创作了 214 首墓志铭诗，于 1915 年汇集出版，取名《匙河集》。诗集出版后获得巨大成功。

《匙河集》之后，马斯特斯先后又出版了几本诗集，如《大山谷》(*The Great Valley*，1916)、《朝向海湾》(*Toward the Gulf*，1918)、《饥饿的岩石》(*Starved Rock*，1919)、《公海》(*The Open Sea*，1921)等。虽然这些诗集的题材依然来自伊利诺伊大草原，但都没有突破《匙河集》的成就。

除了诗歌之外，马斯特斯还创作了一些小说和传记。小说题材基本都是他在伊利诺伊的成长故事，如《米奇·米勒 》(*Mitch Miller*，1920)、《斯基特斯·科比》(*Skeeters Kirby*，1923)和《吉特·奥布莱恩》(*Kit O'Brien*，1927)；传记作品有《维切尔·林赛：一位美国诗人》(*Vachel Lindsay：A Poet in America*，1935)、《惠特曼》(*Whitman*，1937)、《林肯：这个人》(*Lincoln：The Man*，1931)和《马克·吐温：肖像》(*Mark Twain：A Portrait*，1938)等。

马斯特斯先后获得了一系列文学大奖：美国诗歌协会奖、雪莱纪念奖、美国诗人学会奖。1950 年马斯特斯在宾夕法尼亚州去世，遗体安葬在伊利诺伊州的奥克兰公墓。

---

① 马库斯·坎利夫：《美国文学》，方杰译，中国对外翻译出版公司，1985，第 242 页。

## Doc Hill

I went up and down the streets
Here and there by day and night,
Through all hours of the night caring for the poor who are sick.
Do you know why?
My wife hated me, my son went to the dogs.
And I turned to the people and poured out my love to them.
Sweet it was to see the crowds about the lawn on the day of my funeral,
And hear them murmur their love and sorrow.
But oh, dear God, my soul trembled, scarcely able
To hold to the railing of the new life
When I saw Em Stanton behind the oak tree
At the grave,
Hiding herself, and her grief.

## 多克·希尔

无论白天还是黑夜
我来往于街头巷尾，
通宵达旦照料生病的穷人。
为何这般?
妻子讨厌，儿子心里只有狗。
于是投身民众将爱撒向他们。
喜欢看到我死后埋葬时人们聚集在草坪，
念叨我对他们的爱，低声诉说他们的哀思。
可是，天啊！猛然发现艾姆·斯坦顿在墓旁的
橡树后，
藏匿着，掩饰着心中的悲痛，
我的心灵开始颤抖，
对新生活的抱怨一扫而尽。

## Abel Melveny

I bought every kind of machine that's known—

Grinders, shellers, planters, mowers,
Mills and rakes and ploughs and threshers—
And all of them stood in the rain and sun,
Getting rusted, warped and battered,
For I had no sheds to store them in,
And no use for most of them.
And toward the last, when I thought it over,
There by my window, growing clearer
About myself, and my pulse slowed down,
And looked at one of the mills I bought—
Which I didn't have the slightest need of,
As things turned out, and I never ran—
A fine machine, once brightly vanished,
And eager to do its work
Now with its paint washed off—
I saw myself as a good machine
That life had never used.

## 艾贝尔·麦尔维尼

我购买了已知的各种机械——
研磨机、脱壳机、播种机、割草机、
磨面机、耙子、犁、打谷机——
因没有存放的棚舍，
而且大多数没有用处，
长期雨淋日晒，
已经生锈、变形、破损。
后来，仔细思量了一下，
就在窗户旁，重新认识了自己，
心情平静了下来，
瞅了瞅买的其中一台磨面机——
结果证明毫无必要，
从来没有用过——
一台好机器，曾经很想干活，
但崭新锃亮就被遗弃

如今漆皮脱落——
我就是一台被生活
遗弃的好机器。

## William Jones

ONCE in a while a curious weed unknown to me,
Needing a name from my books;
Once in a while a letter from Yeomans.
Out of the mussel-shells gathered along the shore
Sometimes a pearl with a glint like meadow rue:
Then betimes a letter from Tyndall in England,
Stamped with the stamp of Spoon River.
I, lover of Nature, beloved for my love of her,
Held such converse afar with the great
Who knew her better than I.
Oh, there is neither lesser nor greater,
Save as we make her greater and win from her keener delight.
With shells from the river cover me, cover me.
I lived in wonder, worshipping earth and heaven.
I have passed on the march eternal of endless life.

## 威廉·琼斯

偶见奇花异草,
需查书籍才知其名;
有时致函请教约曼斯①。
海边堆集的蚌壳
不时藏有一颗唐松草般闪亮的珍珠:
偶然间收到英格兰丁铎尔②的来信,
信封上贴着匙河镇邮票。
我,大自然的恋人,因钟情于她而受宠,

---

① 约曼斯:伦敦著名的花商。
② 丁铎尔:(John Tyndall,1820—1893)英国物理学家。

与比我更了解她的大师
隔空交流。
哦，没有卑微也没有尊贵，
只有让她变的更加伟大而且从她的巨大的喜悦中受益。
用河里的贝壳盖住我，盖住我。
我一生好奇尚异，尊天敬地。
旅程中我得到了无尽生命的永恒。

# 维切尔·林赛
# (Vachel Lindsay，1879—1931)

林赛 1879 年出生于伊利诺伊州的斯普林菲尔德(Springfield)。父亲是乡间医生，母亲酷爱艺术，两人信奉基督教，是“福音派”的忠实信徒。父母希望林赛能子承父业，于是送他到俄亥俄州的希拉姆学院(Hiram College)学习医学，但后来林赛放弃了医学，转而学习艺术。先后就读于芝加哥艺术学院和纽约艺术学院。在大学期间，林赛没有展露出众的才华，他的志向高远，一心要成为“青年会救世军的伟大歌手；要既有书卷气概，又有男子风度；要做 1905 年芝加哥最伟大的人物”①。但他毕业后相当长一段时间的生活却不尽人意，所画的插图无人问津，所作的诗没人愿意出版。为了生计，时常被迫外出干一些体力活。后来他决定做个“流浪诗人”，漫游美国，描写普通大众的日常生活，述说他们的欢乐与忧愁，用诗歌“换取面包”。经过多年的艰苦努力，著名的美国现代诗刊物《诗刊》1913 年刊登了他的一首诗《威廉·布思将军进天堂》(*General William Booth Enters into Heaven*)。诗歌发表后立刻引起广泛关注，林赛名声大振，请他吟唱或诵读诗歌的邀请纷至沓来。1914 年《刚果河》(*The Congo*)和《圣菲路》(*The Santa Fe Trail*)以及 1917 年《中国夜莺及其他》的出版为林赛在美国诗坛赢得了“现代游吟诗人”的美名；然而随后他的诗歌创作便开始走下坡路。1931 年，由于理想和信念的破灭以及个人生活和身体诸方面的原因，林赛在寓舍里以极端的方式结束了年仅 52 岁的生命。

受父母福音派基督教思想影响，林赛一生坚持走平民化道路。他的诗歌创作在积极宣扬福音派教义的基础上，坚持贴近人民大众的实际生活，反映社会底层人民的民主需求，深受美国普通民众的喜爱。

林赛的诗歌继承发扬了惠特曼的传统：通俗易懂、自由、奔放、口语化。在诗歌形式上，他有意识借鉴民歌和爵士乐元素，特别是黑人圣歌、民谣以及民族管乐，创立了一种节奏感强、特别适合朗诵吟唱的四重音格律诗行。

## Abraham Lincoln Walks at Midnight

It is portentous, and a thing of state
That here at midnight, in our little town
A mourning figure walks, and will not rest,

① 马库斯·坎利夫：《美国的文学》，方杰译，中国对外翻译出版公司，1985，第 239 页。

Near the old court-house pacing up and down,

Or by his homestead, or in shadowed yards
He lingers where his children used to play,
Or through the market, on the well-worn stones
He stalks until the dawn-stars burn away.

A bronzed, lank man! His suit of ancient black,
A famous high top-hat and plain worn shawl
Make him the quaint great figure that men love,
The prairie-lawyer, master of us all.

He cannot sleep upon his hillside now.
He is among us—as in times before!
And we who toss and lie awake for long,
Breathe deep, and start, to see him pass the door.

His head is bowed. He thinko on men and kings.
Yea, when the sick world cries, how can he sleep?
Too many peasants fight, they know not why;
Too many homesteads in black terror weep.

The sins of all the war-lords burn his heart.
He sees the dreadnaughts scouring every main.
He carries on his shawl-wrapped shoulders now
The bitterness, the folly and the pain.

He cannot rest until a spirit-dawn
Shall come; —the shining hope of Europe free:
A league of sober folk, the Workers' Earth,
Bringing long peace to Cornland, Alp and Sea.

It breaks his heart that kings must murder still,
That all his hours of travail here for men
Seem yet in vain. And who will bring white peace

That he may sleep upon his hill again?

## 亚伯拉罕·林肯午夜漫步

真是意想不到，而且还是国家大事
深更半夜，在我们这座小城里，
一位悲痛忧伤的身影不肯安歇，
徘徊踟蹰在古老的法院建筑附近，

或者他的宅地旁，或者阴影笼罩的院落，
盘桓在孩子们曾经的游玩之地，
或者穿过市场，悄然行走在年代久远的
石头路上，直到启明星的余晖慢慢隐去。

古铜色的皮肤，瘦高的身材！身穿过时的黑色西装，
头戴名牌大礼帽，脖子系着朴素的旧围巾，
他就是人民爱戴的奇特伟人，
草原律师，我们大家的领袖。

他在山坡上无法安睡，
来到我们中间——一如既往！
长期彻夜难眠、辗转反侧的我们，
看他路过无不震动惊愕。

他低垂着头，挂念人民，想起君王。
是呵，患病的世界在呐喊，他怎能安睡?
无数农民无的放矢地在打斗；
众多家庭在黑色恐怖中哭泣。

军阀们的孽行令他勃然大怒。
他看到无畏战舰在海洋上驰骋。
他裹着围巾的肩上承受着
苦难、过错和疼痛。

他不会入睡，在等充满朝气的黎明；

——自由欧洲前景灿烂的心愿，
觉醒者的联盟，劳动者的大地，
把和平带到玉米地、高山和海洋。

君王们嗜血本性难改，他毕生在此为人民的
辛勤付出即将化为乌有，
这一切使他心碎。谁能带来和平
让他在山坡上可以重新安睡?

## Heart of God

O great heart of God,
Once vague and lost to me,
Why do I throb with your throb tonight,
In this land, eternity?

O little heart of God,
Sweet intruding stranger,
You are laughing in my human breast,
A Christ-child in a manger.

Heart, dear heart of God,
Beside you now I kneel,
Strong heart of faith. O heart not mine,
Where God has set His seal.

Wild thundering heart of God
Out of my doubt I come,
And my foolish feet with prophets' feet,
March with the prophets' drum.

## 上帝之心

啊，仁慈宽厚的上帝之心，
曾经令我茫然不解，

今夜我的心为何随着您的脉搏一起跳动，
在这片土地上，永远？

啊，细微弱小的上帝之心，
扰乱人心的可爱陌生人，
您在我尘世的胸中开怀大笑，
马槽中的基督小孩。

心啊，仁慈的上帝之心，
现如今我跪拜在您的身旁，
永不动摇的信仰之心。啊，那颗已经不属我的心，
上面盖上了上帝的印章。

隆隆作响的上帝之心
让我不再疑惑，
使我不明就里的脚步紧随先知的脚步，
踩着先知的鼓点前行。

## The Merciful Hand

(*Written to Miss Alice L. F. Fitzgerald*, *Edith Cavell memorial nurse*, *going to the front*.)
Your fine white hand is Heaven's gift
To cure the wide world, stricken sore,
Bleeding at the breast and head,
Tearing at its wounds once more.

Your white hand is a prophecy,
A living hope that Christ shall come
And make the nations merciful,
Hating the bayonet and drum.

Each desperate burning brain you soothe,
Or ghastly broken frame you bind,
Brings one day nearer our bright goal,
The love-alliance of mankind.

## 仁慈之手

*（献给奔赴前线的艾迪丝·卡维尔纪念医院护士爱丽丝·L. F. 菲茨杰拉尔德小姐）*
上帝赐予你精巧的洁白之手
治愈广袤大地，受难场所，
流血的心胸，
再次撕开它的伤口。

你的洁白之手让人看到希望，
基督一定会到来
让世间充满慈悲，
永无刺刀和战鼓。

你安抚的每个绝望的灵魂，
或包扎的每个恐怖的伤口，
使他们日益走近我们的美好目标，
让爱充满人间。

## Ghosts in Love

"Tell me, where do ghosts in love
Find their bridal veils?"

"If you and I were ghosts in love
We'd climb the cliffs of mystery,
Above the sea of wails.
I'd trim your gray and streaming hair
With veils of fantasy
From the tree of memory.
"Tis there the ghosts that fall in love
Find their bridal veils."

## 恋爱中的鬼魂

“你知道相爱中的鬼魂
在哪里找到婚纱?”

“假如你我是相爱中的鬼魂
我们会攀上哭泣海洋
之上的神秘悬崖。
我会用从记忆之树
采摘的奇幻面纱
为你修整飘逸的灰发
在那儿相爱的鬼魂
会找到婚纱。”

## Crickets on a Strike

The foolish queen of fairyland
From her milk-white throne in a lily-bell,
Gave command to her cricket-band
To play for her when the dew-drops fell.

But the cold dew spoiled their instruments
And they play for the foolish queen no more.
Instead those sturdy malcontents
Play sharps and flats in my kitchen floor.

## 罢工的蟋蟀

愚昧无知的仙境女王
坐在百合花冠里的乳白御座上,
号令她的蟋蟀乐队
露水降落之际为她奏唱。

而冰冷的露珠损坏了乐器

它们无法再给蠢货女王弹奏。
那帮满腹牢骚的彪悍艺术家
却来到我家厨房肆意演唱。

## In Praise of Songs that Die

(*AFTER HAVING READ A GREAT DEAL OF GOOD CURRENT POETRY IN THE MAGAZINES AND NEWSPAPERS*)

Ah, they are passing, passing by,
Wonderful songs, but born to die!
Cries from the infinite human seas,
Waves thrice-winged with harmonies.
Here I stand on a pier in the foam
Seeing the songs to the beach go home,
Dying in sand while the tide flows back,
As it flowed of old in its fated track.
Oh, hurrying tide that will not hear
Your own foam children dying near
Is there no refuge-house of song,
No home, no haven where songs belong?
Oh, precious hymns that come and go!
You perish, and I love you so!

## 赞美消亡的诗篇

(*阅读报纸和杂志上大量现代优秀诗篇有感*)
啊，诗篇如流星般划过、划过，
精彩无限但注定要消亡！
茫茫人海发出的呼喊，
三翼波浪演奏的和谐曲。
现今我站在泡沫淹没的码头
目睹诗篇返回岸边的家园，
然后随潮而去消失在沙滩，
按照命运早已安排的轨迹。
啊，匆忙的潮汐不会理会

自己的泡沫之子就在附近死去。
难道没有属于诗篇的庇护之所?
安放之家? 保存之地?
啊，绵延不绝的珍贵赞歌啊，
你虽然流逝但我对你的爱永驻!

# 哈莱姆文艺复兴

20世纪20年代末30年代初，以纽约黑人聚居区哈莱姆为中心，出现了现代美国黑人文学艺术的第一次高潮，史称“哈莱姆文艺复兴”，主要表现为一大批优秀的黑人作家、音乐家、艺术家相继出现，促使了美国黑人文学和艺术史无前例的繁荣与发展，展现出前所未有的创造力和生命力，对20世纪初的美国文学和文化产生了极其重大的影响。其中引人注目的诗人有克劳德·麦凯、琼·图默、康蒂·卡伦和兰斯顿·休斯等。

# 克劳德·麦凯
## (Claude McKay, 1889—1948)

克劳德·麦凯 1889 年出生在牙买加山区一个贫苦的农民家庭。

1906 年，获得牙买加政府奖学金资助，麦凯离开家乡到外地学习木工，但他很快对这个工作失去了兴趣，改行当了警察，结果也只干了 8 个月便离职回到了山区老家。

麦凯从小喜欢诗歌。在做小学教师的哥哥及当地一位侨居牙买加的英国人帮助下，他先后阅读了米尔顿、蒲柏、济慈、雪莱、拜伦以及但丁、歌德、波德莱尔等著名诗人的诗歌作品。1912 年，麦凯的第一本诗集《牙买加之歌》(*Songs of Jamaica*)出版，因此获得牙买加文艺科学院的奖学金。他拿着这笔钱只身来到美国求学，先在黑人办的杜斯克基科技学校学习，几个月后去了堪萨斯州立大学学习农学；两年后离开堪萨斯州到纽约哈莱姆谋生，先后当过门房、饭店服务员、听差，也在火车上的茶房做过各种杂活。

1917 年底，麦凯的两首十四行诗《哈莱姆的舞女》(*The Harlem Dancer*)和《祈祷》(*Pray*)发表，引起了广泛关注。随后，《七艺》(*Seven Arts*)、《皮尔逊》(*Pearson*)、《解放者》(*Liberator*)等杂志连续刊发了他的一些作品。

1919 年，麦凯去了英国。在英国期间，他在《剑桥杂志》先后发表了 23 首诗。1920 年，诗集《新罕布什尔的春天》(*Spring in New Hanpshire*)在英国出版。1921 年，诗集《哈莱姆的暗影》(*Harlem Shadows*)在美国出版。

1923 年，他来到巴黎，期间因身患肺病在医院住了几个月，后来在朋友的资助下，他转到马赛、土伦等地疗养。

1931 年，在离开美国大约 12 年后，麦凯回到了哈莱姆区。1940 年他的最后一部作品《哈莱姆：黑人大都会》(*Harlem: Negro Metropolis*)出版。1948 年 5 月 22 日，麦凯在芝加哥一家医院病逝，结束了他颠沛流离、贫困潦倒的一生。

除了诗歌写作外，麦凯还写了一些其他形式的文学作品，如小说《回到哈莱姆》(*Home to Harlem*)，《班卓》(*Banjo*)，《香蕉谷》(*Banana Bottom*)；短篇小说集《姜镇》(*Gingertown*)以及回忆录《远离家乡》(*A Long Way from Home*)等。麦凯的文学作品主题基本围绕着牙买加乡村和哈莱姆区的黑人生活，描写生活在社会底层人们的辛酸经历或悲惨遭遇。

## The Snow Fairy

I

Throughout the afternoon I watched them there,
Snow-fairies falling, falling from the sky,
Whirling fantastic in the misty air,
Contending fierce for space supremacy.
And they flew down a mightier force at night,
As though in heaven there was revolt and riot,
And they, frail things had taken panic flight
Down to the calm earth seeking peace and quiet.
I went to bed and rose at early dawn
To see them huddled together in a heap,
Each merged into the other upon the lawn,
Worn out by the sharp struggle, fast asleep.
The sun shone brightly on them half the day,
By night they stealthily had stol'n away.

## 雪精灵

一

我一个下午待在那儿瞧着他们，
雪精灵们飘落，从空中飘落而下，
在雾蒙蒙的空中神奇地翻转，
激烈争夺空中霸权。
夜间飞舞更加急速，
仿佛天堂发生暴乱，
他们，弱小之物急忙飞向
平静的大地寻求和平与安宁。
我就寝入睡，黎明醒来
看见他们挤成一堆，
相互交织在草坪上，

激烈搏斗精力耗尽，很快入睡。
享受了半天火红的太阳，
夜间他们悄无声息地溜走。

## Spring in New Hampshire

Too green the springing April grass,
Too blue the silver-speckled sky,
For me to linger here, alas,
While happy winds go laughing by,
Wasting the golden hours indoors,
Washing windows and scrubbing floors.

Too wonderful the April night,
Too faintly sweet the first May flowers,
The stars too gloriously bright,
For me to spend the evening hours,
When fields are fresh and streams are leaping,
Wearied, exhausted, dully sleeping.

## 新罕布什尔的春天

生机勃勃的四月青草葱绿，
湛蓝色的天空下白云朵朵，
欢快的风儿乐呵呵吹过，
我却停留在这儿，唉，
在室内浪费这金色的时光，
清洗窗户，擦拭地板。

四月的夜晚奇妙无穷，
五月的早花吐出丝丝芬芳，
星星璀璨夺目、晶莹剔透，
田野清新，溪水欢唱，
如此美好的夜晚，
而我精疲力竭，昏昏入睡。

## The Barrier

I must not gaze at them although
  Your eyes are dawning day;
I must not watch you as you go
  Your sun-illumined way;

I hear but I must never heed
  The fascinating note,
Which, fluting like a river reed,
  Comes from your trembling throat;

I must not see upon your face
  Love's softly glowing spark;
For there's the barrier of race,
  You're fair and I am dark.

## 界限

我不能注视你的眼睛
  虽然它们犹如黎明的曙光;
我不能凝望你
  当你走在阳光和煦的大路上;

我听到但从未留意
  那迷人的音符,
笛声如同河边的芦苇,
  发自你颤动的喉音;

我不能瞅你脸上
  温柔地闪现出爱的火花;
因为有种族界限,
  你的皮肤白皙而我的黝黑。

## The Tropics in New York

Bananas ripe and green, and ginger-root
  Cocoa in pods and alligator pears,
And tangerines and mangoes and grape fruit,
  Fit for the highest prize at parish fairs,

Set in the window, bringing memories
  Of fruit-trees laden by low-singing rills,
And dewy dawns, and mystical blue skies
  In benediction over nun-like hills.

My eyes grow dim, and I could not more gaze;
  A wave of longing through my body swept.
And, hungry for the old, familiar ways,
  I turned aside and bowed my head and wept.

## 纽约的热带地区

成熟的青色香蕉还有姜根
  豆荚里的可可和鳄梨，
还有橘子、芒果和西柚，
  教区集市的珍贵商品，

摆放在橱窗，令人想起
  潺潺溪水旁结满果实的树木，
白露湿草的黎明，还有如修女的山丘上
  赐下福泽的神秘蓝天。

我双眼模糊，无法再看下去；
  一阵渴望涌上心头。
渴望回到曾经熟悉的生活，
  于是转身低头哭泣。

## The Tired Worker

O whisper, O my soul! The afternoon
Is waning into evening, whiper soft!
Peace, O my rebel heart! For soon the moon
From out its misty veil will swing aloft!
Be patient, weary body, soon the night
Will wrap thee gently in her sable sheet,
And with a leaden sigh thou wilt invite
To rest thy tired hands and aching feet.
The wretched day was theirs, the night is mine;
Come tender sleep, and fold me to the breast.
But what steals out the gray clouds red like wine?
Oh dawn! O dreaded dawn! O let me rest.
Weary my veins, my brain, my life! Have pity!
No! Once again the harsh, the ugly city.

## 疲倦的工人

啊，小点声，我的天啊！
白昼渐去夜幕降临，轻点声！
静一静，不安分的心！月亮很快就要
揭开朦胧面纱高挂空中！
别急，疲倦的身躯，夜晚马上
就要把你温柔地裹进黑色的床被，
而你怅然若失地叹口气
将你疲惫的双手和疼痛的双脚歇息。
难熬的白昼已过去，夜晚属于我自己；
来吧，温柔的睡意，将我拥抱进你的胸膛。
可灰蒙蒙的云中露出的血红如酒的是什么?
啊，黎明！该死的黎明啊，让我休息吧。
我的身体、大脑、生活疲惫不堪！饶了我吧！
休想！又是那座严酷、丑陋的城市。

## Truth

Lord, shall I find it in Thy Holy Church,
Or must I give it up as something dead,
Forever lost, no matter where I search,
Like dinosaurs within their ancient bed?
I found it not in the years of unbelief,
In science stirring life like budding trees,
In revolution like a dazzling thief—
Oh, shall I find it on my bended knees?

But what is truth? So pilate asked thee, Lord,
So long ago when thou wert manifest,
As the eternal and incarnate word,
Chosen of God and by him singly blest:
In this vast world of lies and hate and greed,
Upon my knees, oh Lord, for truth I plead.

## 真理

主啊，在你的圣堂会找到它吗，
还是如死亡之物将它抛弃?
天南海北都永远无法寻见，
犹如远古河床上的恐龙。
困惑的岁月里不见踪影，
恰似萌芽的树木催生生命的科学中无法得到，
近同眼花缭乱的盗贼般的革命中难以遇见——
啊，难道只有奴颜婢膝才能获取?

然而何为真理? 彼拉多①如是问你，主，
长久以来你被当作

① 彼拉多：指 Pontius Pilate，罗马帝国犹太行省的执政官。根据新约圣经所述，曾多次审问耶稣，原本他不认为耶稣犯了什么罪，却在仇视耶稣的犹太宗教领袖的压力下，判处耶稣被钉死在十字架。

不朽之词、化身之道，
上帝所选，独享他的恩赐：
茫茫世间充满谎言、仇恨和贪婪，
主啊，我卑躬屈膝祈求真理。

# 琼·图默
# (Jean Toomer，1894—1967)

琼·图默 1894 年 12 月出生于华盛顿特区。父亲以务农为生，但在琼出生后不久便离家出走。为了生计，母亲不得不将他寄养在外祖父家。在外祖父的照看下，图默在当地学校完成了小学、中学学业。中学毕业后他先后进入威斯康星大学和纽约市立大学学习，所学专业繁杂，包括体育、医学、历史、社会学、农学等，期间曾在各地打过零工。读书期间，图默对写作产生了浓厚兴趣，积极参加各种文艺活动，结识了一些文坛翘楚，如批评家肯尼斯·伯克(Kenneth Burke)、摄影家阿尔弗莱德·施泰格利茨(Altred Steiglitz)、诗人哈特·克莱恩(Hart Crane)等，并在《解放者》《小评论》等期刊开始发表诗歌和短文。

1921 年，图默来到佐治亚州，在当地一所学校教书；但没过多久便辞职去了芝加哥。图默一生结过两次婚，妻子均为白人，为此经常受到亲朋好友或普通民众的诟病。图默于 1967 年 3 月去世。

就诗歌创作说来，图默具有影响力的作品数量并不多。他一生只写了两部长诗：《蓝色子午线》(*Blue Meridian*)和《甘蔗》(*Cane*)。《蓝色子午线》是他对超越种族界限、各个民族间平等相待的期盼和深思；而《甘蔗》通过对诗人在佐治亚地区亲身经历的农村生活的描写，塑造了集美与健康于一身的黑人形象，同时也展现了受种族身份困扰的“黑白混血儿”这一边缘人物复杂的内心感受。

## November Cotton Flower

Boll-weevil's coming, and the winter's cold,
Made cotton-stalks look rusty, seasons old,
And cotton, scarce as any southern snow,
Was vanishing; the branch, so pinched and slow,
Failed in its function as the autumn rake;
Drouth fighting soil had caused the soil to take
All water from the streams; dead birds were found
In wells a hundred feet below the ground—
Such was the season when the flower bloomed.
Old folks were startled, and it soon assumed
Significance. Superstition saw

Something it had never seen before:
Brown eyes that loved without a trace of fear,
Beauty so sudden for that time of year.

## 十一月的木棉花

棉铃象鼻虫来了，冬天寒冷，
让棉杆锈迹斑斑，季节老去，
而棉花稀稀拉拉犹如南方的雪，
渐渐消失；枝条皱缩生机不再，
就像秋天的耙子已无用场；
肆虐大地的干旱迫使土壤
吸干溪流里的水；地下
百尺深的井中发现鸟儿的尸体——
这样的时节棉花竟绽放花朵。
老人们为之震惊，继而就琢磨
此中的深意。迷信让人们看到
某些长久被熟视无睹的东西：
爱得没有一丝恐惧的棕色眼睛，
那段时光里突如其来的美。

## Reapers

Black reapers with the sound of steel on stones
Are sharpening scythes. I see them place the hones
In their hip-pockets as a thing that's done,
And start their silent swinging, one by one.
Black horses drive a mower through the weeds,
And there, a field rat, startled, squealing bleeds,
His belly close to ground. I see the blade,
Blood-stained, continue cutting weeds and shade.

## 收割者

钢铁在石头上霍霍作响

那是黑人收割者在磨长柄大镰刀。
磨好之后他们将磨刀石装进裤子后袋，
一声不吭挥起大镰刀，一下又一下。
黑马拉着割草机在草丛中穿行，
被惊起的一只田鼠身上流着血，
肚皮贴地、尖叫不止。沾满鲜血的
刀锋持续挥向杂草和阴影。

## Evening Song

Full moon rising on the waters of my heart,
Lakes and moon and fires,
Cloine tires,
Holding her lips apart.

Promises of slumber leaving shore to charm the moon,
Miracle made vesper-keeps,
Cloine sleeps,
And I'll be sleeping soon.

Cloine, curled like the sleepy waters where the moon-waves start,
Radiant, resplendently she gleams,
Cloine dreams,
Lips pressed against my heart.

## 黄昏之歌

心的水域冉冉升起一轮圆月，
湖泊、明月、大火，
柯罗英困乏劳累，
嘴唇微微张启。

答应离岸睡觉来魅惑月亮，
夜幕低垂奇妙无比
柯罗英就寝歇息，

我也马上入睡。

柯罗英，身体卷曲宛如月光下波浪起伏的寂静水域，
容光焕发、光彩夺目，
柯罗英酣然入梦，
嘴唇紧贴在我的胸膛。

## The Gods Are Here

This is no mountain
But a house,
No rock of solitude
But a family chair,
No wilds
But life appearing
As life anywhere domesticated,
Yet I know the gods are here,
And that if I touch them
I will arise
And take majesty into the kitchen.

## 神灵在此

这不是高山
而是房子，
不是寂寞的石头
而是家中的座椅，
不是荒野
而是生命的显现
犹如到处被驯化的生命，
我知道神灵依然在此，
而且如若扰动他们
我就要起身
将他们送进灶间。

## Beehive

Within the black hive to-night
There swarm a million bees;
Bees passing in and out the moon,
Silver bees intently buzzing,
Silver honey dripping from the swarm of bees
Earth is a waxen cell of the world comb,
And I, a drone,
Lying on my back,
Lipping honey,
Getting drunk with silver honey,
Wish that I might fly out past the moon
And curl forever in some far-off farmyard flower.

## 蜂巢

黑色的蜂巢今夜
挤满百万只蜜蜂;
月光下蜂儿飞进飞出,
荧光闪闪、嗡嗡叫个不停,
蜂群滴下亮晶晶的蜜
大地是世间蜂巢的蜡制巢房,
而我,一只雄蜂,
仰身而躺,
吮吸蜂蜜,
明亮的糖蜜将我灌醉,
我愿在月光下飞向遥远的农家庭院
在那里的花朵上永远飞绕。

## A Poem from Transatlantic

Stretch sea
Stretch away sea and land

We are following thee
Thy lead is dangerous
And glorious
Stretch thyself and us
And make us live
To mount the ladder of horizons
Until we step upon the radiant plateau.

## 一首来自大西洋彼岸的诗歌

绵绵海洋
无边的水域和广袤的陆地
我们跟随着你
由你领导实属光荣
但充满危机
伸展一下你自己和我们的身体
让我们活着
登上地平线的阶梯
最终踏上光芒四射的高原。

## A Portrait in Georgia

Hair-braided chestnut,
coiled like a lyncher's rope
Eyes-fagots,
Lips-old scars, or the first red blisters,
Breath-the last sweet scent of cane,
And her slim body, white as the ash
of black flesh after flame.

## 佐治亚州的一幅画像

梳成辫的棕色头发，
卷曲着如同私刑者手中的绳索，
眼睛干巴，

嘴唇上的旧伤疤，或最初的红水疱，
气息清香如甘蔗适才散发出的芳香，
身材纤细，苍白如
黑色肉体燃烧后的灰烬。

## People

To those fixed on white,
White is white,
To those fixed on black,
It is the same,
And red is red,
Yellow, yellow—
Surely there are such sights
In the many colored world,
Or in the mind.
The strange thing is that
These people never see themselves
Or you, or me.

Are they not in their minds?
Are we not in the world?
This is a curious blindness
For those that are color blind.
What queer beliefs
That men who believe in sights
Disbelieve in seers.

O people, if you but used
Your other eyes
You would see beings.

## 人们

就那些被定格为白色的人说来，

白色就是白色，
就那些被定格为黑色的人说来，
也是如此，
而且红色就是红色，
黄色就是黄色——
的确在许多有色人的眼里，
或者心中，
情况就是这样，
令人诧异的是
这些人永远看不到自己
或者你，或者我。

难道他们的心中没有自己?
这世界没有我们?
对于那些色盲症患者
这可是个让人好奇的盲区。
相信表象的人
不会相信预言家
实在荒唐怪异。

哎，人啊，你只要用一下
另外一只眼睛
就会看到真相。

# 康蒂·卡伦
## （Countee Cullen，1903—1946）

康蒂·卡伦 1903 年 5 月出生于纽约哈莱姆区。15 岁时父母相继离开人世，随后他被哈莱姆区卫理公会一名白人牧师收养。高中毕业后，卡伦进入纽约大学学习，获得学士学位后又到哈佛大学攻读文学硕士学位。他的学习成绩一贯优秀，非常喜欢诗歌，不时有诗歌发表。早在中学时期他便在纽约市的诗歌大赛中获过奖。1925 年卡伦的第一部诗集《肤色》(*Color*)出版。出版后赢得了社会各界的好评，这极大地激励了卡伦的诗歌创作热情。到 1929 年卡伦已有四部诗集出版，一些作品还被收进美国黑人诗歌选集，蜚声美国诗坛，卡伦瞬间成为 20 世纪 20 年代哈莱姆文艺复兴的风云人物之一。

受 20 世纪 30 年代经济危机的影响，出版行业日渐式微，文学创作特别是诗歌创作受严重影响。为了生计，卡伦受聘到纽约一所初级中学担任法语教师。期间，他很少有新的诗歌作品发表，但创作了一些其他体裁的作品，如小说《通往天堂的一条路》(*One Way to Heaven*，1934)、儿童文学《失去的动物园》(*The Lost Zoo*，1940)、音乐剧《圣路易斯的女人》(*St. Louis Woman*，1946)等。1946 年初，卡伦因患尿毒症在纽约去世。

卡伦在诗歌中所表达的主题首先是种族问题；但是，与当时许多黑人作家一样，他的作品也经常带有一些相互矛盾的思想特征。他一生追寻深深植根于非洲大地的黑人文化，但作品的主题和背景却是 20 世纪初的美国现代城市；他虽然对种族歧视深恶痛绝，但坚决反对使用暴力手段加以改变，却常常幻想通过加强民族团结，以和平方式获得种族平等。除了种族问题，卡伦也有一些涉及宗教信仰、爱情婚姻、道德伦理、生存死亡等主题的诗歌。诗歌创作中，卡伦着力效法英国浪漫主义诗歌传统，诗歌抒情色彩浓厚，形式工整严谨。

### Atlantic City Waiter

With subtle poise he grips his tray
  Of delicate things to eat;
Choice viands to their mouths half way,
  The ladies watch his feet

Go carving dexterous avenues
  Through sly intricacies;

Ten thousand years on jungle clues
  Alone shaped feet like these.

For him to be humble who is proud
  Needs colder artifice;
Though half his pride is disavowed,
  In vain the sacrifice.

Sheer through his acquiescent mask
  Of bland gentility,
The jungle flames like a copper cask
  Set where the sun strikes free.

## 亚特兰大城的侍者

他神情自若、机巧灵敏地端着
  盛满鲜美食品的托盘;
贵妇们停下了送到嘴边的食物
  眼睛瞅着他的脚看

走过错综复杂的诡异地带
  神定气闲地穿梭于餐桌过道;
世代与丛林无法割舍的关系
  造就了这双无以伦比的脚板。

他自豪无比
  卑躬屈膝需要更为冷酷的技巧;
虽然过半的尊严被剥夺,
  但舍弃必是枉然。

透过他那淡漠、斯文
  顺从的面纱,
丛林之火在熊熊燃烧
  就像太阳恣意照射的铜质酒桶。

## Black Majesty

These men were kings, albeit they were black,
Christophe and Dessalines and L'Ouverture;
Their majesty has made me turn my back
Upon a plaint I once shaped to endure.
These men were black, I say, but they were crowned
And purple-clad, however brief their time.
Stifle your agony; let grief be drowned;
We know joy had a day once and a clime.

Dark gutter-snipe, black sprawler-in-the-mud,
A thing men did a man may do again.
What answer filters through your sluggish blood
To these dark ghosts who knew so bright a reign?
"Lo, I am dark, but comely," Sheba sings.
"And we were black," three shades reply, "but kings."

## 黑人陛下

虽然皮肤黝黑，但他们是国王，
克里斯托弗①、德萨林②，还有卢维杜尔③；
他们让我不再对过去
时常遭受的苦难哀叹。
我说，他们是黑人但受封为王
紫袍加身，无论任期多么短暂。
抑制痛苦；丢掉悲伤；
我们知道历史上曾经有过欢乐。

黑色流浪儿，泥土里的黑爬虫，

---

① 亨利·克里斯托弗：(Henry Christophe，1807—1811)海地总统。

② 让·雅克·德萨林：(Jean-Jacques Dessalines，1758—1806)，又译让-雅克·德萨利纳。海地革命的领袖。海地总统、皇帝。

③ 杜桑·卢维杜尔：(Toussaint L'Ouverture，1801—1802)法属圣多明戈总督。

前有古人，后有来者。
经过你们缓缓流动的血液的过滤
你们呈交给
这些深知英明统治的黑色幽灵怎样的回答?
“嘿，我是黑人，但我美丽，”希巴女王①唱到。
“我们是黑人，”三个幽灵回答，“但是国王。”

## For A Lady I Know

She even thinks that up in heaven
Her class lies late and snores

While poor black cherubs rise at seven
To do celestial chores

## 写给我认识的女士

她甚至想在天堂她们这些人
可以很晚起床，鼾声如雷

而可怜的黑人天使七点
就要起床干天堂的杂务。

## Yet Do I Marvel

I doubt not God is good, well-meaning, kind
And did he stoop to quibble could tell why
The little buried mole continues blind,
Why flesh that mirrors him must some day die,
Make plain the reason tortured Tantalus
Is baited by the fickle fruit, declare

---

① 希巴女王：又称示巴女王，是《圣经·旧约》中略用文字提及的人物，在传说中，她是一位阿拉伯半岛的女王，在与所罗门王见面后，慕其英明及刚毅，与所罗门王有过一场甜蜜的恋情，并孕有一子。传说中的希巴女王有两种形象，一是惊艳绝伦，一是丑陋无比。希巴女王首见于《圣经·旧约》的“列王记”。

If merely brute caprice dooms Sisyphus
To struggle up a never-ending stair.
Inscrutable his ways are, and immune
To catechism by a mind too strewn
With petty cares to slightly understand
What awful brain compels his awful hand.
Yet do I marvel at this curious thing:
To make a poet black, and bid him sing!

## 但我感到惊奇

我不怀疑上帝的仁慈、善良和好意，
他屈尊迂贵分辨为何埋在地下的
小鼹鼠的眼睛还是瞎的，
体现他存在的肉体为何总有一天要死去，
阐明坦塔罗斯①受折磨的原因
是他禁不住变化多端的果实的引诱，
宣称野蛮的任性就让西西弗斯②，
注定艰辛地攀上永无止境的阶梯。
上帝之道高深莫测，
对人们的诘问置之不理，
他们的头脑塞满鸡毛蒜皮
难以理解操纵他可怕之手的神奇智慧。
但我对这件怪事感到惊奇：
将诗人肤色变黑，令他赞美！

## To Certain Critics

Then call me traitor if you must,
Shout reason and default!
Say I betray a sacred trust

---

① 坦塔罗斯：即 Tantalus，希腊神话中宙斯之子，因泄露天机被罚永世站在上有果树的水中，口渴想喝水时水即减退，腹饥想吃果子时树枝即升高。

② 西西弗斯：即 Sisyphus，希腊神话中古时的暴君，死后堕入地狱，被罚推石上山，但石头在近山顶时又滚下，于是重新再推，如此往复不息。

Aching beyond this vault.
I'll bear your censure as your praise,
For never shall the clan
Confine my singing to its ways
Beyond the ways of man.

No racial option narrows grief,
Pain is not patriot,
And sorrow plaits her dismal leaf
For all as lief as not.
With blind sheep groping every hill,
Searching an oriflamme①,
How shall the shepherd heart then thrill
To only the darker lamb?

## 致某些批评家

那么如果你能说出理由，
指出错误就叫我叛徒好了！
说我背离了神圣的责任
令我伤心落泪。
你们的斥责权当赞誉，
因为我真正感觉到
这帮人对我的要求
史无前例。

种族选项无法弥合忧伤，
痛苦不是爱国，
懊悔交织为郁闷
没人感到乐意。
双目失明的羊群在山间摸索，
寻找头羊，
牧者的心怎么只会

① oriflamme：（诗/文）历史上用来指红色王旗；骑士的军旗。

为那只黑色的羔羊而兴奋不已?

## Simon the Cyrenian Speaks

He never spoke a word to me,
  And yet he called my name;
He never gave a sign to me,
  And yet I knew and came.

At first I said, "I will not bear
  His cross upon my back;
He only seeks to place it there
  Because my skin is black."

But He was dying for a dream,
  And he was very meek,
And in his eyes there shone a gleam
  Men journey far to seek.

It was himself my pity brought;
  I did for Christ alone
What all of Rome could not have wrought
  With bruise of lash and stone.

## 萨仁尼安人西蒙说

他没同我讲过一句话,
  而知道我姓甚名谁;
他没给我任何暗示,
  而我知道就赶过来。

首先我说,"我不想
  背他的十字架;
但他一定要放在那儿
  因为我的皮肤黑。"

他心怀一个梦想，
　于是温和善良，
眼睛露出敞亮之光
　人生旅程慢慢悠长。

是他令我产生恻隐之心，
　我只怜悯过基督
究竟怎样才不会招致
　皮鞭和石头的伤痕。

## To John Keats, Poet at Spring Time

I cannot hold my peace, John Keats;
There was never a spring like this;
It is an echo, that repeats
My last year's song and next year's bliss.
I know, in spite of all men say
Of Beauty, you have felt her most.
Yea, even in your grave her way
Is said. Poor, troubled, lyric ghost,
Spring never was so fair and dear
As beauty makes her seem this year.

I cannot hold my peace, John Keats,
I am as helpless in the toil
Of Spring as any lamb that bleats
To feel the solid earth recoil
Beneath his puny legs. Spring beats
Her tocsin call to those who love her,
And lo! The dogwood petals cover
Her breast with drifts of snow, and sleek
White gulls fly screaming to her, and hover
About her shoulders, and kiss her neck,
While white and purple lilacs muster

A strength that bears them to a cluster
Of color and odor; for her sake
All things that slept are now awake.

And you and I, shall we lie still,
John Keats, while beauty summons us?
Somehow I feel your sensitive will
Is pulsing up some tremulous
Sap road of a maple tree, whose leaves
Grow music as they grow, since your
Wild voice is in them, a harp that grieves
For life that opens death's dark door.
Though dust, your fingers still can push
The vision splendid to a birth,
Though now they work as grass in the hush
Of the night on the broad sweet page of the earth.

"John Keats is dead," they say, but I
Who hear your full insistent cry
In bud and blossom, leaf and tree,
Know John Keats still writes poetry.
And while my head is earthward bowed
To read new life sprung from your shroud,
Folks seeing me must think it strange
That merely spring should so derange
My mind. They do not know that you,
John Keats, keep revel with me, too.

## 致约翰·济慈，春天的诗人

我心怎能平静，约翰·济慈；
这样的春天世间少有；
它是我去年歌声的回音，
来年福佑吉祥的共鸣。
虽然人人都在述说美

但我知道只有你更懂。
是的，即使你已入土
但还在讲述美的途径。
可怜、不安、抒怀的幽灵啊，
美将今春妆点得无比秀美迷人。

我心怎能平静，约翰·济慈；
春天的劳碌让我难以应付，
犹如咩咩叫的羔羊感受到了
柔弱的腿下坚硬大地的颤动。
那是春天对宠爱她的人发出的警信。
瞧！山茱萸花瓣雪花般洒落在她的胸脯，
洁白光滑的海鸥欢叫着向她飞来，
在她的肩头盘旋，
亲吻她的脖颈；
而白色和紫色的丁香花
聚集力量绽开缤纷色彩
吐出浓郁馨香；
沉睡的万物现在因她而苏醒。

约翰·济慈，美在呼唤我们
你我怎能无动于衷?
不知何故在颤动着树液的枫树纹路
我感到了你的脉动，
枫叶转绿，哗哗作响，
那是你发出的豪迈声音，
是为打开死亡黑暗之门的生命而悲伤的竖琴声。
虽然已为灰尘，你的手指化作青草
在寂静的夜晚，
在亲切辽阔的大地，
依然绘出如画的风景。

“约翰·济慈已然故去，”他们说，
而我在花蕊和鲜花，叶子和树木中
听到了你清晰热切的呼喊，

知道约翰·济慈还在做诗。
我低头沉思
你寿衣中迸发出的新生命，
众人见我一定无法理解
春天尽然使我精神错乱。
他们哪能知道你，
约翰·济慈，也让我沉溺迷恋。

# 兰斯顿·休斯
## (Lanston Hughs，1902—1967)

休斯1902年生于密苏里州的乔普林(Joplin，Missouri)。出生后不久父母离异，父亲去了墨西哥，他便跟随母亲来到外祖母家。13岁时母亲改嫁到伊利诺伊州的林肯市，后来他随继父家定居俄亥俄州的克利夫兰市(Cleveland)。中学毕业后，休斯去墨西哥寻找亲生父亲，在那里得到了一份英文教职的工作。1922年他回到美国，进入哥伦比亚大学学习，期间做过各种临时工作，如助理厨师、洗衣工、餐厅勤杂工等，1923年辍学，随后在一艘远洋货轮上当水手，曾到达西非海岸。后来他流落巴黎，当过夜总会看门人和旅馆侍者。休斯1924年返回美国，居住在华盛顿特区。在此期间，他积极参加黑人组织的文化活动，在黑人主办的刊物上发表了一系列诗歌。休斯在餐馆打工时，诗人维切尔·林赛恰巧前来就餐，休斯惴惴不安地将自己写的几首诗放在林赛的餐盘旁。林赛看后被作者的才华深深打动，于是便在餐厅大声朗读了起来，随后经他人引荐，认识了休斯。休斯大受鼓舞，此后便更加努力地投入到诗歌创作中。1926年休斯的第一部诗集《萎靡的布鲁斯》(*The Weary Blues*)出版。1929年，休斯进入林肯大学继续学习，三年后毕业。1930年出版了第一部小说《不是没有笑声》(*Not Without Laughter*)，并获得哈蒙文学金质奖①。

受20世纪30年代美国经济危机和臭名昭著的诬害黑人案件“思科茨伯勒案”②的影响，休斯的意识形态逐渐转向左倾。1932年他出访苏联，后来以记者身份参加西班牙内战，路过巴黎时出席了第二届国际作者大会。第二次世界大战后，他写了大量歌颂工人运动、反对种族歧视的作品。20世纪50年代初，麦卡锡主义在美国大肆横行，休斯因其左倾思想和行为而被传讯，为了防止再次遭受迫害，从此以后他在写作中尽量避免沾染任何激进思想，力图走为艺术而艺术的道路。1967年5月休斯因病在纽约去世。

休斯不仅写诗歌，而且写小说、戏剧、音乐剧、散文、传记等多种文体作品。他还将许多西班牙语或法语的诗歌翻译成了英语，除此之外，他还编辑出版过其他黑人作家的文选，但主要以诗歌作品著称，被誉为“黑人的桂冠诗人”(*Luarel Poet of Black*

---

① 哈蒙文学金质奖：威廉·E. 哈蒙1962年设立，用于奖励做出杰出成就的黑人，特别是在以下几个领域：文学、音乐、美术、商业和实业、科技创新、教育、宗教服务、种族关系。

② 思科茨伯勒案：1931年，在亚拉巴马州的思科茨伯勒，9位非洲裔美国男孩被指控在火车上强奸两名美国白人妇女。这起案件从起诉到审判，甚至陪审团都由白人承担。在匆忙做出审判结果前，9位被告已受尽了各种私刑的折磨。这起带有种族偏见的案件通常被引证为美国司法系统误判的一个例子。

Race)。他的主要作品还有诗集《犹太人的好衣服》(*Fine Clothes to the Jew*, 1927)、《可爱的死亡》(*Dear Lovely Death*, 1931)、《梦乡人及其他》(*The Dream Keeper and Other Poems*, 1932)、《哈莱姆的莎士比亚》(*Shakespeare in Harlem*, 1942)、《奇妙之地》(*Fields of Wonder*, 1947)、《单程票》(*One-Way Ticket*, 1949)、《迟到梦的蒙太奇》(*Montage of a Dream Deferred*, 1951)、《问你的妈妈：爵士乐的十二种情调》(*Ask Your Mama*: *12 Moods for Jazz*, 1961)等；小说《白人的行径》(*The Ways of White Folks*, 1934)、《辛普勒讲出心里话》(*Simple Speaks His Mind*, 1950)、《辛普勒娶妻》(*Simple Takes a Wife*, 1953)、《辛普勒孤注一掷》(*Simple Stakes a Claim*, 1957)、《共同的东西及其他故事》(*Something in Common and Other Stories*, 1963)、《辛普勒的山姆大叔》(*Simple's Uncle Sam*, 1965)等；自传《我飘泊，我思考》(*I Wonder as I Wander*, 1956)等等。

与同时代其他黑人作家一样，休斯诗歌的主题常常与黑人的文化和生活息息相关。但与他们不同，休斯从来不隐瞒自己的非裔身份，相反常常为此而深感自豪。他的抒情诗中常常充满黑人爵士乐和布鲁斯的节奏和叠句。

## The Weary Blues

Droning a drowsy syncopated tune
Rocking back and forth to a mellow croon,
  I heard a Negro play.
Down on Lenox Avenue the other night
By the pale dull pallor of an old gas light
  He did a lazy sway...
  He did a lazy sway...
To the tune o' those Weary Blues.
With his ebony hands on each ivory key
He made that poor piano moan with melody.
  O Blues!
Swaying to and fro on his rickety stool
He played that sad raggy tune like a musical fool.
  Sweet Blues!
Coming from a black man's soul.
  O Blues!
In a deep song voice with a melancholy tone
I heard that Negro sing, that old piano moan—

"Ain't got nobody in all this world,
Ain't got nobody but ma self.
I's gwine to quit ma frownin'
And put ma troubles on the shelf."

Thump, thump, thump, went his foot on the floor.
He played a few chords then he sang some more—
"I got the Weary Blues
And I can't be satisfied.
Got the Weary Blues
And can't be satisfied—
I ain't happy no mo'
And I wish that I had died."
And far into the night he crooned that tune.
The stars went out and so did the moon.
The singer stopped playing and went to bed
While the Weary Blues echoed through his head.
He slept like a rock or a man that's dead.

## 忧郁的布鲁斯

低沉的切分曲调郁闷压抑，
柔和的低吟摇来摆去，
我听过黑人的演唱。
利诺克斯大道旁的另一个夜晚
在昏暗苍白的旧汽灯下
他懒散地摇摆……
他懒散地摇摆……
伴着那忧郁的布鲁斯曲调。
他用乌黑的双手触动乳白色的琴键
破旧钢琴呻吟着发出悦耳的旋律。
啊布鲁斯！
他在晃动的琴凳上来回摇摆
像个乐盲演奏那悲伤破碎的曲子。
甜蜜的布鲁斯！

来自黑人的灵魂深处。
　噢布鲁斯！
深沉的歌声带着忧郁的音调
我听过黑人的吟唱，那台破钢琴呻吟着……
　“这个世界罕有人迹，
　只剩下我自己。
　我打算不再蹙眉
　把烦恼置于案几。”

咚，咚，咚，他的脚跺着地板。
他弹了几个和弦然后又唱了起来——
　“我听到忧郁的布鲁斯
　但心愿没有满足。
　听到忧郁的布鲁斯
　但心愿没有满足——
　闷闷不乐
　死了多好。”
低沉的曲子在深夜回荡。
月亮隐去，星光黯淡。
歌声停止，歌手入睡
脑际回响着忧郁的布鲁斯。
他沉沉入睡，渐入梦乡。

## Merry-Go-Round

Colored child at carnival

Where is the Jim Crow section
On this merry-go-round,
Mister, cause I want to ride?
Down South where I come from
White and colored
Can't sit side by side.
Down South on the train
There's a Jim Crow car.
On the bus we're put in the back—

But there ain't no back
To a merry-go-round!
Where's the horse
For a kid that's black?

## 旋转木马

狂欢节里的黑孩子

这旋转木马
黑人区域在哪儿?
先生，我想坐。
我从南方来
那里白人黑人
不能坐在一起
在南方，火车上
有黑人车箱，
公共汽车黑人坐后面……
可是旋转木马
分不出前后。
哪一个木马
黑孩子可以骑?

## As I Grew Older

It was a long time ago.
I have almost forgotten my dream.
But it was there then,
In front of me,
Bright like a sun—
My dream.

And then the wall rose,
Rose slowly,
Slowly,

Between me and my dream.
Rose until it touched the sky—
The wall.

Shadow.
I am black.

I lie down in the shadow.
No longer the light of my dream before me,
Above me.
Only the thick wall.
Only the shadow.

My hands!
My dark hands!
Break through the wall!
Find my dream!
Help me to shatter this darkness,
To smash this night,
To break this shadow
Into a thousand lights of sun,

Into a thousand whirling dreams
Of sun!

## 我长大的时候

那是很久以前。
我的梦现在都快被遗忘。
但那时它在那里，
在我面前，
光明如太阳——
我的梦。

然后就升起了这堵墙，

慢慢地升起，
慢慢地，
横亘于我和我的梦中间。
高耸直抵苍穹……
这堵墙。

阴影。
我是黑人。

我躺倒在这阴影里。
眼前没了梦的光辉，
不在我的头上。
只有这厚厚的墙。
只有这阴影。

我的双手！
我黑色的双手！
砸开这堵墙！
找回我的梦！
帮我冲破这黑暗，
捣毁这黑夜，
打破这阴影
把它变成太阳的万丈光芒，

把它变成太阳千万个飞旋的
梦想！

## Dreams

Hold fast to dreams
For if dreams die
Life is a broken-winged bird
That cannot fly.
Hold fast to dreams
For when dreams go

Life is a barren field
Frozen with snow.

## 梦

紧紧地抓住梦，
梦若是消亡
生命就像鸟儿折了翅膀
再也不能飞翔。
紧紧抓住梦，
梦若是消失
生命就像贫瘠的荒野，
雪覆冰封，万物不再生长。

## Mother to Son

Well, son, I'll tell you:
Life for me ain't been no crystal stair.
It's had tacks in it,
And splinters,
And boards torn up,
And places with no carpet on the floor—
Bare.
But all the time
I'se been a-climbin' on,
And reachin' landin's,
And turnin' corners,
And sometimes goin' in the dark
Where there ain't been no light.
So, boy, don't you turn back.
Don't you set down on the steps.
'Cause you finds it's konder hard.
Don't you fall now—
For I'se still goin', honey,
I'se still climbin',

And life for me ain't been no crystal stair.

## 母亲写给儿子

哎，孩子，听妈妈说：
生活对我来说不是水晶建造的楼梯。
它布满荆棘，
鸡零狗碎，
木板破裂，
有些地方没有铺地毯——
裸露无遗。
但妈妈从来没有气馁，
一个劲儿往上爬，
爬到梯台拐角处，
拐个弯又继续，
时而需要摸黑前行，
没有一丝光亮，
所以孩子，不要放弃。
哪怕历经千辛万苦，
在人生的阶梯上永不停留。
不能甘心放弃。
妈妈还在辛苦跋涉，好孩子，
妈妈还在奋力攀登。
生活呀，对我来说不是水晶建造的楼梯。

## Luck

Sometimes a crumbfalls
From the tables of joy,
Sometimes a bone
Is flung.

To some people
Love is given,
To others

Only heaven.

## 运气

有时欢乐的餐桌
掉下一片面包屑，
有时抛下
一块骨头。

对有些人
爱是给予，
对他人
可是天堂。

## Peace

We passed their graves:
The dead men there,
Winners or losers,
Did not care.

In the dark
They could not see
Who had gained
Their victory.

## 和平

我们穿过了他们的坟墓:
已故的人葬在那里，
成功者或者失败者，
已不在乎。

黑暗中
他们无法看到

谁获得了
胜利。

## Warning

Negroes,
Sweet and docile,
Meek, humble, and kind:
Beware the day
They change their mind!

Wind
In the cotton fields,
Gentle breeze:
Beware the hour
It uproots trees!

## 警告

黑人,
亲切、温顺、
柔和、谦恭、友好:
当心有朝一日
他们改变主意!

风儿
在棉田,
轻轻吹:
当心某一时刻
它将树木连根拔起!

# 马娅·安杰卢
# （Maya Angelou，1928—2014）

马娅·安杰卢1928年生于美国密苏里州的圣路易斯，原名Marguerite Annie Johnson。她3岁时父母离异，被寄养到外祖母家，她13岁在旧金山一所劳工学校学习舞蹈与戏剧表演。马娅16岁时怀孕，中学毕业后不久生下一子。因生活所迫，曾经做过电车售票员，餐馆里的侍者和厨师、夜总会的舞女和歌女。

1952年，马娅与希腊水手托什·安杰洛斯（Tosh Angelos）结婚，但很快以分手告终。离婚后，马娅带着孩子离开旧金山去纽约寻找工作。在这期间，马娅涉足演艺行业，受邀参与歌剧《波吉与贝丝》（*Porgy and Bess*）的表演，并于1954和1955年参加了去欧洲的巡演。为了提高演技，她拜美国现代舞创始人之一马萨·格林汉姆（Martha Graham）为师学习现代舞，与著名黑人舞蹈家阿尔文·艾利（Alvin Ailey）一起参加电视舞蹈综艺节目，1957年她还发行了自己的第一张唱片。

在纽约期间，马娅与来自南非的民权斗士乌苏姆齐·L·梅克（Vusumzi L. Make）相爱。1960年，两人带着她的儿子移居开罗。在开罗，她担任英语周刊《阿拉伯观察家》的编辑。后来，全家又搬到加纳。她担任了加纳大学音乐舞蹈学院的老师兼助理教务长，还担任一家杂志的编辑，为《加纳时报》和加纳广播公司撰稿。期间，她如饥似渴地阅读各种书籍，学习法语、西班牙语、意大利语、阿拉伯语和西非语言凡提语（Fanti）。美国黑人民权运动领袖马尔科姆（Malcolm）访问加纳时，她有幸与他相见，并同他建立起了良好关系。

1964年，马娅回到美国，住在纽约哈莱姆区。在那里她结识了另一位民权运动领袖马丁·路德·金。在这期间，她还认识了作家朋友詹姆斯·鲍德温（James Baldwin）。在鲍德温的鼓励和指导下，她开始了写作。1969年马娅的自传体小说《我知道笼中鸟儿为何歌唱》出版，立刻引起广泛关注，获得如潮的好评。此后，她的新作品不断出现，形式持续翻新，不仅有自传，还有小说、诗歌、戏剧、散文等。同她的第一部作品一样，这些作品不仅在美国赢得读者的普遍喜爱，而且在国外也广受欢迎。

由于她在文学领域以及社会活动方面的杰出表现，多位美国总统曾邀请她参加各种活动。福特总统任命她为“庆祝美国革命二百周年委员会”的成员；卡特邀请她担任“国际妇女年总统委员会”成员；比尔·克林顿1993年元月的就职仪式上邀请她撰写并朗诵了《清晨的脉搏》这首诗；2011年奥巴马总统授予她美国公民的最高奖“总统自由勋章”。

2014年5月28日，马娅在位于北卡罗莱纳州的家中去世，享年86岁。时任总统奥巴马在一份声明中说，“今天，米歇尔和我与全世界数百万人一起怀念我们这个时代最耀眼的一颗明星——一位才华横溢的作家、一个忠贞不渝的朋友、一名真正杰出的女性。”

马娅·安杰卢是位才华横溢、作品丰富的作家。主要作品包括传记《我知道笼中鸟儿为何歌唱》(*I Know Why the Caged Bird Sings*, 1969)、《以我之名相聚》(*Gather Together in My Name*, 1974)、《唱啊，跳啊，就像过圣诞节一样快乐》(*Singin' and Swingin' and Gettin' Merry Like Christmas*, 1976)、《女人心语》(*The Heart of a Woman*, 1981)、《上帝的孩子都需要旅游鞋》(*All God's Children Need Traveling Shoes*, 1986)、《歌声飞入云霄》(*A Song Flung up to Heaven*, 2002)、《妈妈、我、妈妈》(*Mom & Me & Mom*, 2013)；诗集《在我死前给我一口凉水吧》(*Just Give Me a Cool Drink of Water' fore I Die*, 1971)、《但求我的翅膀能合身》(*Oh Pray My Wings Gonna Fit Me Well*, 1975)、《我仍将奋起》(*And Still I Rise*, 1978)、《调酒器，为何没有声音?》(*Shaker, Why Don't You Sing?* 1983)、《现在，希巴女王唱这首歌》(*Now Sheba Sings the Song*, 1987)、《我不为所动》(*I Shall Not Be Moved*, 1990)、《清晨的脉搏》(*On the Pulse of Morning*, 1993)、《马娅·安杰卢诗歌全集》(*The Complete Collected Poems of Maya Angelou*, 1994)、《一个大胆而惊奇的真理》(*A Brave and Startling Truth*, 1995)、《不同寻常的女人：四首赞美女人的诗》(*Phenomenal Woman: Four Poems Celebrating Women*, 1995)、《诧异的和平》(*Amazing Peace*, 2005)；散文集《生活感悟》(*Lessons in Living*, 1993)、《此刻不再小视我的行程》(*Wouldn't Take Nothing for My Trip Now*, 1993)、《即使星星也会寂寞》(*Even the Stars Look Lonesome*, 1997)、《母亲：我的摇篮》(*Mother: A Cradle to Hold Me*, 2006)、《写给女儿的信》(*Letter to My Daughter*, 2008)等。

马娅作品的题材丰富，涉及日常生活的方方面面。在谈及生活和写作时，她说："我的所有作品，我的全部生活，我做的一切，都是为了生活，不仅仅是简单地、委曲求全地生存，而是充满了优雅与信仰的生存。虽然我们每个人都可能会遭受多种失败，但决不能败下阵来！"

## I Know Why the Caged Bird Sings

The free bird leaps
on the back of the wind
and floats downstream
till the current ends
and dips his wings
in the orange sun rays
and dares to claim the sky.

But a bird that stalks
down his narrow cage
can seldom see through
his bars of rage
his wings are clipped and
his feet are tied
so he opens his throat to sing.

The caged bird sings
with fearful trill
of the things unknown
but longed for still
and his tune is heard
on the distant hill
for the caged bird
sings of freedom

The free bird thinks of another breeze
and the trade winds soft through the sighing trees
and the fat worms waiting on a dawn-bright lawn
and he names the sky his own.

But a caged bird stands on the grave of dreams
his shadow shouts on a nightmare scream
his wings are clipped and his feet are tied
so he opens his throat to sing

The caged bird sings
with a fearful trill
of things unknown
but longed for still
and his tune is heard
on the distant hill
for the caged bird
sings of freedom.

## 我知道笼中鸟儿为何歌唱

那只自由的鸟儿
乘风飞翔
接着顺风飘浮而下
到风的尽头
将羽翼浸渗在
橙红色的阳光中
天空任它遨游。
但有一只鸟
在窄小的笼里气冲冲地踱步
残暴的笼条
将它困住
双翼被剪
双足被缚
于是放声高唱。

笼中鸟儿的歌声
凄厉震颤
忌惮未知
叫声回荡在
远处的山丘
因为笼中鸟儿
在歌唱自由。

自由的鸟儿想起另一股清风
轻轻穿过哀嚎树木的信风
还有晨光下草坪上等待的圆滚蠕虫
它将天空归为己有。

笼中鸟站立在梦的坟墓之上
它的幽灵噩梦中一声尖叫
双翼被剪，双足被缚
于是放声高唱。

笼中鸟儿的歌声
凄厉震颤
忌惮未知
但渴望依旧
叫声回荡在
远处的山丘
因为笼中鸟儿
歌唱的是自由。

## Phenomenal Woman

Many people wonder where my secret lies.
I'm not cute or built to suit a fashion model's size.
When I start to tell them,
They think I'm telling lies.
I say,
It's in the reach of my arms,
The span of my hips,
The stride of my step,
The curl of my lips.
I'm a woman
Phenomenally.

I walk into a room
Just as cool as you please,
And to a man,
The fellows stand or
Fall down on their knees.
Then they swarm around me,
A hive of honey bees.
I say,
It's the fire in my eyes,
The flash of my teeth,

The swing in my waist,
The joy in my feet.
I'm a woman
Phenomenally.

Men themselves have wondered
What they see in me.
They try so much
But they can't touch
My inner mystery.
When I try to show them
They say they still can't see.
I say,
It's in the arch of my back,
The sun of my smile,
The ride of my breasts,
The grace of my style.
I'm a woman
Phenomenally

Now you understand
Just why my head's not bowed.
I don't shout or jump about
Or have to talk real loud.
When you see me passing
It ought to make you proud.
I say,
It's in the click of my heels,
The bend of my hair,
The palms of my hands,
The need for my care,
Because I'm a woman
Phenomenally.

## 不同寻常的女人

许多人不理解我的秘密在哪里。
相貌平平、身材也不出众。
当我告诉他们，
以为我在撒谎。
我说，
它在我伸出的手臂，
在我的臀围
在我迈出的脚步，
在我噘起的嘴唇。
我是女人
不同寻常。

我步入房间
以你喜欢般的酷，
来到男人面前，
伙伴们要么站立，
要么跪倒在地。
随后聚拢在我周围，
一窝蜂。
我说，
它是我眼里的激情，
是我闪亮的牙齿，
是我扭动的蛮腰，
是我欢快的脚步。
我是女人
不同寻常。

男人们自己深感困惑
我身上有什么。
他们苦思冥想
无法触及
我内心的秘密。

我尝试告诉他们，
结果说依旧无法理解。
我说，
它在我弓起的背部，
在我灿烂的笑容，
在我丰满的乳房，
在我优雅的身姿。
我是女人
不同寻常。

如今你知道
我为何昂首挺胸。
我不用喊、不用跳，
也不用大声念叨。
见我经过
你应感到自豪。
我说，
它在我鞋跟的咔嗒声里，
在我卷曲的头发里，
在我的掌心，
在我需要的呵护里，
因为我是女人
不同寻常。

## Alone

Lying, thinking
Last night
How to find my soul a home
Where water is not thirsty
And bread loaf is not stone
I came up with one thing
And I don't believe I'm wrong
That nobody,
But nobody

Can make it out here alone.

Alone, all alone
Nobody, but nobody
Can make it out here alone.

There are some millionaires
With money they can't use
Their wives run round like banshees
Their children sing the blues
They've got expensive doctors
To cure their hearts of stone.
But nobody
No, nobody
Can make it out here alone.

Alone, all alone
Nobody, but nobody
Can make it out here alone.

Now if you listen closely
I'll tell you what I know
Storm clouds are gathering
The wind is gonna blow
The race of man is suffering
And I can hear the moan,
'Cause nobody,
But nobody
Can make it out here alone.

Alone, all alone
Nobody, but nobody
Can make it out here alone.

## 独自一人

昨晚，
躺着、思考，
怎样让心能够安稳，
水不再是诉求，
面包片不再像石头那样坚硬。
我领悟到了一点，
而且我坚信没错，
那就是没有人，
绝对没有人，
独自一人说清楚。

独自一人，完全不依靠别人，
没有人，绝对没有人，
独自一人说清楚。

一些百万富翁，
有钱不会用，
妻子像个妖精四处游荡，
儿女怨声载道、满腹牢骚，
为了医治他们的铁石心肠，
他们花重金聘请医生。
但是没有人，
绝对没有人，
独自一人说清楚。

独自一人，完全不依靠别人，
没有人，绝对没有人，
独自一人说清楚。

如果你仔细倾听，
我来告诉你我所知，
乌云在聚集，

暴风就要来临，
人类在遭受苦难，
我听到了呻吟，
因为没有人，
绝对没有人，
独自一人说清楚。

独自一人，完全不依靠别人，
没有人，绝对没有人，
独自一人说清楚。

## Song for the Old Ones

My Fathers sit on benches
their flesh counts every plank
the slats leave dents of darkness
deep in their withered flanks.

They nod like broken candles
all waxed and burnt profound
they say understanding
that makes the world go round.

There in those pleated faces
I see the auction block
the chains and slavery's coffles
the whip and lash and stock.

My Fathers speak in voices
that shred my fact and sound
they say our submission
that makes the world go round.

They used the finest cunning
their naked wits and wiles

the lowly Uncle Tomming
and Aunt Jemima's smiles.

They've laughed to shield their crying
then shuffled through their dreams
and stepped ' n' fetched a country
to write the blues with screams.

I understand their meaning
it could and did derive
from living on the edge of death
they kept my race alive.

## 赞美长辈

父辈们坐在长椅上，
身体紧贴木板，
木条在干瘪的双侧，
留下深深的凹陷。

他们面色蜡黄，风烛残年，
如同毁坏的蜡烛在打盹，
他们常说只有理解
世界才能够运转。

他们布满皱纹的脸上，
我看到了拍卖、
锁链、绑在一起的奴隶、
皮鞭、抽打、囤积。

父辈们说话的嗓门
击碎了我的证据，
淹没了我的声音，
他们说我们屈服
世界才能够运转。

他们绝顶聪明，
坦诚机智、能言善辩，
逆来顺受的汤姆叔叔，
还有和蔼可亲的杰迈玛大婶①。

他们用笑声掩盖痛苦，
在梦境中艰难跋涉，
步入一个国家，
写下触目惊心的郁闷。

我清楚他们的用意，
一定是为了
死亡边缘的生存，
延续我们种族的生命。

## Recovery

A Last love,
proper in conclusion,
should snip the wings
forbidding further flight.
But I, now,
reft of that confusion,
am lifted up
and speeding toward the light.

## 重生

近期的爱，
彻底结束，
将要剪断双翼
不能飞得更远。

① 杰迈玛大婶：指热情好客、身系围裙、头裹印花大手帕、职业为厨师的黑人女性。

但我，如今，
没有了困惑，
昂起头来，
向着光明奋进。

## Woman Work

I've got the children to tend
The clothes to mend
The floor to mop
The food to shop
Then the chicken to fry
The baby to dry
I got company to feed
The garden to weed
I've got shirts to press
The tots to dress
The can to be cut
I gotta clean up this hut
Then see about the sick
And the cotton to pick.
Shine on me, sunshine
Rain on me, rain
Fall softly, dewdrops
And cool my brow again.

Storm, blow me from here
With your fiercest wind

Let me float across the sky
'Til I can rest again.

Fall gently, snowflakes
Cover me with white
Cold icy kisses and

Let me rest tonight.

Sun, rain, curving sky
Mountain, oceans, leaf and stone
Star shine, moon glow
You're all that I can call my own.

## 女人的工作

我要照看小孩，
缝补衣裳，
擦拭地板，
购买食物，
接着炸鸡，
给婴儿换尿布，
给客人做饭，
给花园除草，
熨烫衣服，
给小孩穿衣，
打开罐头，
打扫房间，
照料病人，
采摘棉花。

阳光啊，向我普照，
雨水啊，洒在我身，
露珠啊，慢慢滴下，
再次凉爽我的额头。

暴风，来得猛烈些吧，
将我吹离这里，
让我在空中漂浮，
直到能够再次休憩。

雪片啊，轻轻落下，

用你那白色寒冷的
冰冻之吻将我覆盖，
让我今夜憩息。

阳光、雨露、苍穹、
山脉、海洋、叶子、石头，
星光闪烁，月光朗照，
但愿我能拥有这一切。

## When I Think About Myself

When I think about myself,
I almost laugh myself to death,
My life has been one great big joke,
A dance that's walked
A song that's spoke,
I laugh so hard I almost choke
When I think about myself.

Sixty years in these folks' world
The child I works for calls me girl—
I say "Yes ma'am" for working's sake.
Too proud to bend
Too poor to break,
I laugh until my stomach ache,
When I think about myself.

My folks can make me split my side,
I laughed so hard I nearly died,
The tales they tell, sound just like lying,
They grow the fruit,
But eat the rind,
I laugh until I start to crying,
When I think about my folks.

## 当我反思自己的时候

当我反思自己的时候，
差点笑得要死，
我的一生是个大笑话，
一段行走的舞蹈，
一首讲述的歌曲，
笑得差点窒息，
当我反思自己的时候。

六十年同这些人在一起，
我为她干活的那个小孩叫我姑娘——
为了工作我说“是的，夫人”。
傲慢不逊，绝不弯腰，
饥寒交迫但绝不示弱，
我笑得肚子疼，
当我反思自己的时候。

众亲令我伤心，
我笑得差点要死，
他们讲的故事听来像是谎言，
他们种植水果，
但吃的是果皮，
我笑得都要哭了，
当我想到我的众亲。

# 丽塔·达夫
# (Rita Dove，1952—)

丽塔·达夫是美国诗坛最受人瞩目的诗人之一。年仅35岁时她就因其诗集《托马斯与比尤拉》(*Thomas and Beulah*，1987)而获普利策诗歌奖。1993年荣获桂冠诗人称号，丽塔时年41岁，成为美国历史上最年轻的桂冠诗人，同时也是第一位黑人女桂冠诗人，并于1995年蝉联此项桂冠。1996年，美国总统克林顿授予达夫美国人文奖章；2011年，奥巴马总统为其颁发国家艺术奖章，成为迄今为止美国唯一接受过两位总统颁发奖章的诗人。

丽塔·达夫1952年出生于俄亥俄州阿克伦一个黑人中产家庭。父亲是化学家，在一家轮胎企业工作。受家庭影响，达夫从小喜欢读书，在校学习成绩突出，1970年高中毕业时荣获总统奖，高中毕业进入迈阿密大学学习。毕业后，她受富布莱特资助到德国图宾根大学(The University of Tubingen)学习。回到美国后达夫在爱荷华大学作家班学习写作，获艺术硕士专业学位(MFA)，随后开始文学创作。曾先后担任美国作家协会主席、美国诗人学会会长、弗吉尼亚大学教授。

达夫发表的主要作品包括短诗集《十首诗》(*Ten Poems*，1977)、《天空唯一的黑点》(*The Only Dark Sport in the Sky*，1980)、《曼陀林》(*Mandolin*，1982)、《傍晚的报春花》(*Evening Primrose*，1998)；诗集《街角的黄房子》(*The Yellow House on the Corner*，1980)、《博物馆》(*Museum*，1983)、《托马斯和比尤拉》(*Thomas and Beula*，1986)、《屋子的那一边》(*The Other Side of the House*，1988)、《魅力笔记》(*Grace Notes*，1989)、《诗选》(*Selected Poems*，1993)、《自由女神与我们同在》(*Lady Freedom Among Us*，1993)、《母爱：诗歌》(*Mother Love：Poems*，1995)、《和罗萨·帕克斯同坐公交车》(*On the Bus with Rosa Parks*，1999)、《美式舞蹈》(*American Smooth*，2004)、《穆拉提克奏鸣曲：诗歌》(*Sonata Mulattica：Poems*，2009)、《诗选：1974—2004》(*Collected Poems*：1974—2004，2016)。除此之外，达夫出版了短篇故事集《第五个星期天》(*Fifth Sunday*，1985，1990)、小说《穿过象牙门》(*Through the Ivory Gate*，1992)、戏剧《地球更黑的一面：一出戏》(*The Darker Side of the Earth：A Play*，1996)、随笔《诗人的世界》(*The Poet's World*，1995)、歌词《屋中奴隶》(*The House Slave*，1990)、《二十世纪之歌》(*Song for the Twentieth Century*，1999)等。

作为黑人作家，达夫的诗歌主题自然涉及种族问题；但与早期的黑人作家不同，她的作品里少了愤怒的情绪、激烈的言辞，语气温和平静，有时和谐风趣。与此同时，她也非常乐于描写女性的主题，关注女性的命运，展现她们细腻的内心世界。达夫的诗歌语言优美，富有极强的音乐性。

## Vacation

I love the hour before takeoff,
that stretch of no time, no home
but the gray vinyl seats linked like
unfolding paper dolls. Soon we shall
be summoned to the gate, soon enough
there'll be the clumsy procedure of row numbers
and perforated stubs—but for now
I can look at these ragtag nuclear families
with their cooing and bickering
or the heeled bachelorette trying
to ignore a baby's wail and the baby's
exhausted mother waiting to be called up early
while the athlete, one monstrous hand
asleep on his duffel bag, listens,
perched like a seal trained for the plunge.
Even the lone executive
who has wandered this far into summer
with his lasered itinerary, briefcase
knocking his knees—even he
has worked for the pleasure of bearing
no more than a scrap of himself
into this hall. He'll dine out, she'll sleep late,
they'll let the sun burn them happy all morning
—a little hope, a little whimsy
before the loudspeaker blurts
and we leap up to become
Flight 828, now boarding at Gate 17.

## 度假

我喜欢起飞前的那段时间，
时间确认，抵达地认定，

眼前只有成排的灰色塑料座椅，
犹如展开的折纸玩偶连在一起。
待会儿我们就要到登机口，
瞬间开始古板地安排登机顺序，
在机票上打孔——但眼下
看看那些乱糟糟的小家庭，
有的在叫，有的在闹；
还有穿高跟鞋的单身女子，
全然不顾婴儿的哭嚎，
身心疲惫的母亲等着快点叫号；
而身强力壮的乘客在静等通知，
一只大手安稳地放在行李箱上，
如同训练有素的海豹伺机下水。
甚至形影孤单的行政领导，
终于等来了夏天，
手拿打印行程单，
公文袋敲打着双膝——
他也要委屈一下自己，
来到大厅享受这种“快乐”。
他会外餐，她会晚起，
要让日光整个早晨幸福地晒着自己，
——一丝小希望，些许遐想，
广播声突然响起，
大家一跃而起，
航班 828，
17 号登机口开始登机。

## The Secret Garden

I was ill, lying on my bed of old papers,
when you came with white rabbits in your arms;
and the doves scattered upwards, flying to mothers,
and the snails sighed under their baggage of stone...

Now your tongue grows like celery between us:

Because of our love-cries, cabbage darkens in its nest;
the cauliflower thinks of her pale, plump children
and turns greenish-white in a light like the ocean's.

I was sick, fainting in the smell of teabags,
when you came with tomatoes, a good poetry.
I am being wooed. I am being conquered
by a cliff of limestone that leaves chalk on my breasts.

## 秘密花园①

我卧病在铺满旧报纸的床上,
你怀抱白兔来到床前;
鸽子四散飞起,飞向妈妈,
蜗牛背负石头发出叹息……

如今你的舌头犹如我们之间的西芹:
由于我们爱的呼唤,甘蓝在巢穴黯淡;
菜花想起她苍白、胖乎乎的小孩,
在阳光下变成海洋的青白。

我病了,被袋泡茶味熏倒,
你带着西红柿、美妙的诗歌来到床前。
向我袒露爱意。我被打动,
石灰岩峭壁在我胸部留下白色粉记。

## The Cane Fields

There is a parrot imitating spring
in the palace, its feathers parsley green.
Out of the swamp the cane appears
to haunt us, and we cut it down. El General

① 《秘密花园》:西方家喻户晓的儿童文学女作家弗兰西斯·霍奇森·伯内特(Frances Hodgson Urnett, 1894—1924)创作的一部儿童小说。

searches for a word; he is all the world
there is. Like a parrot imitating spring,
we lie down screaming as rain punches through
and we come up green. We cannot speak an R—
out of the swamp, the cane appears
and then the mountain we call in whispers Katalina.
The children gnaw their teeth to arrowheads.
There is a parrot imitating spring.
El① General has found his word: perejil②.
Who says it, lives. He laughs, teeth shining
out of the swamp. The cane appears
in our dreams, lashed by wind and streaming.
And we lie down. For every drop of blood
there is a parrot imitating spring.
Out of the swamp the cane appears.

## 甘蔗地

宫殿里有只鹦鹉在模仿春天，
羽毛翠绿如欧芹。
沼泽地里长出甘蔗令人不可思议，
我们将其砍倒。
El 将军搜寻单词；
他可是了不起的人物。
就像模仿春天的鹦鹉，
我们躺下尖叫，
雨水侵打我们的身体，
起来全身透绿。
我们无法说出来自沼泽地的 R——，
甘蔗出现，接着我们拜访大山，

① El：墨西哥著名导演路易斯·布努埃尔(Luis Bunue)1953 年导演的电影《他》。这是一部娱乐性的黑色喜剧作品，讽刺了宗教、贵族的虚伪，强调了社会规范压抑人性的主题。

② Perejil：也可译为佩雷·吉尔，地中海一个无人居住的小岛，摩洛哥和西班牙都宣称对其拥有主权。

大山轻声呼唤卡塔利娜①。
孩子们咬牙切齿。
El 将军找到了单词：欧芹。
谁说谁活命。他哈哈大笑，
牙齿在沼泽地熠熠生辉。
甘蔗在梦中出现，被风和溪流抽打。
我们躺着。为了每一滴血，
有只鹦鹉模仿春天。
从沼泽地长出了甘蔗。

## "I Have Been a Stranger in a Strange Land"

It wasn't bliss. What was bliss
but the ordinary life? She'd spend hours
in patter, moving through whole days
touching, sniffing, tasting... exquisite
housekeeping in a charmed world.
And yet there was always

more of the same, all that happiness,
the aimless being there.
So she wandered for a while, bush to arbor,
lingered to look through a pond's restive mirror.
He was off cataloging the universe, probably,
pretending he could organize
what was clearly someone else's chaos.

That's when she found the tree,
the dark, crabbed branches
bearing up such speechless bounty,
she knew without being told
this was forbidden. It wasn't
a question of ownership—

① 卡塔利娜：电影《他》的女主人公。

who could lay claim to
such maddening perfection?

And there was no voice in her head,
no whispered intelligence lurking
in the leaves—just an ache that grew
until she knew she'd already lost everything
except desire, the red heft of it
warming her outstretched palm.

## “身在异乡为异客”

那不是幸福。除了平凡的生活，幸福还有什么?
她没完没了地唠唠叨叨，
日复一日地东摸西摸，
闻闻这，尝尝那……
魅力无穷的世界里的精细管家。
然而同样的事情总是没法做完，

所有幸福，
都在这些漫无目的的事情里。
于是她随意走了走，从灌木丛到乔木，
停在池塘边欣赏波光粼粼的水面。
他外出采集宇宙资料，也许，
自以为他能够把他人已确定的
混乱整理得井然有序。

就在这时她发现了那棵树，
黑色、蓬乱的枝条，
挂满这些无言的奖品，
不用说她明白
那是禁果。
这不是所有权的问题——
谁能够要求
拥有如此令人发狂的完美之物?

她内心一无所求，
树叶中也没有隐藏嘀嘀咕咕的智慧，
只有日益增长的痛苦，
后来幡然醒悟，
她除了欲望已经一无所有，
欲望的烈火，
温暖着她伸开的手心。

## Chocolate

Velvet fruit, exquisite square
I hold up to sniff
between finger and thumb—

how you numb me
with your rich attentions!
If I don't eat you quickly,

You'll melt in my palm.
Pleasure seeker, if i let you
you'd liquefy everywhere.

Knotted smoke, dark punch
of earth and night and leaf,
for a taste of you

any woman would gladly
crumble to ruin.
Enough chatter: I am ready

to fall in love!

## 巧克力

天鹅绒般光滑的果品，

做成精美的方块
我用食指和拇指拿起闻了闻——

你味道醇美，
沁人心脾！
如果不立即吃掉，

你会融化在我手心。
享乐追求者，如果给你自由，
你会遍地融化。

锁住烟雾，给地面、
夜晚和树叶打上黑色的洞，
为了尝一口你，

哪怕粉身碎骨
每个女人都乐意。
再不絮叨：我已做好准备

坠入爱河！

## Exit

Just when hope withers, the visa is granted.
The door opens to a street like in the movies,
clean of people, of cats; except it is your street
you are leaving. A visa has been granted,
'provisionally'—a fretful word.
The windows you have closed behind
you are turning pink, doing what they do
every dawn. Here it's gray. The door
to the taxicab waits. This suitcase,
the saddest object in the world.
Well, the world's open. And now through
the windshield the sky begins to blush

as you did when your mother told you
what it took to be a woman in this life.

## 出口

希望就要破灭，签证获批。
通往大街的大门打开，
如电影里的街道，没人没猫；
不过它正是你要离开的那条街。
获批的签证上令人不安地写着“临时”。
你随手关上的窗户正变成粉红，
每个黎明都是这般景象。
现在是灰色。通向出租车的门等着。
行李箱，世上最伤心之物。
好啦，世界之门打开。
当你母亲告诉你
今生今世如何做个女人，
你做到了，
透过挡风玻璃，空中出现红色。

## Heart to Heart

It's neither red
nor sweet.
It doesn't melt
or turn over,
break or harden,
so it can't feel
pain,
yearning,
regret.

It doesn't have
a tip to spin on,
it isn't even

shapely—
just a thick clutch
of muscle,
lopsided,
mute. Still,
I feel it inside
its cage sounding
a dull tattoo:
I want, I want—
but I can't open it:
there's no key.
I can't wear it
on my sleeve,
or tell you from
the bottom of it
how I feel. Here,
it's all yours, now—
but you'll have
to take me,
too.

## 坦诚相待

既不流血,
也不愉快。
不会溶化,
或者翻转,
或破裂,
或僵硬,
所以没有疼痛,
渴望,
遗憾。

它没有经验
可以仿照,

甚至没有
任何章法——
只要紧紧
攥住肌肉，
倾斜一下，
别出声。虽然如此，
我感到它
在笼子里响动，
无聊的纹身：
我要、我要——
但无法打开：
没有钥匙。
我无法用
言语表达，
或者告诉你
我的真实感受。
此时，
它全是你的，现在——
但你也不得不
接受我。

# 垮掉派

“垮掉派”或称“垮掉的一代”(Beat Generation)是指第二次世界大战后在美国出现的一个文学流派。它是西方文学领域后现代主义文学的重要组成部分，也是美国文学史上的重要流派之一。

“垮掉派”文学首先以否定高雅文化为特点，拒绝接受艾略特式僵化的形式主义、保守主义和“古典主义”传统，反对含混、艰涩、朦胧、封闭的诗歌文体，标榜“开放性诗体”；主张文学作品以自由的文体风格、大众化的语言，真实地将个人的经验和情感以极其放任的、摆脱理性和艺术规律束缚的方式记录于纸面。由于笃行自由主义，“垮掉派”的文学创作理念往往是自发的。他们的作品通常违背传统创作规律，结构和形式杂乱无章，语言粗糙，时常为世人所诟病。

“垮掉派”诗人主要有艾伦·金斯伯格、劳伦斯·弗林盖蒂、格雷戈里·柯索等。

# 艾伦·金斯伯格
## (Allen Ginsburg，1926—1997)

艾伦·金斯伯格 1926 年出生于新泽西州纽瓦克一个保守的犹太知识分子家庭。受家庭影响，金斯伯格少年时期就开始诗歌写作。高中毕业后，金斯伯格进入哥伦比亚大学学习。在那里他结识了“垮掉派”的核心人物威廉·S·巴勒斯(William S. Burroughs,1914—1997)和杰克·克鲁亚克(Jack Kerouac，1922—1969)，并与他们建立了终身友谊。

青年时期的金斯伯格曾做过各种杂役，先后到欧洲、亚洲和南美等地旅游，潜心研读惠特曼和布莱克的诗歌作品；与此同时，金斯伯格积极参与各种“垮掉派”成员组织的活动。他支持民权运动，反对战争，抨击中央情报局，成为 20 世纪 50 年代抵抗美国主流文化的主要代表人物之一。

1954 年，金斯伯格移居旧金山。当年秋天在旧金山著名诗人组织的诗歌朗诵会上，金斯伯格朗诵了他振聋发聩的代表作《嚎叫》，不仅震动了美国诗坛，也引起了世界诗坛的广泛关注。金斯伯格一夜之间名闻天下，先后受邀到耶鲁大学、普林斯顿大学、哈佛大学等著名学府举办诗歌朗诵会。

20 世纪六七十年代，金斯伯格的兴趣转向东方文化，特别是以禅宗为主的佛教文化。作为“垮掉派”的核心人物，他积极参与当时各种反抗政府的激进活动，如反对战争、言论自由、女权运动等等。

1979 年，金斯伯格荣获“美国国家艺术基金会”(the National Endowment for the Arts)学术奖；1993 年荣获法国文化部颁发的“艺术与文学骑士勋章”(the Chevalier des Arts et des Lettres)。晚年，他受聘为布鲁克林学院教授。1997 年因肝炎并发症在纽约去世。

除了《嚎叫及其他》之外，金斯伯格的主要诗集包括：《空镜：早期诗歌》(*Empty Mirror*：*Early Poems*，1961)、《卡第绪及其他》(*Kaddish and Other Poems*，1961)、《现实三明治，1953—1967》(*Reality Sandwiches*，1953—1960，1963)、《行星新闻，1961—1967》(*Planet News*，1961—1967，1968)、《铁马》(*Iron Horse*，1972)、《美国的衰落：关于这些州的诗》(*The Fall of America*：*Poems of these States*，1973)、《心灵气息》(*Mind Breaths*，1978)、《冥界赞美诗：1977—1980 的诗》(*Plutonian Ode*：*Poems 1977—1980*，1982)、《白色寿衣：1980—1985 的诗》(*White Shroud*：*Poems*，1980—1985，1986)、《世界性的问候：1986—1993 的诗》(*Cosmopolitan Greetings*：*Poems*，1986—1993，1994)、《死亡与荣耀：1993—1997 的诗》(*Death and Fame*：*Poems 1993—1997*，1999)、《等我死后：没有收录的诗》(*Wait Till I'm Dead*：*Uncollected Poems*，2016)等。

金斯伯格是一位风格独特的诗人，他的思想激进、行为超俗。他诗中充满对社会不满而发出的声嘶力竭的呐喊以及自残式的狂欢，令全球为之瞠目。就诗歌形式说来，金斯伯格自称师承惠特曼，其作品语言通俗、节奏自由、句式具有明显的散文化特色。

## A Desolation

Now mind is clear
as a cloudless sky.
Time then to make a
home in wilderness.

What have I done but
wander with my eyes
in the trees? So I
will build: wife,
family, and seek
for neighbors.

Or I
perish of lonesomeness
or want of food or
lightning or the bear
(must tame the hart
and wear the bear).

Or maybe make an image
of my wandering, a little
image—shrine by the
roadside to signify
to traveler that I live
here in the wilderness
awake and at home.

## 孤寂

眼下大脑清楚
就像晴朗的天空。
趁此在
野外建个家。

除了
用眼在树间
四处徘徊，我还做了什么？于是
我就要组建：妻子，
家庭，还要
寻找邻居。

或者因
孤独而消亡
或者饿死或者
被雷劈或被熊吃掉
(必须驯服牡鹿
教训一下灰熊)

或许为我来此
做一幅画像，一幅小小
的画像——路边的
神龛告诉
游客我住在这里
生活在荒野之中
神清智明，感觉舒适。

## A Supermarket in California

What thoughts I have of you tonight, Walt Whitman, for I walked down the streets under the trees with a headache self-conscious looking at the full moon.

In my hungry fatigue, and shopping for images, I went into the neon fruit supermarket, dreaming of your enumerations!

What peaches and what penumbras! Whole families shopping at night! Aisles full of husbands! Wives in the avocados, babies in the tomatoes! —and you, Garcia Lorca, what were you doing down by the watermelons?

I saw you, Walt Whitman, childless, lonely old grubber poking among the meats in the refrigerator and eyeing the grocery boys.

I heard you asking questions of each: Who killed the pork chops? What price bananas? Are you my Angel?

I wandered in and out of the brilliant stacks of cans following you, and followed in my imagination by the store detective.

We strode down the open corridors together in our solitary fancy tasting artichokes, possessing every frozen delicacy, and never passing the cashier.

Where are we going, Walt Whitman? The doors close in an hour. Which way does your beard point tonight?

(I touch your book and dream of our odyssey in the supermarket and feel absurd.)

Will we walk all night through solitary streets? The trees add shade to shade, lights out in the houses, we'll both be lonely.

Will we stroll dreaming of the lost America of love past blue automobiles in driveways, home to our silent cottage?

Ah, dear father, graybeard, lonely old courage-teacher, what America did you have when Charon quit poling his ferry and you got out on a smoking bank and stood watching the boat disappear on the black waters of Lethe?

## 加利福尼亚超市

今晚，您在我的脑海中萦绕，沃尔特·惠特曼，因为我漫步在树荫下的街道上，头痛不已，特意举头望着那一轮满月。

我又饿又累，想买些意象时，走进霓虹灯闪烁的水果超市，想起你曾在这里逐一挑选！

多好的桃子！多美妙的安魂曲！全家人都在晚上购物！过道站满了丈夫！妻子在买牛油果，小孩在看西红柿！——而你，加西亚·洛尔卡[①]，你站在西瓜堆旁干什么？

我看见了您，沃尔特·惠特曼，没有孩子，孜孜不倦工作的孤独老人，扒拉着冰

---

① 加西亚·洛尔卡：(Garcia Lorca，1898—1936)，西班牙戏剧家，诗人。

柜里的肉，打量着食品售货员。

我听见您一个个地问：谁杀的猪排？香蕉多少钱？你是我的天使吗？

我跟随您在闪闪发亮的罐头堆中进进出出，心想身后跟着店面侦探。

我们一起大步流星地穿过宽敞的走廊，拿着自己喜欢的怪味朝鲜蓟，带着各种冰冻美味，从来不在收银员面前经过。

我们要去哪里，沃尔特·惠特曼？超市一小时后关门。您的胡子今晚指向哪里？

(我摸了摸您的书，想着我们在超市的奇幻历险，感觉荒唐可笑。)

我们要整夜穿行在这孤寂的街道吗？树木使街上的阴影更加浓重，屋子里的灯已熄灭，我们两人都会感到孤独。

我们经过车道上的蓝色汽车，梦想着那已逝去的充满爱的美国，回我们冷清的小屋？

啊，亲爱的父亲，灰胡子、孤独而勇敢的老导师，当冥府渡神不再摆渡，你来到烟雾缭绕的河岸，站在那里看着小船在黑水的遗忘河上消失，在您心目中美国是什么样子？

## Making the Lion for All It's Got—A Ballad

I came home and found a lion in my room...

A lion met America
in the road
they stared at each other
two figures on the crossroads in the desert.

America screamed
The lion roared
They leaped at each other
America desperate to win
Fighting with bombs, flamethrowers,
knives forks submarines.

The lion ate America, bit off her head
and loped off to the golden hills
that's all there is to say
about america except

that now she's
lionshit all over the desert.

## 让狮子尽其所能——一首民谣

回到家，发现屋子里有一头狮子……

一头狮子
在路上遇到美国
他们相互对望
两者在沙漠的十字路口。

美国大声尖叫
狮子发出怒吼
他们一跃而起扑向对方
美国渴望获胜
扔下炸弹，投入火焰喷射器，
刀、叉、潜水艇。

狮子吃了美国，咬下了她的头
大步流星奔向金山
这就是我对美国的看法
除此之外
她现在是
沙漠中随处可见的狮子屎。

## The Blue Angel

Marlene Dietrich is singing a lament
for mechanical love.
She leans against a mortarboard tree
on a plateau by the seashore.

She's a life-sized toy,
the doll of eternity;

her hair is shaped like an abstract hat
made out of white steel.

Her face is powdered, whitewashed and
immobile like a robot.
Jutting out of her temple, by an eye,
is a little white key.

She gazes through dull blue pupils
set in the whites of her eyes.
She closes them, and the key
turns by itself.

She opens her eyes, and they're blank
like a statue's in a museum.
Her machine begins to move, the key turns
again, her eyes change, she sings.

—you'd think I would have thought a plan
to end the inner grind,
but not till I have found a man
to occupy my mind.

## 蓝天使

马琳·黛德丽①斜靠在
一棵四方帽状的树上，
在海边高地唱起一首
老气横秋的爱情挽歌。

她是真人大小的玩具，
永恒的玩偶；
她的发式宛如一顶

① 玛琳·黛德丽：(Marlene Dietrich，1901—1992)，生于德国柏林，德裔美国演员兼歌手。

白钢制成的抽象派礼帽。

她的脸抹了粉，涂了脂，
像个机器人一动不动。
一只眼睛旁，从太阳穴伸出
一个小白键。

她透过眼白上
呆滞的蓝色瞳孔凝视。
眼睛闭上，
小键自动旋转。

睁开眼睛，双眼空白
如同博物馆雕塑的眼睛。
她这机器开始运行，钥匙
再次转动，眼睛变化，她歌唱。

——你以为我会有个计划
终结内心的痛苦。
除非找到一个男人
占据我的心。

# 格雷戈里·柯索
## (Gregary Corso，1930—2001)

格雷戈里·柯索是“垮掉派”代表性诗人之一。与其他“垮掉派”诗人一样，他生活放荡不羁，性格刚直不阿，但一生穷困潦倒，小小年纪流浪街头，依靠天赋自学成为广受同仁崇拜的优秀诗人，被誉为“诗人中的诗人”。

柯索1930年生于纽约格林威治村。幼年父母离异，16岁因偷窃被判入狱三年。服刑期间，他阅读了大量经典文学作品，作家包括费多尔·陀思妥耶夫斯基、司汤达、雪莱、克里斯托弗·马娄等的作品，并开始尝试写作。1950年他刑满释放回到纽约打工，后来到洛杉矶做记者，最后又做船员，先后去了非洲和南美洲。柯索在纽约与金斯伯格初次相遇，他们一起探讨诗歌写作。金斯伯格鼓励他要敢于大胆创新，不要囿于某一固定的模式。

1954年，柯索去了波士顿。在那里结识了一群以新方法写作的诗人。而真正对他产生诱惑力的是哈佛大学的图书馆。他每天置身图书馆，埋头于浩瀚的书籍之中，认真研读历史上伟大诗歌作品，汲取营养、积淀知识，为自己诗歌创作做准备。一年以后，他的第一本诗集《布拉特尔街的贞洁夫人及其他诗歌》(*The Vestal Lady on Brattle and Other poems*，1955)与读者见面。

1956年，柯索来到了“垮掉派”的大本营旧金山，与“垮掉派”核心人物克鲁亚克、金斯伯格等会合，与他们一起讨论文学，在咖啡馆和酒吧间朗诵自己创作的新作品，很快成为“垮掉派”的核心人物之一。1957年至1958年，柯索在巴黎生活期间完成了他的第二本诗集《汽油》(*Gasoline*)，出版之后引起热烈反响。有评论认为该诗集无论是内容，还是句式和措辞都有金斯伯格诗风的痕迹。而金斯伯格则认为诗集中的诗节奏感强，波普爵士乐①特色明显。他说，写诗时柯索经常以正规的词汇和节奏开始，然后慢慢地再把这些各不相同的成分消解成自己的声音。其结果构成一种声音和节奏极其不易调节的复杂语言模式。因此，有人指出在柯索看来优秀的诗歌必须要有完全出人意料的表达方式。这样一来，诗歌创作就不会再枯燥乏味，反而成了一种愉快的创新游戏。

20世纪70年代柯索几乎没有任何作品出版。1981年《原住民精神的先驱》(*Herald of the Autochthonic Spirit*)问世，其内容比前两本要少得多，因此除了其中的几首诗外，

---

① 波普爵士乐：(Bebop或Bop)，源于美国，是一种兴起于20世纪40年代初中期的爵士乐演奏形式，相较大乐团时期的爵士乐，波普爵士乐在垂直的和声上采用许多延伸音(Tension)，水平的旋律构筑除与和声的延伸音相应外，也运用许多邻接音与半音来即兴。节奏运用许多重音错置手法造成特殊的律动。

这本书并没有引起批评界的关注。柯索的主要诗集还有《炸弹》(*Bomb*, 1958)、《死亡的快乐生日》(*The Happy Birthday of Death*, 1960)、《万岁人》(*Long Live Man*, 1962)、《思想领域：新诗选》(*Mindfield: New and Selected Poems*, 1989)等。

除了写作之外，柯索曾经分别在纽约州立大学水牛城分校(the State University of New York, Buffalo)和位于科罗拉多州博尔德的那罗巴学院(the Naropa Institute in Boulder, Colorado)短期任教。柯索2001年去世，享年71岁。

## The Mad Yak

I am watching them churn the last milk they'll ever get from me.
They are waiting for me to die;
They want to make butters out of my bones.
Where are my sisters and brothers?
That tall monk there, loading my uncle, he has a new cap.
And that idiot student of his—I never saw that muffler before.
Poor uncle, he lets them load him.
How sad he is, how tired!
I wonder what they'll do with his bones?
And that beautiful tail!
How many shoelaces will they make of that!

## 疯牦牛

我瞧着他们搅动从我身上挤下的最后一滴牛奶。
他们在等我死;
想从我的骨头里榨出黄油。
我的兄弟姐妹哪儿去了?
那边那个高个子和尚，在给我叔叔背上载装货物，他戴了一顶新帽子。
还有他那个痴傻的弟子——以前没见过那个呆滞的家伙。
可怜的叔叔，任凭他们给他身上载装。
他该多难受，多累呀!
不知道他们会用他的骨头做什么?
还有那条漂亮的尾巴!
他们用它能做多少根鞋带!

## Destiny

They deliver the edicts of God
without delay
And are exempt from apprehension
from detention
And with their God-given
Petasus, Caduceus, and Talaria
ferry like bolts of lightning
unhindered between the tribunals
of space and time

The Messenger-Spirit
in human flesh
is assigned a dependable,
self-reliant, versatile,
thoroughly poet existence
upon its sojourn in life

It does not knock
or ring the bell
or telephone
When the Messenger-Spirit
comes to your door
though locked
It'll enter like an electric midwife
and deliver the message

There is no tell
throughout the ages
that a Messenger-Spirit
ever stumbled into darkness

## 命运

他们传达上帝的旨意
毫不迟疑
因此不用担心
被拘役
上帝赐予他们
宽边帽、使者杖、翼靴、
快如闪电的渡船
在时空的法庭间
畅通无阻

信使精灵
化成肉身
在它生命的旅程中
被委以诚实可信、
自食其力、无所不知、
纯粹诗人的使命

当信使精灵来到门前
虽然锁着
它不用敲
也不用按门铃
不用打电话
它会像电动助产士一样破门而入
传达信息

古往今来
无法确认
一个信息精灵
曾经跌入黑暗之中

## Many Have Fallen

In 1958 I took to prophecy

the heaviest kind: Doomsday
It was announced in a frolicy poem called *BOMB*
and concluded like this:
know that in the hearts of men to come
more bombs will be born
... yea, into our lives a bomb shall fall

Well, 20 years later
not one but 86 bombs, A-Bombs, have fallen
we bombed Utah, Nevada, New Mexico,
and all survived
... until two decades later
when the dead finally died

## 许多人已经倒下

1958 年我开始迷上了预言
最沉重的一类：世界末日
一首叫《炸弹》的滑稽诗扬言
那首诗断定：
相信未来人们的心中
期盼生产更多炸弹
……是的，投向我们的居住地

那么，二十年后
投下的就不是一颗而是八十六颗原子弹
我们轰炸过犹他、内华达、新墨西哥，
但都活了下来
……直到二十年后
死了的彻底死去

## Humanity

What simple profundities
What profound simplicities

To sit down among the trees
and breathe with them
in murmur brool and breeze—

And how can I trust them
who pollute the sky
with heavens
the below with hells

Well, humankind,
I'm part of you
and so my son

But neither of us
will believe
your big sad lie

## 人类

多么简单的深奥
多么深奥的简单
坐在树林里
用小声吼叫和微风——
与他们交流

他们污染了
拥有天堂的苍穹
污染了地狱所在的下界
让我如何相信他们

啊，人类，
我是你的一员
我儿子也是

但我们俩

谁都不会相信
你那令人伤心的大谎言

## Writ on the Steps of Puerto Rican Harlem

There's a truth limits man
A truth prevents his going any farther
The world is changing
The world knows it's changing
Heavy is the sorrow of the day
The old have the look of doom
The young mistake their fate in that look
That is truth
But it isn't all truth

Life has meaning
And I do not know the meaning
Even when I felt it were meaningless
I hoped and prayed and sought a meaning
It wasn't all frolic poesy
There were dues to pay
Summoning Death and God
I'd a wild dare to tackle Them
Death proved meaningless without Life
Yes the world is changing
But Death remains the same
It takes man away from Life
The only meaning he knows
And usually it is a sad business
This Death

I'd an innocence I'd a seriousness
I'd a humor save me from amateur philosophy
I am able to contradict my beliefs
I am able able

Because I want to know the meaning of everything
Yet sit I like a brokenness
Moaning: Oh what responsibility
I put on thee Gregory
Death and God
Hard hard it's hard

I learned life were no dream
I learned truth deceived
Man is not God
Life is a century
Death an instant

## 波多黎各哈莱姆台阶之令状

真理约束人
让他固步自封
世界正在改变
世界清楚它在变化
每日悲哀沉沉
老人面露厄运之相
年轻人误以为他们的命运就是那样
这就是真理
但这大都是假象

生命具有意义
而我不理解其中之意
甚至心想它毫无意义
但我依然希望、期盼、寻找一种意义
它不全是戏谑的诗歌
需要付费
召唤死亡和上帝
我斗胆冒险同它们交涉
没有生命，死亡毫无意义
是的，世界正在改变

但死亡依然如故
它夺走人的生命
这是他知道的唯一意义
而且总是令人心碎
该死的死亡

我可能天真幼稚，我或许严肃古板
或许为了避免处世的浅薄而略带幽默
我能背叛我的信仰
我能、我能
因为我想弄清每件事情的意义
然而如同一个心灰意懒之人
我坐地悲叹：格雷戈里啊
我赋予你什么责任
死亡和上帝
难、难、难

我知道人生并不是梦想
我明白真理就是欺骗
人不是上帝
人生百年
草木一秋

## Birthplace Revisited

I stand in the dark light in the dark
street
and look up at my window, I was
born there.
The lights are on; other people are
moving about.
I am with raincoat; cigarette in
mouth,
hat over eye, hand on gat.
I cross the street and enter the
building.

The garbage cans haven't stopped
smelling.
I walk up the first flight; Dirty Ears
aims a knife at me...
I pump him full of lost watches.

## 重游出生地

幽暗的街道，
我站在昏暗的灯光下
抬头仰望我出生的那间屋子的
窗户。
灯亮着：有人在
走来走去。
我穿着雨衣；
叼着烟卷，
帽子遮住眼睛，手按着手枪。
穿过街道，进了
大楼。
垃圾桶依然散发着
臭味。
上了一楼；肮脏的耳朵①
拿刀对着我……
我给他塞了一大堆丢失的手表。

① 肮脏的耳朵：提喻，指违法之人。

# 加里·斯奈德
# (Gary Snyder，1930—)

加里·斯奈德 1930 年 5 月 8 日出生在加利福尼亚州的旧金山，童年时期在西雅图郊区的农场度过，成年后进入俄勒冈的里德学院读大学，在那里他结识了菲利普·沃伦(Philip Warren)和卢·韦尔奇(Lew Welch)等"垮掉派"诗人。青年时期的斯奈德做过森林防火观察员、油轮水手等工作。一次偶然机会，斯奈德看到了一张中国古代水墨画，对此产生了浓厚兴趣，从画中他发现了中国人对待自然的态度。为了进一步了解东方文化和印第安文化，斯奈德离开工作岗位，到印第安纳大学专门学习语言学和印第安文化。20 世纪 60 年代初斯奈德回到旧金山，在加利福尼亚大学伯克利分校学习东方语言。在肯尼斯·雷克斯罗斯的举荐下，斯奈德在"六号艺术馆"朗诵了自己的诗歌《浆果宴》(*A Berry Feast*)。与同在"六号艺术馆"朗诵诗歌的金斯伯格直白的狂呼呐喊不同，斯奈德的诗以大自然为题材，语气平缓、沉稳，表达的思想意蕴深厚。因此，他的朗诵立刻引起轰动，为斯奈德在当地文学界赢得了广泛声誉。在获得"美国第一禅堂"(The First Zen Institute of America)奖学金之后，斯奈德去日本学习禅宗佛教，一年之后回到美国。此后，特别是 1956 年到 1959 年期间，斯奈德时常往返于加州和日本之间，一边学习、翻译禅宗经文，一边写作、发表诗歌。1959 年他的第一部诗集《砌石》(*Riprap*)出版；第二年另一本汇集了他 1950 年以来作品的诗集《神话与文本》(*Myths & Texts*)出版。1958 年，斯奈德在《常青评论》(*Evergreen Review*)上发表了自己翻译的 24 首中国唐代僧人寒山的诗。1975 年，斯奈德的代表作品之一《龟岛》(*Turtle Island*)荣获普利策诗歌奖。1984 年，斯奈德作为美国作家代表团的成员访问中国，实现了他多年的梦想。1985 年至 2001 年，斯奈德受聘为加利福尼亚大学戴维斯分校的写作教授，与此同时继续到世界各地游历、读书、讲学，特别是致力于各种环境保护工作。

1996 年，斯奈德出版了诗集《山水无尽》(*Mountains and Rivers Without End*)。该书以诗意的象征，将情感和叙述紧紧地融合在一起，赞美歌颂了栖息在地球一隅的生活。出版后立刻引起强烈反响，为他先后赢得了"博林根诗歌奖"(Bollingen Prize for Poetry)、《洛杉矶时报》"罗伯特·寇什终身成就奖"(Robert Kirshi Lifetime Achievement Award)、"约翰·黑自然写作奖"(John Hay Award for Nature Writing)，以及 1997 年度"山川平原书店联盟"(Mountains & Plains Booksellers Association)诗歌作品奖。斯奈德于 2003 年当选美国诗人学院院士，2004 年，他出版了新诗合集《高处不胜寒》(*Dangers on Peaks*)。

斯奈德是位非常勤奋的作家，他先后出版的诗文集已达十六卷之多。除了以上提到的诗集外，斯奈德的主要诗集还包括，《砌石与寒山诗》(*Riprap and Cold Mountain Poems*，1965)、《留在雨中：1947 至 1985 年未发表的诗》(*Left out in the Rain：New Poems 1947—1985*，1986)、《癖野》(*The Back Country*，1968)、《观浪》(*Regarding Wave*，1970)、《斧柄》(*Axe Handle*，1983)、《没有自然：新诗选》(*No Nature：New Poems*，1993)、以及诗、文、翻译合集《加里·斯奈德读本》(*The Gary Snyder Reader*，1999)等。主要散文集有《真正的工作：1964 年至 1997 年间的访谈》(*The Real work：Interview & Talks 1964—1979*，1980)、《荒野实践》(*The Practice of the Wild*，1990)、《大地家族：对即将到来的佛教革命的叩问与记录》(*Earth House Hold：Technical Notes and Queries for Fellow Dharma Revolution*，1999)等。

斯奈德一生钟情自然，痴迷佛教。他的文学创作不仅与他的生活经历密切相关，而且大部分都没有离开自然和佛教的主题。斯奈德的诗风深受东方文化，特别是唐代诗人寒山的影响，对禅宗有着无比深厚的兴趣，但他的文学写作并不仅仅拘泥于佛教。在谈到斯奈德诗歌作品的特质时，斯奈德研究专家鲍勃·斯托丁(Bob Steuding)在他的专著《加里·斯奈德》(*Gary Snyder*，1976)里总结出了以下几点，1. 荒野或东方背景；2. 避免抽象，强调具体；3. 简单有机的形式，诗行里一般都有意象；4. 使用口语；5. 深奥的引喻；6. 偶尔带色情的描写。①

## Hay for the Horses

He had driven half the night
From far down San Joaquin
Through Mariposa，up the
Dangerous mountain roads，
And pulled in at eight a. m.
With his big truckload of hay
behind the barn.
With winch and ropes and hooks
We stacked the bales up clean
To splintery redwood rafters
High in the dark，flecks of alfalfa
Whirling through shingle-cracks of light，
Itch of haydust in the
sweaty shirt and shoes.

---

① 张子清：《二十世纪美国诗歌史》，吉林教育出版社，1991，第 569 页。

At lunchtime under black oak
Out in the hot corral,
—The old mare nosing lunchpails,
Grasshoppers crackling in the weeds—
"I'm sixty-eight" he said,
"I first bucked hay when I was seventeen.
I thought, that day I started,
I sure would hate to do this all my life.
And dammit, that's just what
I've gone and done."

## 喂马的干草

从遥远的圣华金
穿过马里波萨，
沿着危险的山路，
他驱车走了大半夜
于早晨八点
将装满干草的车
停在了马厩后面。
我们用绞车、绳子和铁杈
把草捆一一堆起
垛子顶部直抵裂开的红木椽条
那里一片昏暗，
屋顶的木板裂开了缝，
光线透了进来，
苜蓿碎粒在光线里打着转，
干草碎屑沾在了
汗水渗透的短袖
或钻进了鞋里
令人浑身发痒。
午餐时间
炎热的马厩外
黑色橡树下，
——那匹老母马用鼻子嗅着饭盒，

蚂蚱在草丛里唧唧叫个不停——
“我六十八了”，他说，
“我十七岁时第一次堆干草。
刚开始干的那天我就想，
这活儿绝不能干一辈子。
该死，偏偏就这活儿
我居然还干了一辈子。”

## Lodgepole Pine: the Wonderful Reproductive

"Lodgepole Pine: the wonderful reproductive
power of this species on areas over which its
stand has been killed by fire is dependent upon
the ability of the closed cones to endure a fire
which kills the tree without injuring its seed.

After fire, the cones open and shed their seeds
on the bared ground and a new growth springs up."
stood straight

...

Hsu Fang lived on leeks and pumpkins.
  goosefoot,
  wild herbs,
  fields lying fallow!

  But it's hard to farm
between the stumps:
  the cows get thin, the milk tastes funny,
the kids grow up and go to college
they don't come back.
  the little fir-trees do

  Rocks the same blue as sky

only icefields, a mile up,
  are the mountain
hovering over ten thousand acres
of young fir.

## 美国黑松：奇妙繁殖（节选）

“美国黑松：矗立在这里的这一物种
有一奇妙的繁殖力，大火焚毁了树杆
种子却没有伤及，依靠没有裂开的球果
生命得以延续。

大火过后，球果裂开将种子撒在
寸草不留的大地，生长出一茬新芽。”
长得笔直。

……

徐芳靠韭葱和南瓜为生。
  藜属植物，
  野生草本植物，
  田地休耕！

  但是树桩间
无法耕种：
  奶牛变瘦，牛奶变味，
孩子们长大后上大学
他们不会再回来。
  小杉树会回来

  岩石和天空一般蓝
只有冰原，向上一英里，
  是山脉
俯瞰着万亩
杉木幼林。

## Pine Tree Tops

In the blue night
frost haze, the sky glows
with the moon
pine tree tops
bend snow-blue, fade
into sky, frost, starlight.
the creak of boots.
rabbit tracks, deer tracks,
what do we know.

## 松树冠

蓝色的夜里
撒下薄薄的霜雾，
明月当空
松树冠
压上了雪白的蓝色，隐没
在空中，冰霜、星光。
靴子的吱嘎声。
兔的足迹，鹿的行踪，
我们知道什么。

## Prayer for the Great Family

Gratitude to Mother Earth, sailing through night and day—
　and to her soil: rich, rare, and sweet
　　(*in our minds so be it*.)

Gratitude to Plants, the sun-facing light-changing leaf
　and fine root-hairs; standing still through wind
　and rain; their dance is in the flowing spiral grain
　　(*in our minds so be it*.)

Gratitude to Air, bearing the soaring swift and the silent
owl at dawn. Breath of our song
clear spirit breeze
(*in our minds so be it.*)

Gratitude to Wild Beings, our brothers, teaching secrets,
freedoms, and ways; who share with us their milk;
self-complete, brave, and aware
(*in our minds so be it.*)

Gratitude to Water: clouds, lakes, rivers, glaciers;
holding or releasing; streaming through all
our bodies salty seas
(*in our minds so be it.*)

Gratitude to the Sun: blinding pulsing light through
trunks of trees, through mists, warming caves where
bears and snakes sleep—he who wakes us—
(*in our minds so be it.*)

Gratitude to the Great Sky
who holds billions of stars—and goes yet beyond that—
beyond all powers, and thoughts
and yet is within us—
Grandfather Space.
The Mind is his Wife.

(*so be it.*)

## 为大家庭祈祷

感恩大地母亲，日夜运转——
还有她的土地：富饶、珍贵、温馨
（*愿我们的心灵就是这样。*）

感恩草木，对着太阳变换光亮的叶子
　还有发达的根系；在风雨中傲然挺立；
　在旋转的气流中翩翩起舞
　　*（愿我们的心灵就是这样。）*

感恩空气，托起翱翔的雨燕
　还有黎明悄无声息的老鹰。我们歌唱的气息
　清爽的微风
　　*（愿我们的心灵就是这样。）*

感恩野生生命体，我们的兄弟，传授奥秘、
　自由和方式；让我们享用它们的乳汁；
　自我完善、勇敢无畏、知情达理
　　*（愿我们的心灵就是这样。）*

感恩水：云彩、湖泊、河流、冰川；
　储存或排放；流经
　我们身体全部的咸海
　　*（愿我们的心灵就是这样。）*

感恩太阳：令人眩目的脉动的光
　透过树干，穿过薄雾，温暖熊和蛇
　睡眠的洞穴——唤醒我们的他——
　　*（愿我们的心灵就是这样。）*

感恩伟大的星空
　容纳亿万星球——已经超过那个数量——
　超越一切力量、思想
　但是就在我们心中——
　空间始祖。
　心灵是他之妻。

　　*（愿这样。）*

## Axe Handles

One afternoon the last week in April
Showing Kai how to throw a hatchet
One—half turn and it sticks in a stump.
He recalls the hatchet—head
Without a handle, in the shop
And go gets it, and wants it for his own
A broken off axe handle behind the door
Is long enough for a hatchet,
We cut it to length and take it
With the hatchet head
And working hatchet, to the wood block.
There I begin to shape the old handle
With the hatchet, and the phrase
First learned from Ezra Pound
Rings in my ears!
"When making an axe handle
the pattern is not far off."
And I say this to Kai
"Look: we'll shape the handle
By checking the handle
Of the axe we cut with—"
And he sees. And I hear it again:
It's in Lu Ji's *Wen Fu*, fourth century A. D.
"Essay on Literature"— in the
Preface: "In making the handle
Of an axe
By cutting wood with an axe
The model is indeed near at hand."
My teacher Shih-hsiang Chen
Translated that and taught it years ago
And I see pound was an axe
Chen was an axe, I am an axe

And my son a handle, soon
To be shaping again, model
And tool, craft of culture,
How we go on.

## 斧柄

四月最后一周的某个下午
指导凯伊投掷短柄小斧
旋转了二分之一，小斧就卡在了树桩上。
他想起那把没有柄的
小斧头，在商店里
于是去拿，想据为己有。
门后一根折断的斧柄，
长度够做一把短柄小斧，
我们砍下一截，把它
和小斧的头，
还有工作斧拿到木板上。
在那里开始将旧斧柄
嵌进小斧，耳边
响起了早期从艾兹拉·庞德那里
学到的那句诗
“操斧
　　　　其则不远。”
于是我对凯伊说
“瞧，我们按照
用来砍的斧子的
柄做斧柄——”
他明白。我又听见：
这是公元四世纪陆机
《文赋》①——序言里的
句子：“至于

① 《文赋》：晋代陆机的文艺理论作品，原文为“至于操斧伐柯，虽取则不远，若夫随手之变，良难以辞逮”。

操斧
伐柯
虽取则不远。”
我的老师陈世骧[1]
多年前就翻译并讲过这句话
于是我明白了：庞德是斧子，
陈是斧子，我是斧子
而我儿子是斧柄，不久
再重新做，模型
和工具，文化的技艺，
就是这样传承下来的。

## Jackrabbit

Jackrabbit,
black-tailed Hare
by the side of the road,
hop, stop.

Great ears shining,
you know me
a little. A lot more than I
know you.

## 长耳朵大野兔

长耳朵大野兔
黑尾巴
在路边，
蹦蹦、停停。

---

① 陈世骧：(1912—1971)，字子龙，号石湘，祖籍河北滦县。1912 年 3 月 7 日生，幼承家学，后入北京大学主修英国文学，1932 年获文学学士。1936 年起任北京大学和湖南大学讲师。1941 年赴美深造，在纽约哥伦比亚大学专攻中西文学理论。1945 年起，陈世骧长期执教于加州大学伯克利分校的(UC Berkeley)东方语文学系，先后任助理教授、副教授和教授，主讲中国古典文学和中西比较文学，并协助筹建该校的比较文学系。

大耳朵闪闪发亮，
你似乎认识我。
我不大
认识你。

## The Bear Mother

She veils herself
　　to speak of eating Salmon
Teases me with
　　"what do you know of my ways".
And kisses me through mountains.
Through and under its layers, its
　　Gullies, its folds;
Her mouth full of blueberries,
　　We share.

## 熊妈妈

她遮掩着自己
　　说起吃鲑鱼
戏弄我说
　　"你知道我有何办法"。
穿越群山亲吻我。
穿过并在岩层下、
　　溪谷中、褶皱里；
她嘴里塞满蓝莓
　　我们一起分享。

# 旧金山文艺复兴

美国文学史上，“旧金山文艺复兴”与“垮掉派”出现于同一时期、同一地点，而且两个流派中的许多代表性人物同属两个流派，因此，“旧金山文艺复兴”时常被认为是从“垮掉派”中衍生出来的一个流派。

“旧金山文艺复兴”主要指第二次世界大战后从美国各地移居旧金山海湾的一批文学家和艺术家。他们厌恶二战后的美国社会现实和僵化的文化体制，不满美国文坛风行的以艾略特为代表的现代主义诗风，在弘扬20世纪20年代的波希米亚文化的基础上，通过借鉴东方文化，恢复已失去的艺术理念和价值追求。与“垮掉派”强调社会问题不同，“旧金山文艺复兴”诗人更加关注自然传统，将大自然作为创作灵感的源泉。旧金山奇异的风光、嶙峋的海岸、周边美丽庄严的山脉是他们情感交流和抒发的最佳对象和素材。

“旧金山文艺复兴”诗人主要包括杰克·斯比塞(Jack Spicer，1925—1965)、加里·斯奈德(Gary Snyder，1930—)、肯尼思·雷克斯罗斯(Kenneth Rexroth，1905—1982)等。他们中的大多数人都同情普通劳动人民。他们的诗歌往往质朴、乐观、易于理解。

# 杰克·斯比塞
# (Jack Spicer，1925—1965)

杰克·斯比塞1925年生于洛杉矶一个小商人的家庭。他幼年离开父母，失去了家庭的温暖和关爱，幼小的心灵留下了终身挥之不去的伤痛。长大后，斯比塞考入加州大学伯克利分校；学习期间，对政治学产生了浓厚兴趣，特别是政治自由化方面的问题。除了课堂学习外，斯比塞积极参加各种讲座、研讨会以及其他相关活动，其人生观和写作思想受到重大影响。校园里的各种文学团体也令他非常着迷。在大学里斯比塞结交认识了一批在当地学习或工作的诗人，同他们建立起了深厚友谊。众多朋友中，罗伯特·邓肯(Robert Duncan)与他的关系最好。通过邓肯，斯比塞结识了一些西海岸的著名诗人。他们一起讨论人生，谈论诗歌创作，并给他们的活动起名"伯克利文艺复兴"(Berkley Renaissance)。大学毕业后，斯比塞留校担任语言学课程助教，但因为拒绝签署效忠美国的"效忠誓言"(Loyalty Oath)不久便被辞退。随后，他去了明尼苏达，在友人的帮助下得到了语言学教师的职位；然而没隔多久他又回到伯克利，继续担任语言学助教，撰写学位论文。

1953年，斯比塞受聘担任加州艺术学院(the California School of Fine Arts)人文系主任，但不久因酗酒被迫辞职，而后他去了东部，供职于波士顿图书馆；没过多久又回到旧金山就职于邓肯的麾下，在邓肯任主任的旧金山州立大学诗歌中心给学生讲授"诗歌与魔力"(*Poetry and Magic*)课程。讲座收到了意想不到的效果，追随者纷至沓来，聆听他的精彩报告，在当地形成了一个不可小觑的"斯比塞圈"。

1965年初，斯比塞应邀到加拿大的不列颠哥伦比亚大学讲学。斯比塞因病于同年8月在旧金山去世。

斯比塞的主要诗歌作品有《效仿洛尔迦》(*After Lorca*，1957)、《致敬克里利》(*Homage to Creeley*，1959)、《比利小子》(*Billy the Kid*，1959)、《哀悼制造商》(*Lament for the Makers*，1962)、《圣杯》(*The Holy Grail*，1964)、《语言》(*Language*，1965)、《杂志诗歌之书》(*Book of Magazine Verse*，1966)、《音乐之书》(*Book of Music*，1969)、《红色手推车》(*A Red Wheelbarrow*，1971)、《15个针对上帝的伪命题》(15 *False Propositions Agains God*，1974)、《告诫》(*Admonitions*，1974)、《一夜看台及其他诗》(*One Night Stand and Other Poems*，1980)、《傀儡》(Golem，1999)等。

斯比塞认为，"诗人是时间的机械师而不是藏尸官。"①所以通过语言，诗人可以将

① David Lehman, *The Oxford Book of American Poetry*, (New York: Oxford University Press, 2006) P. 725.

现实生活中瞬间即逝的事物转化为永恒，这也是他进行诗歌创作追求的最高目标。

## Thing Language

This ocean, humiliating in its disguises
Tougher than anything.
No one listens to poetry. The ocean
Does not mean to be listened to. A drop
Or crash of water. It means
Nothing.
It
Is bread and butter
Pepper and salt. The death
That young men hoped for. Aimlessly
It pounds the shore. White and aimless signals. No
One listens to poetry.

## 物语

这海洋，看上去卑微懦弱
比世间万物都要坚强。
没有人听诗。海洋
并不是用来倾听。一滴水
或者排山倒海之水。它
什么都不是。
它
是面包和黄油
胡椒和盐巴。年轻人
期待的死亡。漫无目的地
它撞击着海岸。白色和随意的信号。没有
人听诗。

## Frog

Like all the novels I've read

My mind is going to a climax
And a climax means a splash in the pool.
j j j
Booing. Booing. Booing.
And your heart is full of water
And your nose can't hardly breathe.
Remember
How black those pine trees were that fire burned.
All that black forest. And the noise
(Splash)
Of a single green needle

## 青蛙

就像读过的每一部小说
思绪正在走向高潮。
高潮如同池中溅起了水花。
唧唧唧
嘘嘘嘘
你的心里充满了水
你的鼻子几乎不能呼吸。
记得
那场大火把那些松树烧得多么黑。
整片黑色森林。还有
一根绿色的针
(溅起)
的噪声

## A Second Train Song for Gary

When the trains come into strange cities
The citizens come out to meet the strangers.
I love you, Jack, he said
I love you, Jack, he said
At another station.

When passengers come in from strange cities
The citizens come out to help the strangers.
I love you too, I said
I love you too, I said
From another station.
The citizens are kind to passing strangers
And nourish them and kiss their lips in kindness.
I walk the unbelieving streets
I walk the unbelieving streets
In a strange city.
At night in cold new beds the welcomed strangers
Achieve in memory the city's promise.
I wake in love with you
I wake in love with you
At last year's station.
Then say goodbye to citizens and city
Admit this much—that they were kind to strangers.
I leave my love with you
I leave my love with you
In this strange city.

## 加里的第二首火车之歌

火车驶入陌生的城市
市民们出来迎接那些陌生人。
我爱你，杰克，他说
我爱你，杰克，他说
在另一个车站。
旅客们从陌生的城市到达
市民们出来帮助那些陌生人
我也爱你，我说
我也爱你，我说
从另一个车站。
市民们对过往的陌生人很友善
滋养他们，亲切地吻他们的嘴唇。

我行走在满腹狐疑的街道
我行走在满腹狐疑的街道
在一个陌生的城市。
夜晚在冰冷的新床上，颇受欢迎的陌生人
在记忆中实现了城市的诺言。
我在与你的爱中醒来
我在与你的爱中醒来
在去年的车站。
然后向市民和城市说再见
绝对承认——他们善待陌生人。
我把我的爱留给你
我把我的爱留给你
在这个陌生的城市。

## Psychoanalysis: An Elegy

What are you thinking about?

I am thinking of an early summer.
I am thinking of wet hills in the rain
Pouring water. Shedding it
Down empty acres of oak and manzanita
Down to the old green brush tangled in the sun,
Greasewood, sage, and spring mustard.
Or the hot wind coming down from Santa Ana
Driving the hills crazy,
A fast wind with a bit of dust in it
Bruising everything and making the seed sweet.
Or down in the city where the peach trees
Are awkward as young horses,
And there are kites caught on the wires
Up above the street lamps,
And the storm drains are all choked with dead branches.

What are you thinking?

I think that I would like to write a poem that is slow as a summer
As slow getting started
As 4th of July somewhere around the middle of the second stanza
After a lot of unusual rain
California seems long in the summer.
I would like to write a poem as long as California
And as slow as a summer.
Do you get me, doctor? It would have to be as slow
As the very tip of summer.
As slow as the summer seems
On a hot day drinking beer outside riverside
Or standing in the middle of a white-hot road
Between Bakersfield and Hell
Waiting for Santa Claus.

What are you thinking now?

I'm thinking that she is very much like California.
When she is still her dress is like a roadmap. Highways
Traveling up and down her skin
Long empty highways
With the moon chasing jackrabbits across them
On hot summer nights.
I am thinking that her body could be California
And I a rich Eastern tourist
Lost somewhere between Hell and Texas
Looking at a map of a long, wet, dancing California
That I have never seen.
Send me some penny picture-postcards, lady,
Send them.
One of each breast photographed looking
Like curious national monuments,
One of your body sweeping like a three-lane highway
Twenty-seven miles from a night's lodging

In the world's oldest hotel.

What are you thinking?

I am thinking of how many times this poem
Will be repeated. How many summers
Will torture California
Until the damned maps burn
Until the mad cartographer
Falls to the ground and possesses
The sweet thick earth from which he has been hiding.

What are you thinking now?

I am thinking that a poem could go on forever.

## 精神分析：一首挽歌

你在想什么?

我在想初夏。
我在想雨中湿润的山丘
倾泻而下的雨水。流淌在
橡树和石兰属植物的空旷之地
进入阳光下交织在一起的古老绿色灌木、
黑肉叶刺茎藜、鼠尾草和春芥。
或者从圣塔安娜吹来①
肆虐山丘的热风，
一种夹杂着些许沙尘的疾风
摧毁了一切，让种子深受欢迎。
或者去城里，那里有
像笨拙的小马一样的桃树，

① 圣塔安娜(风)：是南加州地区一种季节性强风。这种风因在干旱条件下加剧了该地区灌木和森林的火灾险情，因而也常常被称为“魔鬼风”。

还有挂在街灯上面
电线上的风筝，
以及塞满枯枝的水沟。

你在想什么?

我想写一首慢如夏日的诗
起始很慢
七月四日大约在第二节中间的某个地方
下了几场罕见的雨之后
加利福尼亚的夏季似乎很长。
我想写首长如加利福尼亚
慢如夏天的诗。
你明白我的意思吗，博士? 它必须很慢
就像夏天的起始。
慢如夏日
热天在河边喝啤酒
或者站在贝克尔斯菲市①和地狱之间的
炙热马路上
等待圣诞老人。

你眼下在想什么?

我在想她很像加利福尼亚。
她站着不动时连衣裙就像一个路标。
高速公路在她的皮肤上来回穿梭
漫长空荡荡的高速公路
炎热的夏夜
月亮在上面追逐着长耳大野兔。
我在想她的身体可能就是加利福尼亚
而我，一位富有的东方游客
迷失在地狱和德克萨斯之间
看着从未见过的一个长长的、潮湿的、舞动的

---

① 贝克尔斯菲市：美国加利福尼亚州中南部城市。

加利福尼亚。
夫人，请给我寄几张廉价的明信片，
发送它们。
一张拍摄的胸部看起来
都要像奇特的国家纪念碑，
一张你的身躯跨度要像一条三车道的高速公路
离夜间寄宿的世界上最古老的酒店
二十七英里之遥。

你在想什么?

我在想这首诗会被重复
多少次。要有多少个夏季
蹂躏加利福尼亚
该死的地图才会燃烧
疯狂的制图师才会
坠落并占有
他一直躲藏的亲切坚实的大地。

你现在想什么?

我在想一首诗可以永远继续下去。

## Sporting Life

The trouble with comparing a poet with a radio is that radios don't develop scar-tissue. The tubes burn out, or with a transistor, which most souls are, the battery or diagram burns out replaceable or not replaceable, but not like that punchdrunk fighter in the bar. The poet
takes too many messages. The right to the ear that floored him in New Jersey. The right to say that he stood six rounds with a champion.
(Then they sell beer or go on sporting commissions, or, if the scar tissue is too heavy, demonstrate in a bar where the invisible champions might not have hit him. Too many of them.)
The poet is a radio. The poet is a liar. The poet is a counterpunching radio.

And those messages (God would not damn them) do not even know they are champions.

## 博彩生涯

把诗人和收音机做比较，麻烦是收音机不会产生疤痕组织。电子管烧坏了，或者晶体管坏了，电池或线路板烧坏了，换掉或者不换，大部分人也都这样；然而酒吧里那个醉醺醺的拳击手不是这样。诗人
收到太多信息。在新泽西，右拳打到他的耳朵而倒地。他可以说他经受了一个冠军六个回合的击打。
(然后他们销售啤酒或者继续进行博彩活动，或者，如果疤痕组织过于明显的话，在酒吧里展示，那些不在场的冠军们可能没有打到他。这些太多了。)
诗人是台收音机。诗人是个骗子。诗人是台抗击打的收音机。
而那些信息(上帝不会诅咒他们)甚至不知道他们是冠军。

# 肯尼斯·雷克斯罗斯
# (Kenneth Rexroth，1905—1982)

肯尼斯·雷克斯罗斯不仅是诗人，也是翻译家、评论家和哲学家。

肯尼斯·雷克斯罗斯 1905 年 12 月出生于美国印第安那州的南本德(South Bend, Indiana)。他 15 岁开始在期刊上发表作品。1927 年雷克斯罗斯移居到旧金山。受当地文化影响，雷克斯罗斯对东方神秘哲学和左派政治产生了浓厚的兴趣，时常同一些思想激进的左翼诗人在一起谈论人生、社会、哲学、诗歌创作等，特别是诗歌如何才能摆脱欧美感伤主义和形式主义桎梏的问题。

雷克斯罗斯中年时期的思想意识发生了一些变化，他的注意力不只局限于文学、哲学等形而上的问题，而开始关注生态、战争、非暴力等与日常生活密切相关的问题。

晚年的雷克斯罗斯垂青东方文学，还特意为自己取了中文名字“王红公”。他翻译了许多日本和中国经典诗歌，后来汇集成了两本册子，《日本诗歌一百首》(*One Hundred Poems from the Japanese*)和《中国诗歌一百首》(*One Hundred Poems from the Chinese*)。1964 年，因在诗歌创作和翻译方面的突出成就，雷克斯罗斯荣获美国文学艺术学会大奖。

雷克斯罗斯 1975 年获得美国诗人学会的最高奖“哥白尼终生成就奖”。1977 年获得“美国艺术基金会”(The National Endowment for the Arts)的资助。1982 年 6 月，雷克斯罗斯在圣巴巴拉去世，享年 77 岁。

雷克斯罗斯的主要作品有：《几点钟》(*In What Hour*，1940)、《凤凰与乌龟》(*The Phoenix and the Tortois*，1944)、《万物的印记》(*The Signiture of All Things*，1949)、《世俗智能的艺术》(*The Art of Worldly Wisdom*，1949)、《龙与独角兽》(*Dragon and Unicorn*，1952)、《保卫地球》(*In Defense of the Earth*，1956)和《自然数》(*Natural Numbers*，1963)等。

雷克斯罗斯的诗歌绝大部分植根于美国西部，西部的独特文化，西部的荒莽景色；书写个人生活经验，歌颂美丽大自然；其中一些作品，特别是后期作品不乏东方的元素和智慧。他的诗歌清新自然、宁静深邃、口语化特色明显。

## The Thin Edge of Your Pride

### I

Later when the gloated water

Burst with red lotus; when perfect green
Enameled grass and tree, "I most solitary,
Boating," rested thoughtful on the moated water;
Where the low sun spread crimson
Interstices in the glowing lotus; aware
Of the coming, deep in the years, of a time
When these lagoons and darkening trees,
This twilight sliding mirror where we have floated,
Would surge hugely out of memory
Into some distant, ordinary evening—
Hugely, in vertigo and awe.

IX

After an hour the mild
Confusion of snow
Amongst the lamplights
Has softened and subdued
The nervous lines of bare
Braches etched against
The chill twilight.
Now behind me, upon the pallid
Expanse of empty boulevard,
The snow reclaims from the darkened
Staring shop windows,
One by one, a single
Line of footprints.

## 锋芒初露

一

傍晚荡漾的水面
铺满红色的莲花;
草地和树木一片深绿,
"我只身一人泛舟湖上,"

在盈盈湖水上停歇沉思；
鲜艳的荷花丛间
撒满夕阳的余辉；
深秋即将来临
泻湖及日渐变黑的树木
黄昏我们曾经漂浮其上的移动镜子，
从记忆中倾泻而出
奔向某个遥远而平凡的夜晚——
汹涌澎湃、眼花缭乱、惊叹不已。

**九**

不久灯光下
纷乱的积雪
开始融化
寒冷的黄昏里
光秃秃的树枝
神经质地排列成
一排排。
身后空旷苍白的林荫大道上，
黑漆漆凝视着的橱窗上，
又积上了雪。
一片片，一行
脚印。

## The Bad Old Days

The summer of nineteen eighteen
I read *The Jungle*① and *The*
*Research Magnificent*②. That fall
My father died and my aunt

---

① *The Jungle*：《丛林故事》(*The Jungle Book*)，是20世纪初英国作家拉迪亚德·吉卜林(Rudyard Kipling，1865—1936)的早期代表作。该书由七个中篇故事结集而成，讲述了"狼孩"莫戈里和其他几种不同动物的故事。

② *The Research Magnificent*：《宏伟的研究》，英国著名作家赫伯特·乔治·威尔斯(Herbert George Wells，1866—1946)的作品。

Took me to Chicago to live.
The first thing I did was to take
A streetcar to the stockyards.
In the winter afternoon,
Gritty and fetid, I walked
Through the filthy snow, through the
Squalid streets, looking shyly
Into the people's faces,
Those who were home in the daytime.
Debauched and exhausted faces,
Starved and looted brains, faces
Like the faces in the senile
And insane wards of charity
Hospitals. Predatory
Faces of little children.
Then as the soiled twilight darkened,
Under the green gas lamps, and the
Sputtering purple arc lamps,
The faces of the men coming
Home from work, some still alive with
The last pulse of hope or courage,
Some sly and bitter, some smart and
Silly, most of them already
Broken and empty, no life,
Only blinding tiredness, worse
Than any tired animal.
The sour smells of a thousand
Suppers of fried potatoes and
Fried cabbage bled into the street.
I was giddy and sick, and out
Of my misery I felt rising
A terrible anger and out
Of the anger, an absolute vow.
Today the evil is clean
And prosperous, but it is

Everywhere, you don't have to
Take a streetcar to find it,
And it is the same evil.
And the misery, and the
Anger, and the vow are the same.

## 郁闷的往日

一九一八年夏天
读了《丛林》和《重大研究》。
秋天父亲辞世
姑母将我带到芝加哥居住。
我做的第一件事
就是乘坐有轨电车到牲畜饲养场。
冬日的午后
浑身散发着臭气
我迈着坚定的步伐走过污秽的积雪，
穿过污垢遍地的街道，
战战兢兢地窥视人们的脸色，
那些白天待在家里的人。
放荡而疲倦的面容，
饥饿和被洗劫一空的大脑，
如同慈善医院老人和精神病人的脸色。
孩童霸道蛮横的表情。
然后，污浊的暮色渐渐暗了下来，
绿色的汽灯和哔哔啪啪作响的紫色弧光灯下，
面前走来了下班回家的人们，他们看上去
有些依然抱有希望的最后一丝冲动或勇气，
有些诡秘痛苦，
有些衣冠楚楚但傻头傻脑，
大多数心灰意冷、头脑空虚、死气沉沉，
只有一望而知的倦怠，
胜过世间所有疲惫的生物。
街头弥漫着晚饭吃的炸土豆和炒白菜的酸味。
令人头晕作呕，

因悲伤而怒不可遏；
因怒不可遏而立下郑重的誓言。
如今罪恶昭然若揭
遍地横行，随处可见，
不用特意坐电车去寻找，
同样的罪恶。
悲伤还在、愤怒依旧，
誓言如故。

## Falling Leaves and Early Snow

In the years to come they will say,
"They fell like the leaves
In the autumn of nineteen thirty-nine."
November has come to the forest,
To the meadows where we picked the cyclamen.
The year fades with the white frost
On the brown sedge in the hazy meadows,
Where the deer tracks were black in the morning.
Ice forms in the shadows;
Disheveled maples hang over the water;
Deep gold sunlight glistens on the shrunken stream.
Somnolent trout move through pillars of brown and gold.
The yellow maple leaves eddy above them,
The glittering leaves of the cottonwood,
The olive, velvety alder leaves,
The scarlet dogwood leaves,
Most poignant of all.

In the afternoon thin blades of cloud
Move over the mountains;
The storm clouds follow them;
Fine rain falls without wind.
The forest is filled with wet resonant silence.
When the rain pauses the clouds

Cling to the cliffs and the waterfalls.
In the evening the wind changes;
Snow falls in the sunset.
We stand in the snowy twilight
And watch the moon rise in a breach of cloud.
Between the black pines lie narrow bands of moonlight,
Glimmering with floating snow.
An owl cries in the sifting darkness.
The moon has a sheen like a glacier.

## 落叶和初雪

未来岁月里他们会说，
“他们就像一九三九年秋季
的叶子一样纷纷落下。”
十一月已经来到森林，
来到了我们采摘仙客来的草甸。
岁末已近，
清晨的草甸朦朦胧胧，褐色莎草覆盖上了白霜，
留下鹿群踏过的黑色踪迹。
背阴的地方结了冰；
凌乱的枫树倒垂在水面；
金色的阳光在快要枯竭的小溪上闪烁。
昏昏欲睡的鳟鱼在棕色和金色的柱子间游荡。
黄色的枫叶在水面上打起了旋涡，
熠熠生辉的三叶杨叶，
柔软的橄榄色桤木叶，
最惹人注目的要数
那血红色的山茱萸叶。

午后的山岭
飘过薄薄的云层；
团团乌云紧随其后；
无风的空中下起蒙蒙细雨。
雨中的森林一片潮湿和寂静。

雨后的云层
紧贴着悬崖和瀑布。
傍晚风向起了变化；
开始下起了雪。
我们站在落雪的暮色中
看着月亮从云隙中升起。
黑色的松林间铺上狭窄的月光带，
随着漂浮的雪花跃动。
猫头鹰在晃动的黑暗中鸣叫。
月亮披上了冰川般的光辉。

## Doubled Mirrors

It is the dark of the moon.
Late at night, the end of summer,
The autumn constellations
Glow in the arid heaven.
The air smells of cattle, hay,
And dust. In the old orchard
The pears are ripe. The trees
Have sprouted from old rootstocks
And the fruit is inedible.
As I pass them I hear something
Rustling and grunting and turn
My light into the branches.
Two raccoons with acrid pear
Juice and saliva drooling
From their mouths stare back at me,
Their eyes deep sponges of light.
They know me and do not run
Away. Coming up the road
Through the black oak shadows, I
See ahead of me, glinting
Everywhere from the dusty
Gravel, tiny points of cold

Blue light, like the sparkle of
Iron snow. I suspect what it is,
And kneel to see. Under each
Pebble and oak leaf is a
Spider, her eyes shining at
Me with my reflected light
Across immeasurable distance.

## 双面镜

月黑之时。
夏末的深夜,
初秋干燥的天空
星光闪烁。
空气中弥漫着
家畜、干草和灰尘味。
老果树园里
梨已成熟。
老根茎上长出了
新枝,果子不能吃。
路过树旁听到
沙沙声和咕噜声
抬头在树枝间搜寻
只见两只浣熊
嘴里流着刺鼻的梨汁和唾液
瞪着水汪汪的眼睛
盯着我看。
它们认识我,因此
并没有跑开。
穿过黑色的橡树林
来到路上看见前边
灰尘覆盖的碎石里
荧光闪闪,犹如
光芒四射的铸铁雪花。
深感困惑便双膝

跪地探个究竟。
每块石头每片橡树叶下
都藏着一只蜘蛛。
无论我在何处看它们
它们的眼睛都对着我熠熠发亮。

## Andree Rexroth

(*Died October* 1940)
Now once more gray mottled buckeye branches
Explode their emerald stars,
And alders smoulder in a rosy smoke
Of innumerable buds.
I know that spring again is splendid
As ever, the hidden thrush
As sweetly tongued, the sun as vital—
But these are the forest trails we walked together,
These paths, ten years together.
We thought the years would last forever,
They are all gone now, the days
We thought would not come for us are here.
Bright trout poised in the current—
The raccoon's track at the water's edge—
A bittern booming in the distance—
Your ashes scattered on this mountain—
Moving seaward on this stream.

## 安德烈·雷克斯劳斯

(*1940年10月去世*)
斑驳的灰色七叶树枝条
又迸发出翠绿色的叶子，
桤树萌发出数不清的幼芽
披上了粉红色盛装。
明媚的春天重返大地，

那只隐藏的画眉
又在鸣啭啁啾，
阳光再次带来勃勃生机——
这些林间小径，
这些小路，
十年前我俩一起走过。
我们以为岁月会绵延不断，
如今那样的时光已经流逝，
我们不曾期盼的日子已然来临。
明亮的鳟鱼在急流中泰然自若——
浣熊在水边留下踪迹——
一只麻鸭在远处嘎嘎乱叫——
你的骨灰撒在这座山上
顺着小溪流向大海。

## Andree Rexroth Elegy

Lonely, caught in the midst of life,
In the chao of the world;
And all the years that we were young
Are gone, and every atom
Of your learned and disordered
Flesh is utterly consumed.

## 安德烈·雷克斯劳斯的挽歌

孤独，人到中年，
身处纷乱的世界;
我们年轻的岁月
一去不复返，你博学
而紊乱的肉体
已经彻底耗尽。

## The Love Poems of Marichiko

I sit at my desk,

What can I write to you?
Sick with love,
I long to see you in flesh.
I can write only,
"I love you. I love you. I love you."
Love cuts my heart
And scars my vitals.
Spasms of longing suffocate me
And will not stop.

**XⅧ**

Spring is early this year.
Laurel, plums, peaches,
Almonds, mimosa,
All bloom at once. Under the
Moon, night smells like your body.

## 摩利支子[①]的情诗

坐在书桌旁。
能给你写点什么?
坠入爱河,
多想看到生灵活现的你。
只能写道,
"爱你,爱你,爱你。"
爱使我心碎
让我伤痕累累。
阵阵渴望令我窒息
今生不会停息。

**十八**

今年春天来得早。
桂树、梨树、桃树、

① 摩利支子:Marichiko,日本女诗人。

杏树、含羞草、
瞬间百花齐放。
月光下的夜晚，
弥漫着你身体的芳香。

## Quietly

Lying here quietly beside you,
My cheek against your firm, quiet thighs,
The calm music of Boccherini
Washing over us in the quiet,
As the sun leaves the housetops and goes
Out over the Pacific, quiet—
So quiet the sun moves beyond us,
So quiet as the sun always goes,
So quiet, our bodies, worn with the
Times and penances of love, our
Brains curled, quiet in their shells, dormant,
Our hearts slow, quiet, reliable
In their interlocked rhythms, the pulse
In your thigh caressing my cheek. Quiet.

## 静静地

静静地躺在你身旁，
脸颊贴着你结实、安静的大腿，
博凯里尼①平静的音乐
在寂静中涤荡着我们的心灵，
当太阳离开屋顶，
来到太平洋上，静静地——
太阳就这样静静地离开，

① 卢伊吉·博凯里尼：(Luigi Boccherini，1743—1805)大提琴家。他于1743年2月19日出生在意大利卢卡。他受乐曲四声部的启发，创造了室内乐的新风格，成为西班牙路易王子喜爱的室内乐音乐家。1787年，普鲁士的弗里德里克·威廉授予他室内乐作曲家的称号。

太阳总是那么静静地运行，
如此安静，我们的身体随着时间的推移
和爱的忏悔而力倦神疲，
我们的大脑安静地蜷缩在壳里，蛰伏，
我们的心在交错的节奏中
缓慢、安静、稳定地跳动，
你大腿上的脉动
抚摸着我的脸颊。静静地。

# 自白派

自白派诗歌也称“坦白派”诗歌，其英文词中的“Confessional”派生于Confession一词，为宗教用语，意思是坦白、忏悔、告解圣事，又称忏悔圣事、修和圣事、和好圣事，为天主教七大圣事之一①。它仅仅是文学创作者以坦诚的态度将长久郁积于自己胸中的苦闷，特别是那些难于启齿的罪恶毫无保留地公布于世，以期达到心灵的解脱。“自白派诗的真正目的是心理现实的一种剖析，剖析自我和自我体验的世界之间的关系。”②

自白派诗人主要包括罗伯特·洛威尔、约翰·贝里曼(John Berryman，1914—1972)、西尔维亚·普拉斯(Sylvia Plath，1932—1963)、安妮·塞克斯顿(Anne Sexton，1928—1974)和莎伦·欧兹(Sharon Olds，1942—)等。

---

① 七大圣事：俗称七礼或七圣礼，是7种被赋予特殊神圣意涵的仪式，是教会一切宗教活动的基础。

② 张子清：《二十世纪美国诗歌》，长春，吉林教育出版社，1995，第614页。

# 罗伯特·洛威尔
# (Robert Lowell，1917—1977)

罗伯特·洛威尔 1917 年 3 月 1 日出生在美国东部历史文化名城波士顿的一个名门望族。中学时期，罗伯特先后就读于波士顿布里默学校(Brimmer Street School)和马萨诸塞州绍斯伯勒圣马克(St. Mark's School in Southborough)预科学校。受诗人艾伦·泰特(Allen Tate，1899—1979)影响，1937 年他转入俄亥俄州的肯庸学院(Kenyon College)，跟随著名文学批评家、诗人、新批评派领军人物约翰·克罗·兰塞姆(John Crowe Ransom，1888—1974)学习古典文学，开始致力于"形式工整而内容坚深"的诗歌创作。在此期间，罗伯特逐渐背离了家族世代信奉的清教主义，改信罗马天主教，并且与信仰天主教的小说家琼·斯特福德(Jean Stafford)结婚。然而从小耳濡目染的清教思想在他身上始终无法彻底销匿，清教传统在他的诗歌中永远是一个无法释怀的文化元素。

1940 年，以优异成绩从肯庸学院毕业后，洛威尔进入路易斯安那州立大学(Louisiana State University)研究生班学习，导师是新批评派大师罗伯特·潘·沃伦(Robert Penn Warren，1905—1989)和柯林斯·布鲁克斯(Cleanth Brooks，1906—1994)。第二次世界大战爆发后，洛威尔曾主动申请入伍服役，但因视力不好而被拒绝。随着战争的深入，数以万计的平民百姓惨死在各个战场，残酷的现实彻底改变了洛威尔对战争的态度。1943 年，他断然拒绝了美国军方的服役通知，为此被监禁了五个多月。服刑期间，洛威尔完成了第一部诗集《不一样的国度》(*Land of Unlikeness*)，诗集于 1944 年正式出版。1946 年《威利爵爷的城堡》(*Lord Weary's Castle*)出版，出版后立刻引起了轰动。诗人兼评论家贾雷尔赞美说，许多评论家认为《威利爵爷的城堡》如同奥登的处女作一样是一部举足轻重的作品；比奥登年轻的诗人中，罗伯特·洛威尔的作品最为出色。[①] 1947 年，《威利爵爷的城堡》获得普利策诗歌奖，如贾雷尔所言，洛威尔一举成为年轻一代诗人的领军人物。

受 20 世纪五六十年代美国西海岸如火如荼的新诗派的吸引，洛威尔 1957 年来到加州，加入"垮掉派"和"新文艺复兴"诗人的行列。新兴诗人的诗歌令他耳目一新，特别是金斯伯格那首近乎撕心裂肺般呐喊的诗《嚎叫》对他触动很大，让他重新认识了惠特曼、威廉·卡洛斯·威廉姆斯式的随意挥洒的自由诗体诗歌的魅力。为了配合心理疾病的治疗，他接受医生的建议开始书写自己的童年生活。这些散文体的回忆录后来

① From the Kingdom of Necessity. No other Book: Jarrell, Randall. Selected Essays, Harper-Collins, 1999.

被结集出版，取名《里维尔街 91 号》(*91 Revere Street*)，其中的大部分诗被收录进《生活研究》(*Life Studies*，1959)。《生活研究》的出版为洛威尔再次赢得了声誉，为他获得了 1960 年的“国家图书奖”。

20 世纪 60 年代美国各地风起云涌的反战和民运活动深刻影响到了洛威尔。这一时期，除了写作外，洛威尔也卷入了各种政治活动。1964 年，洛威尔出版了著名的反战诗集《献给联邦死难者》(*For the Union Dead*)。1967 年出版的《大洋附近》(*Near the Ocean*)以及 1969 年出版的《笔记 1967—68》(*Notebook* 1967—68)中的主题也都与美国当时的社会历史事件紧密相连，特别是《笔记 1967—68》真实地记录了洛威尔对当时世界、历史事件以及家庭生活的深刻思考。围绕《笔记 1967—68》的主题，1973 年出版了三本诗集《历史》(*History*)、《献给莉兹和哈丽特》(*For Lizzie and Harriet*)和《海豚》(*The Dolphin*)。《历史》收录了《笔记 1967—68》里一些大众话题的诗歌；《献给莉兹和哈丽特》汇集了《笔记 1967—68》里一些与描写他妻子和女儿的诗，还有一些述说他与第二任妻子哈德威克婚姻破裂的新诗；《海豚》中的诗描写的是他与第三任妻子、英国女作家卡罗琳·布莱克伍德(Caroline Blackwood)的婚姻生活，该诗集获得 1974 年度普利策诗歌奖。

晚年的洛威尔大部分时间陪同妻儿住在英国。1977 年 9 月 12 日，洛威尔去纽约看望前妻哈德威克，结果因路上心脏病发作逝世。最后一部作品《日复一日》(*Day by Day*)在他去世后不久出版。

## Beyond the Alps

### I

(On the train from Rome to Paris)

Reading of how the Swiss have thrown the sponge①
In once again and Everest is still
Unscaled, I watch our Paris Pullman lunge
Mooning across the fallow Alpine snow;
O bella Roma! It's against my will,
Like the tri—lingual Roman cooks who go
Forward on tiptoe, banging on their gongs.

① have thrown the sponge：译为认输放弃。根据拳击比赛规则，拳手每打完三分钟一个的回合，都要休息一分钟，用海绵或者毛巾擦去身上汗水准备再战。假如拳手眼看要被对方击倒了，那么他的教练或者副手可以把擦身用的海绵或者毛巾扔进拳击场里，表示自己一方认输了，请裁判终止比赛。所以，throw in the sponge 现在往往引伸为“认输”“放弃”的意思。

I leave the city of God where it belongs.
O gods, when the breast—thumping blimp unfurled
The eagle of Caesar, he was one of us
Only, pure prose, and less miraculous
Than those grand tours that our grand parents made
Immortal, when the artist followed trade,
While breezing on his trust fund through the world.

Ⅶ

My mountain-climbing train has come to earth.
Tired by the querulous hush-hush of the wheels,
The blear-eyed ego, kicking in my berth,
Lies still, and sees Apollo plant his heels
On terra firma through Aurora's thigh—
Fire-branded socket of the cyclop's eye.
O Machiavellian vision charged with good,
Dog-star of Athens, when the Goddess stood—
Prince, Pope, philosopher and golden bough,
Pure mind and murder at the scything prow—
Minerva, the miscarriage of the brain:
Decipher Europe! Vibrate through my pane...
Now Paris, our black classic, breaking up
Like killer kings on an Etruscan cup.

## 越过阿尔卑斯山

一

（罗马开往巴黎的火车上）
我一边翻阅着瑞士人再次放弃
攀登珠穆朗玛峰的报道，一边注视着
开往巴黎的普尔曼客车
在阿尔卑斯山白雪覆盖的休耕大地上奔驰；
啊，美丽的罗马！这并非我心所盼，
就像会三种语言的罗马厨师

敲着锣踮起脚尖前行。
我离开了属于上帝之城的地方。
天啊，那捶胸顿足的胖子①放飞了
凯撒②之鹰，他与我们没有什么不同
只是，过于无聊，这位艺术家以信誉资源
轻而易举地在世界各地推行他的事业
比起我们先辈们流芳百世的
宏伟旅行实在平淡无奇。

**七**

盘山而上的火车来到了地面。
厌倦了怨声载道呼哧呼哧的车轮，
睡眼惺忪的我，在铺位上乱踹乱蹬，
静静地躺着，看着阿波罗③穿过奥罗拉④的大腿
把他的踵种在了陆地之上——
眼窝烙下火的印记的独眼巨人⑤。
啊，当幸运女神站立，眼前出现无数
雅典卓越的马基亚维利式⑥的天狼星⑦——
王子、教皇、哲学家和金枝，
脑瓜单纯和割草船头的凶杀——
密涅瓦⑧，大脑误判：
解读欧洲！通过窗户颤动……
现在的巴黎，我们的黑色经典，分崩离析
就像伊特鲁里亚⑨杯子上的杀人国王。

---

① 捶胸顿足的胖子：暗指墨索里尼。

② 恺撒：(Gaius Julius Caesar，公元前 102 年—公元前 44 年)，史称恺撒大帝，罗马共和国末期杰出的军事统帅、政治家，散文学家，罗马帝国的奠基者。

③ 阿波罗：Apollo，宙斯和勒托之子，希腊神话中的太阳神。

④ 奥罗拉：Aurora，古罗马神话里的黎明之神。

⑤ 独眼巨人：Cyclop，希腊神话中的巨人，海神波塞冬的儿子。

⑥ 马基亚维利：(Niccolò Machiavelli，1469—1527)，意大利政治思想家和历史学家，其思想被概括为马基亚维利主义，常常被看作是不择手段、无视道德而侧重权术与谋略的现实政治的代名词。

⑦ 天狼星：除太阳外最亮的恒星。

⑧ 密涅瓦：Minerva，智慧和技术及工艺之神

⑨ 伊特鲁里亚：(Etruscan) 亦译埃特鲁斯坎人，是古代意大利西北部伊特鲁里亚(Etruria)地区古老的民族，其居住地处于台伯河和亚努河之间。公元前 6 世纪时，其都市文明达于顶峰。伊特拉斯坎文化的许多特点，曾被继伊特拉斯坎人之后统治这个半岛的罗马人所吸收。

## Waking in the Blue

The night attendant, a B. U. sophomore,
rouses from the mare's-nest of his drowsy head
propped on *The Meaning of Meaning*.
He catwalks down our corridor.
Azure day
makes my agonized blue window bleaker.
Crows maunder on the petrified fairway.
Absence! My hearts grows tense
as though a harpoon were sparring for the kill.
(This is the house for the "mentally ill".)

What use is my sense of humour?
I grin at Stanley, now sunk in his sixties,
once a Harvard all-American fullback,
(if such were possible!)
still hoarding the build of a boy in his twenties,
as he soaks, a ramrod
with a muscle of a seal
in his long tub,
vaguely urinous from the Victorian plumbing.
A kingly granite profile in a crimson gold-cap,
worn all day, all night,
he thinks only of his figure,
of slimming on sherbert and ginger ale—
more cut off from words than a seal.
This is the way day breaks in Bowditch Hall at McLean's;
the hooded night lights bring out "Bobbie",
Porcellian' 29,
a replica of Louis XVI
without the wig—
redolent and roly-poly as a sperm whale,
as he swashbuckles about in his birthday suit

and horses at chairs.
These victorious figures of bravado ossified young.

In between the limits of day,
hours and hours go by under the crew haircuts
and slightly too little nonsensical bachelor twinkle
of the Roman Catholic attendants.
(There are no Mayflower
screwballs in the Catholic Church.)

After a hearty New England breakfast,
I weigh two hundred pounds
this morning. Cock of the walk,
I strut in my turtle-necked French sailor's jersey
before the metal shaving mirrors,
and see the shaky future grow familiar
in the pinched, indigenous faces
of these thoroughbred mental cases,
twice my age and half my weight.
We are all old-timers,
each of us holds a locked razor.

## 郁闷中醒来

夜班服务员，一位本科二年级学生，
头枕《意义之意义》①打着盹儿
从梦乡中苏醒过来。
沿着走廊轻手轻脚地漫步。
蔚蓝的天
将我沉闷的蓝色窗户衬托得愈加凄凉。
乌鸦在高尔夫球场石化的平坦球道上游逛。
不见了！我的心一下提到了嗓子眼上
犹如鱼叉投向了猎物。

① 《意义之意义》指 C. K. 奥格登和 I. A. 理查兹的 *The Meaning of Meaning*，1923 年出版。

(这里是“精神病患者”的家。)

我的幽默感有何用?
我朝斯坦利咧嘴笑了笑，他已经60多岁了，
曾经是哈佛大学全美联赛的后卫，
(如果真是这样就太厉害了!)
体格依旧壮如20多岁的小伙子，
他泡澡时，宛如一只肌肉结实的海豹
躺在长长的浴缸中，
维多利亚时代的管道散发出淡淡的尿骚味。
一尊高贵的花岗岩雕像，
从早到晚戴着一顶深红色金帽，
他只考虑他的身材，
喝果汁牛奶和姜汁汽水减肥——
沉默寡言。
这就是麦克莱恩市鲍迪奇大厅黎明时分的景象;
带罩的夜灯下走出“博比”，
1929年的“波斯廉俱乐部”①成员，
路易十六的复制品
没戴假发——
像头胖嘟嘟的抹香鲸散发出浓浓的香味，
他穿着生日礼服，骑跨在椅子上
一幅趾高气扬的神态。
这些装腔作势的胜利者僵化了年轻人。

从早到晚
全体船员花了数个小时理发，
而罗马天主教的侍从们
傻头傻脑地眨巴着眼睛。
(天主教堂没有

---

① “波斯廉俱乐部”：始建于1794年的哈佛大学，是美国最古老和著名的秘密学生社团。“Porcellian”由拉丁语“porcus”转化而来，有“猪”的意思，所以“猪”成为该俱乐部的主要象征和会员崇拜的对象。该俱乐部奉行享乐主义，每年只招收10名新会员。会员每年缴纳的会费高得令人瞠目结舌，因此，该俱乐部严格按照家庭背景挑选会员，其成员均为男性，并且是终身制。每年秋天，俱乐部都会从二年级学生中挑选“贵族血脉”，邀请他们参加活动。

五月花号上的疯子。)

吃了顿丰盛的新英格兰早餐,
今早体重到了两百磅。
穿着高领法国水手衫
我大摇大摆地大步
走到金属剃须镜前,
在这些纯土著血统的精神病患者
消瘦的脸上
看见熟悉的摇摇欲坠的未来,
他们年龄是我的两倍,
体重只有我的一半。
我们都是迂腐守旧之人,
每人拿着一把没有打开的剃刀。

## 91 Revere Street

...

I can hear my father trying to explain his resignation from the Navy to Cousin Ledyard or Commander Billy. Talking with an unnatural and importunate jocularity, he would say, "Billy Boy, it's a darned shame, but this state of Massachusetts doesn't approve of the service using its franchise and voting by mail. I haven't had a chance to establish residence since our graduation in '07. I think I'll put my blues in mothballs① and become a cit② just to prove I still belong to the country. The directors of Lever Brothers' Soap③ in Cambridge... I guess for cits, Billy, they've really got something on the ball, because they tell me they want me on their team."

Or father, Cousin Ledyard, Commander Billy, and I would be sitting on after dinner at the dining-room table and talking man to man. Father would say, "I'm afraid I'll grow dull

---

① Put my blues in mothballs：blues 指美国海军礼服；in mothballs，长期搁置不用。

② Cit：市民；老百姓服装。

③ Lever Brothers："利华兄弟公司"于 1885 年在英国创建。1930 年，利华兄弟公司与成立于 1920 年的荷兰"玛格瑞乃公司"(Margarine Unie)合并，组成"英荷联合利华公司"，生产食品和饮料以及洗涤品、洁肤品、护发品等，目前已成为全世界最成功的日用消费品的生产商之一。旁氏(Ponds)、力士(Lux)、夏士莲(Hazeline)、洁诺(Signal)、立顿(Lipton)、多芬(Dove)都是其著名的品牌。

and drab with all this goldbricking① ashore. I am too old for tennis singles, but too young for that confirmed state of senility known as golf."

Cousin Ledyard and Commander Billy would puff silently on their cigars. Then father would try again and say pitifully, "I don't think a naval man can ever on the outside replace the friends he made during his years of wearing the blue."

Then Cousin Ledyard would give Father a polite, funeral look and say, "Speaking of golf, Bob, you've hit me below the belt. I've been flubbing away at the game for thirty years without breaking ninety."

Commander Billy was blunter. He would chaff Father about becoming a "beachcomber" or "purser for the Republican junior chamber of commerce." He would pretend that Father was in danger of being jailed for evading taxes to support "Uncle Sam's circus." Circus was Commander Billy's slang for the Navy. The word reminded him of a comparison, and once he stood up from the table and bellowed solemnly: "Oyez, Oyez! Bob Lowell, our bright boy, our class baby, is now on a par with 'Rattle-Ass Rats'."

Richardson, who resigned from us to become press agent for Sells-Floto Circus, and who writes to me: "Bilgy Dear—Beating the drum ahead of the elephants and the spangled folk, I often wonder why I run into so few of my classmates."

Those dinners, those apologies! Perhaps I exaggerated their embarrassment because they hover so gravely in recollection and seem to anticipate ominously my father's downhill progress as a civilian and Bostonian. It was to be expected, I suppose, that Father should be in irons for a year or two, while becoming detached from his old comrades and interests, while waiting for the new life.

...

## 里维尔街 91 号

……

我能听到父亲试图向莱迪亚德表哥或者比利中校解释他从海军辞职的原因。他说话怪里怪气、诙谐风趣，"比利小子，太丢人了，但在马萨诸塞州服役不靠特权和邮件来投票。零七年(1907年)毕业后我一直漂泊不定。我之所以脱下海军军装，当个平民百姓，是想证明我仍然属于这个国家。剑桥利华兄弟肥皂公司的董事们……我认为，比利，作为普通市民他们的确有一手，因为他们想让我入他们的伙。"

或者，父亲、莱迪亚德表哥、比利中校和我晚饭后继续坐在餐桌旁聊聊天。父亲

① Goldbrick：(装病)逃避责任。

会说，“这样逃避到岸上，我担心会越来越反应迟钝、萎靡不振。我这年龄，打网球太老，而打高尔夫又太年轻，那是老态龙钟之人才玩的项目。”

莱迪亚德表哥和比利中校一声不吭地抽着雪茄。于是父亲再次向他们解释，可怜兮兮地说，“我想海军服役期间结交的朋友，退役之后应该依然是朋友。”

莱迪亚德表哥礼貌、伤心地看了看父亲说，“提起高尔夫，鲍勃，你算说到了我的痛处。我打了三十年，从没有破过九十杆。”

比利中校讲话从来不拐弯抹角。他开玩笑说父亲是个“海滩流浪汉”，或者“共和党青年商会的事务长。”他郑重其事地说父亲会面临坐牢之灾，因他逃避“山姆大叔的马戏”税。“马戏”是比利中校的口头禅，意指海军。这个词使他想到了与此类似的一件事。一次吃饭时他突然站起，郑重其事地大声说：“肃静，肃静！鲍勃·洛威尔，聪明的小伙，我们出类拔萃的宠儿，现如今混得同‘摇头乞怜的鼠辈’没什么两样。”

理查森离开我们后去了塞尔斯-弗洛多马戏团做新闻经纪人。他给我写信说，“亲爱的比尔吉——敲着鼓行走在大象和身着银光闪闪的条状服饰的演员队伍之前，我常常想怎么遇不到几个同学呢。”

讨厌的晚宴，无聊的致歉！我也许夸大了他们的窘迫之情，因为心中时刻记挂着他们，他们好像都有一种不好的预感，父亲无论作为一介平民还是一个波士顿人都大不如前。我想父亲应该再被关上一两年，摆脱他的老朋友和兴趣爱好，重新开始新生活。

……

## Fall 1961

Back and forth, back and forth
goes the tock, tock, tock
of the orange, bland, ambassadorial
face of the moon
on the grandfather clock.

All autumn, the chafe and jar
of nuclear war;
we have talked our extinction to death.
I swim like a minnow
behind my studio window.

Our end drifts nearer,
the moon lifts,
radiant with terror.
The state
is a diver under a glass bell.

A father's no shield
for his child.
We are like a lot of wild
spiders crying together,
but without tears.

Nature holds up a mirror.
One swallow makes a summer.
It's easy to tick
off the minutes,
but the clock hands stick.

Back and forth!
Back and forth, back and forth—
my one point of rest
is the orange and black
oriole's swinging nest!

## 1961 年秋天

滴答、滴答、滴答
桔黄色、和缓、大使般
圆形表面
落地式大摆钟
来回摆动。

整个秋天，核战争的
冲突；
我们一直在谈论人类灭绝。

我像一条米诺鱼
在我工作室的窗户后面徘徊。

我们的末日越来越近，
月亮升起，
发出恐怖的亮光。
国家
是个玻璃罩下的潜水者。

父亲无法作为
孩子的盾牌。
我们就像众多
一起哭泣的野蜘蛛，
但没有泪水。

大自然拿起一面镜子。
一燕成夏。
分钟显示
容易，
但时钟的指针粘住不动。

来来回回！
来来回回，来来回回——
我停歇的一个地方
是桔黄加黑色的
黄鹂鸟悬荡的巢！

## History

History has to live with what was here,
clutching and close to fumbling all we had—
it is so dull and gruesome how we die,
unlike writing, life never finishes.
Abel was finished; death is not remote,
a flash-in-the-pan electrifies the skeptic,

his cows crowding, like skulls against high-voltage wire,
his baby crying all night like a new machine.
As in our Bibles, white-faced, predatory,
the beautiful, mist-drunken hunter's moon ascends—
a child could give it a face: two holes, two holes,
my eyes, my mouth, between them a skull's no-nose—
O there's a terrifying innocence in my face
drenched with the silver savage of the mornfrost.

## 历史

历史必须与这里过去的一切共存,
紧扣和尽量寻找我们曾经拥有的一切——
我们的死亡无聊透顶、阴森恐怖,
不像写作,生命永远不会终结。
亚伯①死了;死亡就在眼前,
昙花一现让无神论者兴奋不已,
他的奶牛挤在一起,就像高压线下的头骨,
他的孩子如同一台新机器整夜哭叫不停。
月亮升起,就像《圣经》所说,她是面无血色、掠夺成性、
卓越多姿、醉意朦胧的猎手——
一个小孩可以给它一张脸:两个洞,两个洞,
我的眼睛、我的嘴巴,它们中间是块没有鼻子的头骨——
啊,我的脸上露出一种恐怖的天真
沐浴在晨霜的银色野性之中。

## Dear Sorrow

The hurt mother sleeps awake like a cat till daybreak
stretched on the mat by the bed of our breathy child...
her cat thrusts its small brown arm through a crack in the door,
then another arm, a brown nose, and the door sticks—
it is this waking daily to the fire of the daybreak,

① 亚伯:《圣经》故事中亚当和夏娃的次子,被其兄该隐所杀。

our twenty years of fractious will and feather...
Do I romanticize if I think I
can be as selfish a father as Karl Marx,
Milton, Dickens, Trotsky, Freud, James Mill,
or George II, a bad son and worse father—
the great lions needed a free cage to roar in...
O when will I sleep out the storm, dear love,
and see at the end of the walk your dress glow
burnt-umber, as if you had absorbed the sun?

## 可亲的悲伤

受伤的母亲像猫一样一夜没睡躺到天亮
匍匐在呼吸急促的孩子床边的垫子上……
她的小猫从门缝里伸出一只棕色的小胳膊，
接着是另一只胳膊，一个棕色的鼻子，把门卡住了——
每天就是这样在晨曦的火焰中醒来，
我们二十年来的喜怒无常……
假如我觉得我要做个自私的父亲
像卡尔·马克思、弥尔顿、狄更斯、托尔斯泰、弗洛伊德、
詹姆斯·米尔、或者乔治二世、坏儿子、坏父亲
那我是不是过于浪漫了——
威猛的狮子需要一个自由的笼子来吼叫……
啊，我何时才能够安稳地睡个觉，亲爱的，
看见你的裙子在路的尽头发出
焦赭色的光彩，难道你并吞了璀璨的阳光?

## Dolphin

My Dolphin, you only guide me by surprise,
a captive as Racine, the man of craft,
drawn through his maze of iron composition
by the incomparable wandering voice of Phèdre.
When I was troubled in mind, you made for my body
caught in its hangman's knot of sinking lines,

the glassy bowing and scraping of my will...
I have sat and listened to too many
words of the collaborating muse,
and plotted perhaps too freely with my life,
not avoiding injury to others,
not avoiding injury to myself—
to ask compassion... this book, half fiction,
an eelnet made by man for the eel fighting

my eyes have seen what my hand did.

## 海豚

我的海豚，你只出人预料地引导我，
一个拉辛①式的俘虏，一个手艺人，
被费德尔②无与伦比的飘逸的声音
诱惑进铁料建成的迷宫。
我心神不宁、身陷死结的时候，
你令我断然屈服，收敛锋芒……
我坐着听了太多
通敌叛国的缪斯的话，
也许我的生活过于自由，
避免不了伤害他人，
避免不了伤害我自己——
恳求同情……这本书，一半虚构，
人类为了制服鳗鱼而制作的鳗鱼网。

---

① 拉辛：(Jean Racine，1639—1699)，法国古典主义戏剧代表作家。他的戏剧创作以悲剧为主，往往创造一种激烈、无法摆脱、伦理上的困境。

② 《费德尔》：是拉辛写得最好、情感最强烈、形式最完美的作品，也是他的最后一部作品。主人公费德尔拥有一切，是个幸福的女人，她是王后，她也是母亲，她花容月貌。可是，她却想方设法躲避世人，想结束自己的生命。因为她知道她心中有一种无法为世人所接受，她又不能承认的激情。她爱上了丈夫的儿子，可是这种爱是不为世人所容的。她对自己的处境有着清醒的认识，但是，尽管如此，萦绕在她心头的顽念仍然会将她引导向一条死路。这是她无法打开的一个死结。拉辛以大师的笔触，向我们表明了一个女人为了自尊而进行的斗争，她在与自我的斗争中极力克制着自己，可是最终，她不得不向周围非理性的压力低头。

我亲眼看到了我这双手做过的事。

## Epilogue

Those blessèd structures, plot and rhyme—
why are they no help to me now
I want to make
something imagined, not recalled?
I hear the noise of my own voice:
The painter's vision is not a lens,
it trembles to caress the light.
But sometimes everything I write
with the threadbare art of my eye
seems a snapshot,
lurid, rapid, garish, grouped,
heightened from life,
yet paralyzed by fact.
All's misalliance.
Yet why not say what happened?
Pray for the grace of accuracy
Vermeer gave to the sun's illumination
stealing like the tide across a map
to his girl solid with yearning.
We are poor passing facts,
warned by that to give
each figure in the photograph
his living name.

## 后记

那些神圣的结构、情节和韵律——
它们为什么现在对我毫无用处
我要写的东西
是想象，而不是回忆?
我要听自己杂乱无章的声音:

画家的视角不是镜头，
它颤动着抚摸光线。
然而有时我用我那落伍的艺术眼光
写下的东西
就像个快照，
苍白、急促、艳丽、混搭，
高于生活，
但虚假得让人难以置信。
全都不伦不类。
但是为何不讲发生过的事？
祈求精确的魅力
维米尔①用它将太阳光线
投射到他那日思夜想的姑娘身上
如同穿越地图的洋流悄无声息。
我们不擅长传递事实，
被警告给
照片上的每个人物
写上他的真实姓名。

## Loneliness

A stone's throw off,
seven eider ducks
float and dive in their watery commune...
a family, though not married—
we have learned not to share.
We were
so by ourselves and calm this summer,
I would wish to live forever,
like the small boy on the wharf
marching alone, far ahead of the others,
still anxiously flapping

① 维米尔：(Johannes Vermeer，1632—1675)，荷兰优秀风俗画家，被看作“荷兰小画派”的代表画家。代表作品有《戴珍珠耳环的少女》《花边女工》《士兵与微笑的少女》。

their parti-colored sails in the calm.

## 孤单

不远处，
七只绒鸭
在它们的水域漂浮、潜水……
一家子，虽然没有成婚——
我们已学会了不去分享。
我们自己
原来就是如此，让这个夏天变得平静，
我多么希望长生不老，
就像码头上的那个小男孩
独自前行，将他人远远抛在身后，
风平浪静时依然急促地摆动
他们那五彩缤纷的风帆。

# 西尔维亚·普拉斯
# (Sylvia Plath，1932—1963)

西尔维亚·普拉斯 1932 年 10 月生于马萨诸塞州的波士顿。父亲为波士顿大学德语和生物学教授，母亲是父亲大学的同学，两人于 1932 年结婚，同年生下西尔维亚·普拉斯。

天性聪颖的普拉斯从小就表现出突出的诗歌创作天赋，十一岁便有诗歌发表在当地的报刊，高中刚刚毕业就在《基督教科学箴言报》上发表了一首诗歌。

高中毕业后，普拉斯进入位于北安普顿市的私立女子学院——史密斯学院学习。她的学习成绩优秀，获得多项奖学金。大学二年级时她因写作才能出色被纽约一家时装杂志邀请担任客座编辑。但同时普拉斯患上了精神分裂症，严重时还需到医院电疗，病痛的折磨使她时刻试图自杀。

大学毕业后，普拉斯获得富布莱特奖学金资助前往英国剑桥纽纳姆学院学习。在剑桥的一次聚会上，普拉斯结识了英国著名诗人泰德·休斯(Ted Hughes，1930—1998)，很快与之坠入爱河，不久便与泰德·休斯结下百年之好。

婚后普拉斯同休斯一起回到马萨诸塞，在斯密斯学院教授英语，并在罗伯特·洛威尔的指导下学习诗歌。1960 年，普拉斯的第一本诗集《巨神像及其他诗歌》(*The Colossus and Other Poems*)在英国出版(两年后在美国出版)。随后普拉斯随同丈夫回到英国，先后生下女儿和儿子。孩子的出生不仅没有给家庭带来欢乐，反而使他们的婚姻走到了尽头。1963 年，普拉斯的半自传体小说《钟形罩》(*The Bell Jar*)出版，发行后反响平平，同年 2 月 11 日，普拉斯扔下嗷嗷待哺的孩子，在伦敦寓所里打开煤气自杀身亡，年仅 31 岁。

虽然在世时仅有两部作品问世，但普拉斯是一位多产的作家。在她去世后，休斯整理出版了她的遗作，包括《爱丽尔》(*Ariel*，1966)、《渡水》(*Crossing the Water*，1971)、《冬树》(*Winter Trees*，1972)，特别是 1981 年出版的《诗歌全集》(*The Collected Poems*)为普拉斯赢得了 1982 年的普利策诗歌奖，使其成为美国文学史上第一位死后获取该殊荣的作家。

普拉斯的诗歌主题多数与她的生活息息相关，家庭、婚姻、生育等等。受其个人人生经历和社会思潮的影响，普拉斯对世界和人生的态度总体上消极和悲观，死亡是她诗歌创作中一个乐此不疲的话题。普拉斯的诗歌观察细腻，表达方式新颖独特；她非常擅长借助意象和象征表达个人情感和诗歌主题，她的绝大多数诗歌中都包含一个或多个意象或象征，因蕴含意义及其丰富，对读者的理解和欣赏带来极大挑战。

## Blue Moles

**1**

They're out of the dark's ragbag, these two
Moles dead in the pebbled rut,
Shapeless as flung gloves, a few feet apart—
Blue suede a dog or fox has chewed.
One, by himself, seemed pitiable enough,
Little victim unearthed by some large creature
From his orbit under the elm root.
The second carcass makes a duel of the affair:
Blind twins bitten by bad nature.

The sky's far dome is sane a clear.
Leaves, undoing their yellow caves
Between the road and the lake water,
Bare no sinister spaces. Already
The moles look neutral as the stones.
Their corkscrew noses, their white hands
Uplifted, stiffen in a family pose.
Difficult to imagine how fury struck—
Dissolved now, smoke of an old war.

## 蓝色鼹鼠

一

从黑暗的杂物堆里爬出来，
这两只鼹鼠死在了铺着鹅卵石的车辙里，
两者相间几英尺，横七竖八就像被扔掉的手套——
蓝色毛皮被狗或狐狸撕咬过。
一只，孤零零的一只，看上去非常凄惨，
小可怜被某个大型动物

从榆树根下它爬行的道上扒出。
第二具尸体为此展开决斗：
凶残的动物咬死了鲁莽的双胞胎。

遥远的天穹明朗开阔。
树叶，毁灭了它们湖水
和道路之间的黄色洞穴，遮盖了
危险的空间。鼹鼠
早已如同石头一样平静。
它们螺旋形的鼻子、白色的爪子
高高抬起，僵硬地摆出怀孕的姿势。
一场古老战争的硝烟业已消散——
难以想象打斗时的激烈景象。

## Frog Autumn

Summer grows old，cold-blooded mother.
The insects are scant，skinny.
In these palustral homes we only
Croak and wither.

Mornings dissipate in somnolence.
The sun brightens tardily
Among the pithless reeds. Flies fail us.
The fen sickens.

Frost drops even the spider. Clearly
The genius of plenitude
Houses himself elsewhwere. Our folk thin
Lamentably.

## 青蛙的秋天

夏天变成苍老、冷血的母亲。
昆虫稀少，瘦小。

在这地处沼泽的家里我们只有
呱呱地叫着衰老。

清晨在睡梦中度过。
太阳在细软的芦苇中
慢慢升起。苍蝇忘记了我们。
没人再喜欢沼泽地。

霜冻甚至打下了蜘蛛。显然
众多天才将自己安置在了
其他地方。我们这些伙计
悲惨地日渐消瘦。

## The Beekeeper's Daughter

A garden of mouthings. Purple, scarlet-speckled, black
The great corollas dilate, peeling back their silks.
Their musk encroaches, circle after circle,
A well of scents almost too dense to breathe in.
Hieratical in your frock coat, maestro of the bees,
You move among the many-breasted hives,

My heart under your foot, sister of a stone.

Trumpet-throats open to the beaks of birds.
The Golden Rain Tree drips its powders down.
In these little boudoirs streaked with orange and red
The anthers nod their heads, potent as kings
To father dynasties. The air is rich.
Here is a queenship no mother can contest—

A fruit that's death to taste: dark flesh, dark parings.

In burrows narrow as a finger, solitary bees

Keep house among the grasses. Kneeling down
I set my eyes to a hole-mouth and meet an eye
Round, green, disconsolate as a tear.
Father, bridegroom, in this Easter egg
Under the coronal of sugar roses

The queen bee marries the winter of your year.

## 养蜂人的女儿

嗡嗡作响的花园。紫色、猩红斑、黑色
巨大的花冠开始膨胀，剥离了它们的丝质外衣。
麝香味扑面而来，一圈又一圈，
浓烈的气味令人窒息。
身穿礼服大衣宛如僧侣，蜜蜂大师，
你来回穿梭在多乳房的蜂巢间。

我的心在你的脚下，石头妹妹。

喇叭状的喉咙对着鸟喙张开。
黄山栾树洒下粉末。
在这些点缀着橙红色条纹的小闺房里
花粉囊点着头，像开创新朝代的
国王般强壮威武。空气中弥漫着香气。
这是至高无上的女王——

一种难以下咽的水果：黑色的果肉，黑色的皮。

窄如手指的洞穴，孤独的蜜蜂
在草丛里筑巢。双腿跪地
我将目光投向一个洞口与一只眼相遇
溜圆、发着绿光、噙着惆怅的泪水。
父亲，新郎，在这只复活节彩蛋里
糖玫瑰花冠之下

蜂后嫁给了你岁月里的冬季。

## Metaphors

I'm a riddle in nine syllables,
An elephant, a ponderous house,
A melon strolling on two tendrils.
O red fruit, ivory, fine timbers!
This loaf's big with its yeasty rising.
Money's new-minted in this fat purse.
I'm a means, a stage, a cow in calf.
I've eaten a bag of green apples,
Boarded the train there's no getting off.

## 隐喻

我是一个九个音节的谜语，
一头大象，一栋笨重的房子，
一颗在两条须上漫步的西瓜。
啊，红色的果实，象牙，精致的木材！
这片面包因发酵而膨大。
这个肥大的钱包里新铸就的钱币。
我是一种手段、一个舞台、一头怀孕的母牛。
我吃了一袋子青苹果，
上了火车就别想返回。

## Ariel

Stasis in darkness.
Then the substanceless blue
Pour of tor and distances.

God's lioness,
How one we grow,
Pivot of heels and knees! —The furrow

Splits and passes, sister to
The brown arc
Of the neck I cannot catch,

Nigger-eye
Berries cast dark
Hooks—

Black sweet blood mouthfuls,
Shadows.
Something else

Hauls me through air—
Thighs, hair;
Flakes from my heels.

White
Godiva, I unpeel—
Dead hands, dead stringencies.

And now I
Foam to wheat, a glitter of seas.
The child's cry

Melts in the wall.
And I
Am the arrow,

The dew that flies
Suicidal, at one with the drive
Into the red

Eye, the cauldron of morning.

## 瞪羚羊

在黑暗中停歇。
随后空灵蓝倾泻出
突岩①和间距。

上帝的母狮，
我们竟然长在一起，
脚踝和膝盖的枢轴！——犁沟

裂开，越过，我抓不住
脖子的棕色
弧形的姊妹，

黑鬼眼
浆果抛出黑色
钩子——

满嘴黑色甜美的血，
阴影。
另有东西

越过空中把我拽住——
大腿、毛发；
从我脚跟剥落。

白色

① 突岩：指英格兰西南部的突岩。

戈黛娃[1]，我没去皮——
毫无生气的手，麻木不仁的紧张。

现在的我
对着闪闪发光的海洋——麦田口吐白沫。
孩子的哭声

融化在墙里。
而我
是那支箭，

飞向自我毁灭的
露水，瞄准一个
进入红色

眼睛的目标，黎明的大锅。

## The Applicant

First, are you our sort of a person?
Do you wear
A glass eye, false teeth or a crutch,
A brace or a hook,
Rubber breasts or a rubber crotch,

Stitches to show something's missing? No, no? Then
How can we give you a thing?
Stop crying.

---

① 戈黛娃：(Lady Godiva)是十一世纪英格兰的一位贵妇。根据传说，她丈夫麦西亚伯爵在考文垂施加重税，戈黛娃多次求情，希望丈夫减免税收，但伯爵不予理会。后来，他宣布如果戈黛娃不穿衣服，骑马在城里环绕一圈，就可以减税。戈黛娃同意了。出于对戈黛娃的尊重，考文垂市民在那天都返回家里，门窗紧闭，挂上厚重的窗帘。戈黛娃在空荡荡的城里环绕一圈。伯爵履行了诺言，免除了考文垂的重税。这是一个美丽的故事，据说当时考文垂城里有一个叫汤姆的年轻人，在窗帘上挖了一个洞，想偷偷窥视，结果，眼睛被一道白色强光给刺瞎。后来英文就有了一个词，叫 peeping-tom，意为“偷窥者”。

Open your hand.
Empty? Empty. Here is a hand

To fill it and willing
To bring teacups and roll away headaches
And do whatever you tell it.
Will you marry it?
It is guaranteed

To thumb shut your eyes at the end
And dissolve of sorrow.
We make new stock from the salt.
I notice you are stark naked.
How about this suit—

Black and stiff, but not a bad fit.
Will you marry it?
It is waterproof, shatterproof, proof
Against fire and bombs through the roof.
Believe me, they'll bury you in it.

Now your head, excuse me, is empty.
I have the ticket for that.
Come here, sweetie, out of the closet.
Well, what do you think of that?
Naked as paper to start

But in twenty-five years she'll be silver,
In fifty, gold.
A living doll, everywhere you look.
It can sew, it can cook,
It can talk, talk, talk.

It works, there is nothing wrong with it.
You have a hole, it's a poultice.

You have an eye, it's an image.
My boy, it's your last resort.
Will you marry it, marry it, marry it.

## 申请者

首先，你和我们是同类吗?
你装着
玻璃眼球、假牙或腋杖，
支架或钩子，
戴着橡胶胸或橡胶胯部，

露出开裂的缝线? 没有，没有? 那么
我们怎么给你东西?
别哭。
手张开。
空的? 空的。这儿有一只手

塞上东西、愿意
端来茶杯、医治头痛
而且照你说的去做。
你愿意娶它为妻吗?
保证最后时刻

用拇指阖上你的眼睛
驱散悲痛。
刺激成了我们的新花样。
我看到你赤裸精光。
这套西装怎么样——

黑色、笔挺，比较合身。
你愿意娶它为妻吗?
它防水、防破碎、
抵御炮火和炸弹从屋顶而入。
真的，它们会把你埋在里边。

对不起，你的大脑是空的。
我有证明书。
过来，亲爱的，别躲在壁橱里了。
好，你觉得怎么样?
起初赤条条宛如白纸

但二十五年后她会变成银，
五十年后成为金。
一个逼真的玩偶，无论从哪个方面看。
它会缝衣，它会做饭，
它会说话、说话、说话。

它干活，不会出任何差错。
你若有个洞，它就是膏药。
你若有一只眼睛，它就是映像。
孩子，它是你唯一的依靠。
你娶了它吧，娶了它，娶了它。

## Morning Song

Love set you going like a fat gold watch.
The midwife slapped your footsoles, and your bald cry
Took its place among the elements.

Our voices echo, magnifying your arrival. New statue.
In a drafty museum, your nakedness
Shadows our safety. We stand round blankly as walls.

I'm no more your mother
Than the cloud that distills a mirror to reflect its own slow
Effacement at the wind's hand.

All night your moth-breath
Flickers among the flat pink roses. I wake to listen:

A far sea moves in my ear.

One cry, and I stumble from bed, cow-heavy and floral
In my Victorian nightgown.
Your mouth opens clean as a cat's. The window square

Whitens and swallows its dull stars. And now you try
Your handful of notes;
The clear vowels rise like balloons.

## 晨歌

爱情使你像一只肥硕的金表在运转。
助产士拍了拍你的脚掌，你单调乏味的叫声
宣告你在尘世的降临。

我们附和着你的叫声，盛赞你的来临。新雕像。
在通风良好的博物馆，你赤裸的身体
遮蔽了我们的安全。我们像墙壁一样呆若木鸡地站立周围。

我这个母亲不过是镜子里的云
烧制出映射自己的器具
在风的手里慢慢隐去。

你整夜飞蛾般的呼吸
在平展的粉色玫瑰间颤动。我起床凝听：
远方的大海在耳边回荡。

一声哭叫，我跌跌撞撞从床上一跃而起，
身着维多利亚睡袍，笨拙如母牛，香气四射。
你嘴巴张开，干净如猫的嘴唇。窗外

泛起白色，吞噬了暗淡的星斗。而你试唱起了
你那少许的音符；
清亮的母音如气球般升起。

## Child

Your clear eye is the one absolutely beautiful thing.
I want to fill it with color and ducks,
The zoo of the new

Whose name you meditate—
April snowdrop, Indian pipe,
Little

Stalk without wrinkle,
Pool in which images
Should be grand and classical

Not this troublous
Wringing of hands, this dark
Ceiling without a star.

## 孩子

你清澈的眼睛绝美无比。
我想给它填上色彩和鸭子，
新物种的植物园

你默想它们叫什么——
四月的雪花莲，水晶兰，
小小的

没褶皱的花梗，
装着壮丽经典
意象的池子

不是这纷乱的
紧紧握手，这没有

星星的黑色顶棚。

## Doomsday

The idiot bird leaps out and drunken leans
Atop the broken universal clock:
The hour is crowed in lunatic thirteens.

Out painted stages fall apart by scenes
While all the actors halt in mortal shock:
The idiot bird leaps out and drunken leans.

Streets crack through in havoc-split ravines
As the doomstruck city crumbles block by block:
The hour is crowed in lunatic thirteens.

Fractured glass flies down in smithereens;
Our lucky relics have been put in hock:
The idiot bird leaps out and drunken leans.

The monkey's wrench has blasted all machines;
We never thought to hear the holy cock:
The hour is crowed in lunatic thirteens.

Too late to ask if end was worth the means,
Too late to calculate the toppling stock:
The idiot bird leaps out and drunken leans,
The hour is crowed in lunatic thirteens.

## 世界末日

白痴鸟跳出，醉醺醺地倚靠在
破碎的通用钟表的顶部:
钟点鸣响了疯狂的十三下。

外部油漆过的舞台因场景倾塌
惊恐万状的演员立刻全部停下：
白痴鸟跳出，醉醺醺地倚靠着。

厄运来袭，城市街区一个个坍塌
街道爆裂成支离破碎的沟壑：
钟点鸣响了疯狂的十三下。

破裂的玻璃碎片纷纷坠落而下；
我们幸运的文物已经做了抵押：
白痴鸟跳出，醉醺醺地倚靠着。

猴子扳手①拧坏了所有机器；
我们从没想过听到神圣的公鸡：
钟点鸣响了疯狂的十三下。

要问结果与手段是否等值已无意义，
估算崩塌的股票为时已晚：
白痴鸟跳出，醉醺醺地倚靠着，
钟点鸣响了疯狂的十三下。

① 猴子扳手：水管工常用的一种工具。

# 安妮·塞克斯顿
## (Anne Sexton，1928—1972)

安妮·塞克斯顿，原名安妮·格雷·哈维，1928 年 11 月生于马萨诸塞州。幼年时，她为了躲避父母的争吵而住在身患精神疾病的姑奶奶家里。后来她在精神病院，遇到了成为她终身治疗师的医生马丁·奥尼。在马丁的鼓励下，她开始致力于写作，报名参加了波士顿地区多个写作班，结识了几位自白派诗人，如罗伯特·洛威尔、W. D. 斯诺德格拉斯、西尔维亚·普拉斯等。

在写作班，塞克斯顿学习掌握了新的写作理论和技巧，特别是与其他自白派诗人的交流不仅提高了她对自白派的理解，而且坚定了她投身自白派诗歌创作的决心。1960 年，塞克斯顿出版了第一本诗集《去精神病院半路折返》(*To Bedlam and Part Way Back*)。诗集的主题围绕诗人本人精神崩溃后在一家私人精神病院治疗的经历，自白特色明显，出版后立刻轰动了当时的美国诗坛，引起了广泛关注，塞克斯顿一举成名，成为自白派的代表诗人之一。她不仅被邀请到哈佛、雷德克里夫、奥柏林、波士顿等大学讲学，而且还受邀到多所中学和精神病院朗读她的作品。

1962 年，塞克斯顿的第二本诗集《所有我可爱的人》(*All My Pretty Ones*)出版。出版后同样引起轰动，特别是在英国诗坛赢得了广泛好评。1964 年，英国诗歌学会从她已出版的两本诗集中挑选了一些诗歌，汇集成册，取名《诗选》(*Selected Poems*)，在英国出版。1965 年她被毫无争议地推举为英国皇家文学学会会员。

1966 年，伴随诗集《生或死》(*Live or Die*)的问世，塞克斯顿的文学创作生涯迎来了高峰。1967 年她不但获得了美国诗歌学会的雪莱纪念奖，而且因《生或死》荣获该年度普利策诗歌奖。1969 年，塞克斯顿的另一部备受瞩目的作品《情诗》(*Love Poems*)出版；同年，她还发表了一部戏剧《怜悯街》(*Mercy Street*)。1972 年，围绕《格林童话集》改写的散文诗《变形》(*Transformations*)出版。《变形》是塞克斯顿第一部将个人主题转向社会主题的诗集。诗中没有个人心路历程及生活经历的描写，而是对社会问题，特别是对女性问题的揭露和批判。时至今日，《变形》仍然是一部女性主义作品的上乘之作。

后来，塞克斯顿的家庭生活发生了一些变故，诗歌创作也遇到了瓶颈。她所创作的一些以宗教为主题的诗歌招致了普遍批评，原来喜爱她的读者群也渐行渐远。在她的生命后期，1972 年《愚蠢之书》(*The Book of Folly*)出版，1974 年《死亡笔记》(*The Death Notebook*)和《向着上帝糟糕的划船》(*The Awful Rowing Toward God*)先后出版。

塞克斯顿的一生可以说是悲惨的一生，这种悲惨不仅源于情感，也来自于心理。作为特色鲜明的自白派诗人之一，塞克斯顿在诗歌创作中对自己的私生活毫无保留地加以披露，她的诗歌主题基本都与自己的个人生活相关。她认为“诗歌的目的不是解释或说明行为，而是让强烈的情感伸手可及。”并且坚持“诗歌应该是感官上的一种震撼，一种伤痛。”①

## Cinderella

You always read about it:
the plumber with the twelve children
who wins the Irish Sweepstakes.
From toilets to riches.
That story.

Or the nursemaid,
some luscious sweet from Denmark
who captures the oldest son's heart.
From diapers to Dior.
That story.

Or a milkman who serves the wealthy,
eggs, cream, butter, yogurt, milk,
the white truck like an ambulance
who goes into real estate
and makes a pile.
From homogenized to martinis at lunch.

Or the charwoman
who is on the bus when it cracks up
and collects enough from the insurance.
From mops to Bonwit Teller.
That story.

Once
the wife of a rich man was on her deathbed

① The Norton Anthology of American Literature: Second Edition, Volume 2, Nina Baym ect, W. W. Norton & Company, New York London, 1985, P2516.

and she said to her daughter Cinderella:
Be devout. Be good. Then I will smile
down from heaven in the seam of a cloud.
The man took another wife who had
two daughters, pretty enough
but with hearts like blackjacks.
Cinderella was their maid.
She slept on the sooty hearth each night
and walked around looking like Al Jolson.
Her father brought presents home from town,
jewels and gowns for the other women
but the twig of a tree for Cinderella.
She planted that twig on her mother's grave
and it grew to a tree where a white dove sat.
Whenever she wished for anything the dove
would dropp it like an egg upon the ground.
The bird is important, my dears, so heed him.

Next came the ball, as you all know.
It was a marriage market.
The prince was looking for a wife.
All but Cinderella were preparing
and gussying up for the event.
Cinderella begged to go too.
Her stepmother threw a dish of lentils
into the cinders and said: Pick them
up in an hour and you shall go.
The white dove brought all his friends;
all the warm wings of the fatherland came,
and picked up the lentils in a jiffy.
No, Cinderella, said the stepmother,
you have no clothes and cannot dance.
That's the way with stepmothers.

Cinderella went to the tree at the grave

and cried forth like a gospel singer:
Mama! Mama! My turtledove,
send me to the prince's ball!
The bird dropped down a golden dress
and delicate little slippers.
Rather a large package for a simple bird.
So she went. Which is no surprise.
Her stepmother and sisters didn't
recognize her without her cinder face
and the prince took her hand on the spot
and danced with no other the whole day.

As nightfall came she thought she'd better
get home. The prince walked her home
and she disappeared into the pigeon house
and although the prince took an axe and broke
it open she was gone. Back to her cinders.
These events repeated themselves for three days.
However on the third day the prince
covered the palace steps with cobbler's wax
and Cinderella's gold shoe stuck upon it.

Now he would find whom the shoe fit
and find his strange dancing girl for keeps.
He went to their house and the two sisters
were delighted because they had lovely feet.
The eldest went into a room to try the slipper on
but her big toe got in the way so she simply
sliced it off and put on the slipper.
The prince rode away with her until the white dove
told him to look at the blood pouring forth.
That is the way with amputations.
They just don't heal up like a wish.
The other sister cut off her heel
but the blood told as blood will.

The prince was getting tired.
He began to feel like a shoe salesman.
But he gave it one last try.
This time Cinderella fit into the shoe
like a love letter into its envelope.

At the wedding ceremony
the two sisters came to curry favor
and the white dove pecked their eyes out.
Two hollow spots were left
like soup spoons.

Cinderella and the prince
lived, they say, happily ever after,
like two dolls in a museum case
never bother by diapers or dust,
never arguing over the timing of an egg,
never telling the same story twice,
never getting a middle-aged spread,
their darling smiles pasted on for eternity.
Regular Bobbsey Twins.
That story.

## 灰姑娘

在书中你经常会读到这样的故事:
有十二个孩子的管道工
赢得爱尔兰彩票。
从厕所到财富。
那个故事。

或者育婴女佣,
来自丹麦的迷人宝贝
俘获了长子的心。
从尿布到迪奥。
那个故事。

或者一个开着如同救护车的白色卡车
为富人投送鸡蛋、乳脂、
黄油、酸奶、牛奶的送奶工、
投身房地产
财源滚滚而来。
午饭时的均质牛奶换成了马丁尼酒。

或者有个钟点女工
乘坐的公交车突然被撞
从保险公司领到足额赔偿金。
从拖把到邦威泰勒。
那个故事。

曾经
一位富人的妻子奄奄一息
于是对女儿灰姑娘说：
要虔敬，要懂事。这样我就会
从天堂的云缝里为你开心。
那位富人另娶了一位妻子，
她有两个女儿，
相貌俊丽但心如盗匪。
她把灰姑娘当女仆使唤。
让她每晚睡在乌黑的炉灶旁
像艾尔·乔森[①]一样来回奔忙。
父亲从城里买来礼物，
给继母和她女儿的是珠宝和礼服
而灰姑娘得到的却是小树枝。
她把树枝栽到母亲的坟头上
树枝长成大树，树上栖息着一只白鸽。
每当她有所需，鸽子就像下蛋一样
将它掉落地上。
注意，宝贝们，小鸟非常关键。

① 艾尔·乔森：(Al Jolson，1886—1950)，出生于俄国，美国歌唱家、表演家。以扮演黑人著称。

众所周知，接下来是舞会。
那是婚姻的市场。
王子正在物色妻子。
除了灰姑娘人人都在准备
精心打扮。
灰姑娘也乞求参加。
继母端来一盆扁豆
洒进煤渣，对她说：
一小时内捡出扁豆才能去。
白鸽带来众多朋友；
地上热心的飞禽都来了，
很快就将扁豆捡出。
继母说，灰姑娘，你不能去，
你没有衣服，怎样跳舞。
世上的继母都这样。

灰姑娘来到墓旁的树前
像福音歌手一样高喊：
妈妈！妈妈！我的斑鸠，
送我去王子的舞会吧！
鸟儿抛下一套金色的裙装
和一双精致的小便鞋。
一般的鸟难以拿起那样的大包。
于是她去了。这并不意外。
脸上没了灰屑，
继母和她的女儿没有认出她
王子当场抓住她的手
她成了他那天唯一的舞伴。

夜幕降临，她要回家。
王子陪她走到家门口
然后她消失在了鸽笼里
王子操起一把斧头
砍开鸟笼，不见她的踪迹。她又成了灰姑娘。

这样的事情接连发生了三天。
但在第三天
王子在宫殿的台阶上抹上鞋蜡
灰姑娘的金鞋粘在了上面。

眼下王子要找能穿这只鞋的姑娘
找到那个奇怪的舞伴。
王子来到她们家，
继母的女儿很高兴，
因为她们都有一双可爱的脚。
大女儿走进房间去试鞋
但大脚趾太大，
于是干脆切掉才穿上。
王子带着她走了
但白鸽告诉他看流出来的血。
那是截肢的结果。
它们没有像期望的那样愈合。
二女儿切下脚后跟
但血使其露出真相。
王子身心疲惫，
心想自己成了卖鞋人。
但他没有放弃最后的尝试。
这次灰姑娘穿上了鞋子
就像情书装进了信封。

婚礼上
姐妹俩向她献殷勤
白鸽啄掉了她们的眼球
留下两个汤勺般的
空眼眶。

他们说灰姑娘和王子
从此幸福地生活在一起，
就像博物馆展柜里的两个玩具娃
再也不为尿布和灰尘烦恼，

再也不为做鸡蛋的时间争吵，
再也不用重复同一件事情，
再也不用吃陈旧的面包，
脸上永远贴着迷人的微笑。
标准的鲍勃西双胞胎①。
这就是那个故事。

## Oysters

Oysters we ate,
sweet blue babies,
twelve eyes looked up at me,
running with lemon and Tabasco.
I was afraid to eat this father-food
and Father laughed and
drank down his martini,
clear as tears.
It was a soft medicine
that came from the sea into my mouth,
moist and plump.
I swallowed.
It went down like a large pudding.
Then I ate one o'clock and two o'clock.
Then I laughed and then we laughed
and let me take note—
there was a death,
the death of childhood
there at the Union Oyster House
for I was fifteen
and eating oysters
and the child was defeated.
The woman won.

---

① 鲍勃西双胞胎：童书出版商爱德华·斯特拉梅耶(Edward Stratemeyer，1862—1930)1904 年出版的系列儿童丛书《鲍勃西双胞胎》《室内室外的快乐日子》中的主人公。

## 牡蛎

我们吃的牡蛎，
可爱的蓝色幼子，
十二只眼睛向上望着我，
佐以柠檬和塔巴斯哥辣酱油。
我不敢吃这种父亲的食物
父亲大笑
喝下他的马丁尼酒，
澄莹如泪水。
它是一种柔软的药物
由大海进入我的嘴里，
湿润丰盈。
我一口吞下。
如同吞下一块大布丁。
接着我一点钟吃，两点钟吃。
然后我笑了，接着我们笑了
让我做个笔记——
有一个死亡，
童年的死亡
在联邦牡蛎馆
我十五岁
吃牡蛎
小孩输了。
那个女人赢了。

## How We Danced

The night of my cousin's wedding
I wore blue.
I was nineteen
and we danced, Father, we orbited.
We moved like angels washing themselves.
We moved like two birds on fire.

Then we moved like the sea in a jar,
slower and slower.
The orchestra played
"Oh how we danced on the night we were wed."
And you waltzed me like a lazy Susan
and we were dear,
very dear.
Now that you are laid out,
useless as a blind dog,
now that you no longer lurk,
the song rings in my head.
Pure oxygen was the champagne we drank
and clicked our glasses, one to one.
The champagne breathed like a skin diver
and the glasses were crystal and the bride
and groom gripped each other in sleep
like nineteen-thirty marathon dancers.
Mother was a belle and danced with twenty men.
You danced with me never saying a word.
Instead the serpent spoke as you held me close.
The serpent, that mocker, woke up and pressed against me
like a great god and we bent together
like two lonely swans.

## 我们这样跳舞

堂弟结婚的那天晚上
我穿着蓝色服装。
那时我十九岁
跳舞，父亲，我们旋转。
我们像洗漱自己的天使一样移动。
我们像两只激动不已的鸟儿一样移动。
随后我们像霎时抖动的大海一样移动，
越来越慢。
乐队演奏

"哦，我们在结婚的那天晚上跳舞跳得多好啊。"
你像转盘一样带我跳华尔兹
非常亲密，
非常亲密。
既然你醉了，
像瞎了眼的狗一文不值，
既然你不再偷偷摸摸，
我脑海响起了那首歌。
纯氧是我们喝的香槟
碰杯，一个对一个。
香槟散发裸潜者的气味
玻璃杯透明，新娘
新郎相拥而睡
就像 1930 年的马拉松舞者。
妈妈是位美女，她与许多男士跳舞。
你一言不发地同我跳。
你紧紧搂着我而那条蛇说。
那条蛇，那个嘲笑者，苏醒并紧紧抵着我
像威严的神，我们弯腰叠在一起
像两只孤独的天鹅。

## Rowing

A story, a story!
(Let it go. Let it come.)
I was stamped out like a Plymouth fender
into this world.
First came the crib
with its glacial bars.
Then dolls
and the devotion to their plactic mouths.
Then there was school,
the little straight rows of chairs,
blotting my name over and over,
but undersea all the time,

a stranger whose elbows wouldn't work.
Then there was life
with its cruel houses
and people who seldom touched—
though touch is all—
but I grew,
like a pig in a trenchcoat I grew,
and then there were many strange apparitions,
the nagging rain, the sun turning into poison
and all of that, saws working through my heart,
but I grew, I grew,
and God was there like an island I had not rowed to,
still ignorant of Him, my arms, and my legs worked,
and I grew, I grew,
I wore rubies and bought tomatoes
and now, in my middle age,
about nineteen in the head I'd say,
I am rowing, I am rowing
though the oarlocks stick and are rusty
and the sea blinks and rolls
like a worried eyebal,
but I am rowing, I am rowing,
though the wind pushes me back
and I know that that island will not be perfect,
it will have the flaws of life,
the absurdities of the dinner table,
but there will be a door
and I will open it
and I will get rid of the rat insdie me,
the gnawing pestilential rat.
God will take it with his two hands
and embrace it.

As the African says:
This is my tale which I have told,

if it be sweet, if it be not sweet,
take somewhere else and let some return to me.
This story ends with me still rowing.

## 划船

一个故事，一个故事！
(让它去。让它来。)
我如同普利茅斯的挡泥板被冲压成型
来到这个世上。
首先是带着
冰冷栅栏的婴儿床。
接下来是玩偶
和送给它们的塑料嘴巴。
然后是学校，
一排排摆放笔直的小椅子，
一遍又一遍地涂抹我的名字，
但一直呆在海底，
一个胳膊肘坏了的陌生人。
随后是生活
拥有令人痛苦的房子
以及虽然只是为了触摸——
但很少触摸过的人们——
然而我在长大，
像一头穿着风衣的猪一样长大，
然后是许许多多奇怪的幽灵，
絮絮叨叨的雨，变成毒药的太阳
所有这些，像把锯锯开我的心脏，
但我在长大，我在长大，
上帝就在那里，就像一个我划船未曾到过的小岛，
我仍然没有理会他，我的胳膊和腿都动了起来，
我在长大，我在长大，
我戴上红宝石，购买西红柿
如今，到了中年，
我想说马上十九岁了，

我在划船，我在划船
尽管船桨生锈粘在了一起
大海如同忧虑的眼珠
闪烁、翻滚，
但我在划船，我在划船，
尽管风把我推了回去
我知道那座小岛或许不够完美，
它会有生命的瑕疵，
餐桌上的荒谬，
但是它会有一扇门
我来打开它
我要摆脱掉身上的老鼠，
那只咬人的带瘟疫的老鼠。
上帝将用双手把它逮住
拥抱它。

正如那个非洲人所说:
这就是我讲过的故事，
假如是愉快的，假如是不愉快的，
带到别的地方去，还给我一些。
这个故事结束时我依然在划船。

## Courage

It is in the small things we see it.
The child's first step,
as awesome as an earthquake.
The first time you rode a bike,
wallowing up the sidewalk.
The first spanking when your heart
went on a journey all alone.
When they called you crybaby
or poor or fatty or crazy
and made you into an alien,
you drank their acid

and concealed it.

Later,
if you faced the death of bombs and bullets
you did not do it with a banner,
you did it with only a hat to
cover your heart.
You did not fondle the weakness inside you
though it was there.
Your courage was a small coal
that you kept swallowing.
If your buddy saved you
and died himself in so doing,
then his courage was not courage,
it was love; love as simple as shaving soap.

Later,
if you have endured a great despair,
then you did it alone,
getting a transfusion from the fire,
picking the scabs off your heart,
then wringing it out like a sock.
Next, my kinsman, you powdered your sorrow,
you gave it a back rub
and then you covered it with a blanket
and after it had slept a while
it woke to the wings of the roses
and was transformed.

Later,
when you face old age and its natural conclusion
your courage will still be shown in the little ways,
each spring will be a sword you'll sharpen,
those you love will live in a fever of love,
and you'll bargain with the calendar

and at the last moment
when death opens the back door
you'll put on your carpet slippers
and stride out.

## 勇气

小处见勇气。
孩子迈出的第一步，
地震般令人惊叹。
你第一次骑自行车，
翻倒在人行道。
第一次被打屁股
你的心孤独可怜。
他们叫你小泪包
或小可怜或小胖墩或小疯子
让你成了他们的外人，
你忍气吞声
不露声色。

之后，
面临枪林弹雨
你没有挥舞旗帜
仅仅拿顶帽子
捂在胸口。
虽然内心胆怯
但你并不喜欢那样。
你的勇气是一小煤块
你一直在吞咽。
如果你的好友救了你
救的时候他自己却死了，
那么他的勇气就不再是勇气，
而是爱；爱像剃须香皂一样简单。

之后，

如果你忍受巨大悲痛，
那么你独自表现出胆量，
从烈火中汲取力量，
揭掉心上的伤痂，
然后像拧袜子一样拧出勇气。
接着，我的亲人，你粉饰悲伤，
按摩它的后背
随后用毯子盖住
它睡了一会儿
醒来后看到玫瑰花瓣
变了样。

之后，
当你面对衰老和它的自然结局
你依然会在一些小事上展现你的勇气，
每个春天都是一把你要磨的剑，
你所爱的人将生活在爱的狂热中，
你会和日历讨价还价
在最后时刻
当死神打开后门
你会穿上地毯上的拖鞋
昂首阔步迈出步伐。

# 纽约诗派

纽约诗派兴起于20世纪50年代，是美国现代最重要的诗歌流派之一。

第二次世界大战结束后，随着美国经济的快速发展，纽约取代英国伦敦迅速成为世界经济文化的中心。先锋派艺术家从世界各地纷纷涌入这个大都会，在这里寻找创作灵感、实验和展示他们独特的艺术才华。艺术家们之间因相同的艺术审美取向而经常聚集在一起，探讨艺术问题。一些在纽约《艺术新闻》(*ARTnews*)杂志编辑部共事的青年诗人，他们不仅是志同道合的朋友，而且在诗歌创作上志趣相投。他们关注大都市的日常生活，钟情欧洲现代诗歌，着迷于先锋派艺术，时常光顾先锋派艺术家画廊，与画家们讨论现代艺术，写文章赞美他们的抽象表现主义画作；而这些诗人的诗歌也经常出现在先锋派画家的画刊中。纽约诗派就是当时发表他们诗作的一位纽约画廊经理对他们的称呼。

纽约诗派认为诗歌创作中语言的物质性远远大于诗歌的意义。在他们的笔下，口头话语是表达情感和思想，甚至诸如意识、身份构成等形而上的概念的行之有效的工具。他们的诗歌表明世间的一切，无论多么普通、平淡无奇，都会成为有趣迷人的诗歌题材。纽约诗派的美学思想对后世诗歌，特别是语言诗歌的出现产生了举足轻重的影响。

纽约诗派主要诗人包括弗兰克·奥哈拉(Frank O'Hara，1926—1966)、约翰·阿什贝利(John Ashbery，1927—2017)、詹姆斯·斯凯勒(James Schuyler，1923—1991)和肯尼斯·柯克(Kenneth Koch，1925—2002)等。

# 弗兰克·奥哈拉
# (Frank O'Hara，1926—1966)

弗兰克·奥哈拉，原名弗兰西斯·拉塞尔·奥哈拉(Francis Russell O'Hara)，1926年6月27日出生于马里兰州的巴尔的摩，出生后不久随全家搬到马萨诸塞州中部城市伍斯特的郊区小镇格拉夫顿(Grafton，Worcester)。奥哈拉少年时期酷爱音乐，曾经立志要成为一个钢琴家。第二次世界大战爆发后曾在美国海军服役，战争结束后退役，进入哈佛大学学习。在纽约游览时，奥哈拉结识了一大批朋友，包括诗人肯尼斯·柯克、詹姆斯·斯凯勒，画家拉里·里维斯(Larry Rivers，1923—2002)、简·弗莱里奇(Jane Freilicher，1924—2014)、费尔菲尔德·皮特(Fairfield Porter，1907—1975)、格雷斯·哈蒂根(Grace Hartigan，1922—2008)等，并与他们成为终身好友。

受画家朋友的影响，奥哈拉对现代派艺术，特别是表现主义绘画兴趣浓厚。20世纪50年代初，奥哈拉来到纽约，在《艺术新闻》杂志社担任编辑助理，期间，他在该杂志上发表了一系列思想独到、主观色彩浓厚的评论文章，成为纽约诗派第一位撰写艺术评论的诗人。后来，奥哈拉就职于纽约现代艺术博物馆，做过咨询员和销售员；虽然没有经过专业训练，但其工作得到了广泛认可，先后被任命为馆长助理和油画雕塑馆副馆长。期间多次组织筹办艺术展览，撰写展览介绍，特别是在欧洲多个城市的“美国新油画”巡回展，让欧洲观众亲眼目睹了美国抽象表现主义画家的作品。纽约现代艺术博物馆的工作不仅为奥哈拉提供了一个展示管理才能的平台，而且也给他提供了与画家、音乐家、舞蹈家、诗人等广泛交流的机会，极大地影响了奥哈拉艺术思想的形成。

1966年7月，奥哈拉到纽约长岛火烧岛(Fire Island)度假，25日在海滩散步时意外被沙滩车撞倒身亡，年仅40岁。

奥哈拉的诗集有《城市冬季及其他诗歌》(*A City Winter and Other Poems*，1952)、《非常时刻的沉思》(*Meditations in an Emergency*，1957)、《颂歌》(*Odes*，1960)、《第二大街》(*Second Avenue*，1962)、《午餐诗》(*Lunch Poems*，1964)、《爱情诗》(*Love Poems*，1965)、《情感回忆》(*In Memory of My Feelings*，1967)、《弗兰克·奥哈拉诗选》(*The Collected Poems of Frank O'Hara*，1971)、《诗选》(*Selected Poems*，2008)和《找回的诗歌》(*Poems Retrieved*，2013)等。

奥哈拉经常被称为“画家中的诗人”。他的诗歌创作灵感和主题常常来自于同他朝夕相处的艺术家朋友，诗风深受绘画、雕塑、音乐等的影响。诗歌作品充满随意的跳跃、松散的关联，还有时而突然的中断。他的诗歌就像“启发式的漫谈”，以口头语的语气表达各个层次、各个领域的经验，如同超现实主义的梦想。正如约翰·阿什贝利指出，“当代音乐和艺术对他的影响远大于当代美国诗坛的影响。”①

## On Seeing Larry Rivers' *Washington Crossing the Delaware* at the Museum of Modern Art

Now that our hero has come back to us
in his white pants and we know his nose
trembling like a flag under fire,
we see the calm cold river is supporting
our forces, the beautiful history.

To be more revolutionary than a nun
is our desire, to be secular and intimate
as, when sighting a redcoat, you smile
and pull the trigger. Anxieties
and animosities, flaming and feeding

on theoretical considerations and
the jealous spiritualities of the abstract
the robot? They're smoke, billows above
the physical event. They have burned up.
See how free we are! as a nation of persons.

Dear father of our country, so alive
you must have lied incessantly to be
immediate, here are your bones crossed
on my breast like a rusty flintlock,
a pirate's flag, bravely specific

and ever so light in the misty glare
of a crossing by water in winter to a shore
other than that the bridge reaches for.

---

① The Norton Anthology of American Literature: Second Edition, Volume 2, Nina Baym ect, W. W. Norton & Company, New York London, 1985, P2471.

Don't shoot until, the white of freedom glinting
on your gun barrel, you see the general fear.

## 在现代艺术馆观看拉利·里维斯[1]《华盛顿横渡特拉华河》[2]一画有感

既然我们的英雄回来了
穿着白色裤子，我们感受到他的鼻子
像一面旗帜在战火中颤抖，
我们瞧见平静冰冷的河水撑浮着
我们的部队，美丽的历史。

我们希望比修女更加激进，
世俗和亲切，
就像你看见英国兵
微笑着扣动扳机。焦虑
和仇恨，点燃、吸收

理论思索和
抽象的嫉妒情绪
机器人吗？它们在冒烟，在物理的层面
浓烟滚滚。它们已经化为灰烬。
瞧我们多么自由！我们这个民族。

亲爱的国父，为了营造紧迫感
你怂恿不断撒谎的场面
历历在目，你的骨头
像一把生锈的明火枪交织在我的胸部，
一面海盗旗，勇敢地

---

① 拉利·里维斯：(Larry Rivers，1923—2002)美国表现主义、波普艺术家。

② 《华盛顿横渡特拉华河》：德国艺术家埃玛纽埃尔·洛伊茨(Emanuel Leutze，1816 年 5 月 24 日—1868 年 7 月 18 日)于 1851 年创作的一副油画。现藏于纽约大都会艺术博物馆。描绘了美国独立战争期间，1776 年 12 月 25 日华盛顿在横渡特拉华河的场景。这次针对黑森雇佣兵的突袭行动是特伦顿战役的第一步。2004 年，该作品成为纽约市大都会艺术博物馆永久收藏的一部分。作品有很多副本，其中的一幅挂在白宫西翼接待区。

特别是如此鲁莽地在冬季
在朦朦胧胧的炫光中不走路桥
而要涉水登岸。
不要开枪，等到自由的白色
在你的枪筒上寒光闪闪，你会看到一片恐慌。

## Why I Am Not a Painter

I am not a painter, I am a poet.
Why? I think I would rather be
a painter, but I am not. Well,

for instance, Mike Goldberg
is starting a painting. I drop in.
"Sit down and have a drink" he
says. I drink; we drink. I look
up. "You have SARDINES in it."
"Yes, it needed something there."
"Oh." I go and the days go by
and I drop in again. The painting
is going on, and I go, and the days
go by. I drop in. The painting is
finished. "Where's SARDINES?"
All that's left is just
letters, "It was too much," Mike says.

But me? One day I am thinking of
a color: orange. I write a line
about orange. Pretty soon it is a
whole page of words, not lines.
Then another page. There should be
so much more, not of orange, of
words, of how terrible orange is
and life. Days go by. It is even in

prose, I am a real poet. My poem
is finished and I haven't mentioned
orange yet. It's twelve poems, I call
it ORANGES. And one day in a gallery
I see Mike's painting, called SARDINES.

## 我为什么不是画家

我不是画家，我是诗人。
为什么？我觉得做个
画家更好，但我不是。唔，

举例来说，迈克·哥德堡
正在画画。我突然到访。
“坐下，喝点”他
说。我喝；我们喝。我抬头
看了一下。“你画里有沙丁鱼。”
“有，那个地方应该画点什么。”
“噢。”我走了，过了几天
又来了。画还没画完，我走了，
几天过去了。我来了。画
完成了。“沙丁鱼怎么不见了？”
留下的只有
字母，“太累赘了，”迈克说。

而我呢？有一天我在构思
一种颜色：橘黄。我写了一行
关于橘黄色的东西。很快就是一整页，
而不是几行。
接着又是一页。还可以写
许多页，不是橘黄色，是
字，是讨厌的橘黄色
和生活。几天过去了。它的形式实际上
是散文，我是真正的诗人。诗
写完了，而我竟然没有提到橘黄色。

是十二首诗，我给它
取名“橘黄色”。有一天在画廊里
看见迈克的油画，我叫它“沙丁鱼”。

## Today

Oh! Kangaroos, sequins, chocolate sodas!
You really are beautiful! Pearls,
harmonicas, jujubes, aspirins! All
the stuff they've always talked about
still makes a poem a surprise!
These things are with us every day
even on beachheads and biers. They
do have meaning. They're as strong as rocks.

## 今日

啊！袋鼠、烫石、巧克力汽水！
你们真美！珍珠、
口琴、果胶软糖、阿司匹林！
他们经常说到的这些东西
依然让一首诗成为一个惊喜！
这些东西与我们每日相随
即使在滩头阵地和棺材里。它们
确实有意义，像磐石一样坚硬。

## Melancholy Breakfast

Melancholy breakfast
blue overhead blue underneath

the silent egg thinks

and the toaster's electrical
ear waits

the stars are in
“that cloud is hid”

the elements of disbelief are
very strong in the morning

## 忧郁的早餐

忧郁的早餐
头顶蓝色，脚踏蓝色

寂静无声的鸡蛋在想

还有烤面包机的电子
耳在等待

星星在
“那片隐藏的云”里

怀疑的元素
在清晨非常强烈

## Song

I am stuck in traffic in a taxicab
which is typical
and not just of modern life

mud clambers up the trellis of my nerves
must lovers of Eros end up with Venus
muss es sein? es muss nicht sein, I tell you

how I hate disease, it's like worrying
that comes true

and it simply must not be able to happen

in a world where you are possible
my love
nothing can go wrong for us, tell me

## 歌曲

我乘坐出租车被堵在路上
这司空见惯
并非只是现代生活的特点

泥巴爬上了我神经的框架
厄洛斯的情人们最终一定会同维纳斯分手
非要这样? 我告诉你，这是不可能的

我非常讨厌生病，就像担心
这是真的
而这绝对不可能发生

在一个你有可能的世界
亲爱的
告诉我，我们不会出问题的

## A Step Away From Them

It's my lunch hour, so I go
for a walk among the hum-colored
cabs. First, down the sidewalk
where laborers feed their dirty
glistening torsos sandwiches
and Coca-Cola, with yellow helmets
on. They protect them from falling
bricks, I guess. Then onto the
avenue where skirts are flipping

above heels and blow up over
grates. The sun is hot, but the
cabs stir up the air. I look
at bargains in wristwatches. There
are cats playing in sawdust.
                                        On
to Times Square, where the sign
blows smoke over my head, and higher
the waterfall pours lightly. A
Negro stands in a doorway with a
toothpick, languorously agitating.
A blonde chorus girl clicks: he
smiles and rubs his chin. Everything
suddenly honks: it is 12:40 of
a Thursday.
                                Neon in daylight is a
great pleasure, as Edwin Denby would
write, as are light bulbs in daylight.
I stop for a cheeseburger at JULIET'S
CORNER. Giulietta Masina, wife of
Federico Fellini, è bell' attrice.
And chocolate malted. A lady in
foxes on such a day puts her poodle
in a cab.
                        There are several Puerto
Ricans on the avenue today, which
makes it beautiful and warm. First
Bunny died, then John Latouche,
then Jackson Pollock. But is the
earth as full as life was full, of them?
And one has eaten and one walks,
past the magazines with nudes
and the posters for BULLFIGHT and
the Manhattan Storage Warehouse,
which they'll soon tear down. I

used to think they had the Armory
Show there.
　　　　　　　　　　　A glass of papaya juice
and back to work. My heart is in my
pocket，it is Poems by Pierre Reverdy.

## 离他们一步之遥

午饭期间，我出来散步
走在呜呜呜叫的五颜六色的
出租车之间。首先，顺着人行道
工人在那里给他们沾满污垢、
油光发亮的躯体填充三明治
和可口可乐，戴着黄色的头盔。
它们保护他们避免
被掉下的砖块砸伤，我想。然后来到
大街上，裙子在鞋跟上面飞舞，在下水道
井盖上面鼓起。太阳烤炙大地，而出租车
搅乱了空气。我瞅着
手表中的廉价货。几只
猫在锯末里嬉戏。
　　　　　　　　　　　步入
时代广场，那里的指示牌
将烟雾从我头顶吹过，
瀑布从高处轻轻倾泻而下。一个
黑人手拿牙签
站在门口，漫不经心地在找乐子。
一个合唱团金发女郎咔哒咔哒地走过来：他
一边笑一边搓着下巴。喇叭声突然
响起：时间是星期四的
十二点四十分。
　　　　　　　　白天的霓虹灯
令人无比兴奋，如同埃德温·丹比①

① 埃德温·奥尔·丹比：(Edwin Orr Denby，1903—1983) 美国舞蹈批评家、诗人、小说家。

写的那样，就像白天的灯泡。
我在朱莉叶角
买了一个芝士汉堡。费德里科·费里尼①
之妻茱莉艾塔·玛西娜②，
一个楚楚动人的女演员。
巧克力麦芽糖。一位在
这样的日子里身穿裘皮大衣的贵妇把她的卷毛小狗
放在出租车里。
　　　　　　　　　　　　　　　　　今天大街上有
几个波多黎各人，给大街
增添了几份景色和激情。先是
邦尼死了，接着是约翰·拉图什③，
然后是杰克逊·波洛克④。但是他们
在地球上到处都有，生活中也随处可见？
一个人吃过，一个人走，
路过那些刊登裸体图片的杂志
还有斗牛的海报
曼哈顿储物仓库，
他们很快就会拆掉。我
曾经以为他们在那里
举办过武库展览。
　　　　　一杯木瓜汁
然后回去工作。我的心在
我的口袋里，它就是皮埃尔·勒韦迪⑤的诗。

## The Day Lady Died

It is 12:20 in New York a Friday

---

① 费德里科·费里尼：(Federico Fellini，1920—1993)，意大利电影导演、编剧、制作人。

② 茱莉艾塔·玛西娜：(Giulietta Masina，1921—1994)，意大利电影和舞台剧女演员。

③ 约翰·特雷维尔·拉图什：(John Treville Latouche，1914—1956)美国音乐剧词作者。

④ 杰克逊·波洛克：(Jackson Pollock，1912—1956)，美国画家，抽象表现主义绘画大师，也被公认为是美国现代绘画摆脱欧洲标准，在国际艺坛建立领导地位的第一功臣。

⑤ 皮埃尔·勒韦迪：(Pierre Reverdy，1889—1960)，20世纪初期法国著名诗人、超现实主义诗歌的先驱之一。

three days after Bastille day, yes
it is 1959 and I go get a shoeshine
because I will get off the 4: 19 in Easthampton
at 7: 15 and then go straight to dinner
and I don't know the people who will feed me

I walk up the muggy street beginning to sun
and have a hamburger and a malted and buy
an ugly NEW WORLD WRITING to see what the poets
in Ghana are doing these days
                                        I go on to the bank
and Miss Stillwagon (first name Linda I once heard)
doesn't even look up my balance for once in her life
and in the GOLDEN GRIFFIN I get a little Verlaine
for Patsy with drawings by Bonnard although I do
think of Hesiod, trans. Richmond Lattimore or
Brendan Behan's new play or *Le Balcon* or *Les Nègres*
of Genet, but I don't, I stick with Verlaine
after practically going to sleep with quandariness

and for Mike I just stroll into the PARK LANE
Liquor Store and ask for a bottle of Strega and
then I go back where I came from to 6th Avenue
and the tobacconist in the Ziegfeld Theatre and
casually ask for a carton of Gauloises and a carton
of Picayunes, and a NEW YORK POST with her face on it

and I am sweating a lot by now and thinking of
leaning on the john door in the 5 SPOT
while she whispered a song along the keyboard
to Mal Waldron and everyone and I stopped breathing

## 戴女士[①]去世的那一天

那是纽约一个星期五的十二点二十分
巴士底狱节[②]后的第三天，对，
是一九五九年，我去擦鞋
因为我要坐四点十九分的车在七点十五分
到东汉普顿下车然后直接去吃晚饭
而我不知道请我吃饭的那些人是谁

我步行在闷热的大街上，天开始放晴
要了一个汉堡一杯麦芽奶，然后买了
一份丑陋的《新世界写作》看看加纳
诗人近期在干什么
　　　　　　　　　　　接着我去了银行
斯蒂尔维根小姐(我曾经听说她的名字叫琳达)
从来不查看我的余额
在“金色狮鹫”[③]我给帕齐买了本袖珍版的魏尔伦[④]
里边配有波纳尔[⑤]的插图，虽然非常
想买里奇曼·拉蒂默尔[⑥]翻译的赫西俄德[⑦]、
布兰登·贝汉[⑧]的新剧本或者热奈[⑨]的《阳台》或
《黑人们》，但我没买，我坚持买魏尔伦
实际上是在反复考虑都快要睡着之后

---

① 戴女士：指比莉·荷莉戴(Billie Holiday，1915—1959)，美国爵士乐坛的天后级巨星歌手，因出版歌集《Lady Day》而获绰号“戴女士”。

② 巴士底狱节：Bastille day，7 月 14 日，法国国庆日。

③ 金色狮鹫：纽约书店，二十世纪七十年代倒闭。

④ 魏尔伦：(Paul Verlaine，1844—1896)，法国象征派诗歌著名诗人。

⑤ 波纳尔：(Pierre Bonnard，1867—1947)，纳比派代表画家。以色彩而闻名，被誉为 20 世纪最伟大的色彩画家之一。

⑥ 奇曼·拉蒂默尔(Richmond Alexander Lattimore，1906—1984)，美国诗人、古典主义学者，以翻译希腊古典作品而闻名，他所翻译的《伊利亚特》和《奥德赛》常常被认为是最好的英文译本之一。

⑦ 赫西俄德：(古希腊文：Ησιοδος，英语：Hesiod)，古希腊诗人。

⑧ 贝汉：(Brendan Francis Aidan Behan，1923—1964)，爱尔兰著名诗人，小说家，剧作家。

⑨ 热奈：(Jean Genet，1910—1986)法国诗人、小说家，也是荒诞派戏剧的著名代表作家之一。

至于迈克，我只是溜进公园巷里的
酒店买了瓶史特雷加①
然后返回出发地第六大道
进入齐格菲剧院的烟草店
随便要了一盒“高卢”和一盒
“半便士”香烟，一份上面印着她头像的“纽约邮报”

现在我已汗流浃背，想起了
她靠在“第五地”②厕所门上
伴随着琴键对马尔·瓦尔德伦③
低声唱了一首歌，我们都深感惊讶

## To the Harbormaster

I wanted to be sure to reach you;
though my ship was on the way it got caught
in some moorings. I am always tying up
and then deciding to depart. In storms and
at sunset, with the metallic coils of the tide
around my fathomless arms, I am unable
to understand the forms of my vanity
or I am hard alee with my Polish rudder
in my hand and the sun sinking. To
you I offer my hull and the tattered cordage
of my will. The terrible channels where
the wind drives me against the brown lips
of the reeds are not all behind me. Yet
I trust the sanity of my vessel; and
if it sinks, it may well be in answer
to the reasoning of the eternal voices,
the waves which have kept me from reaching you.

---

① 史特雷加：一种意大利葡萄酒。
② 第五地：纽约一家爵士乐酒吧。
③ 马尔·瓦尔德伦：(Malcolm Earl Waldron，1925—2002) 美国爵士乐演奏家、著名钢琴演奏家和作曲家，曾经是比莉·荷莉戴生命后期的钢琴伴奏。

## 致港务长

我要确保到你那里；
虽然我的船在途中因几次停泊
而延误。我总是刚把船停下
然后又决定离开。在风暴中和
日落时，潮水的金属线圈
缠绕着我深不可测的双臂，我难以
理解自己虚荣心的神态
或者太阳正在下沉时
我艰难地掌着波兰船舵背风而行。
向你献出船体和我意志的破烂绳索。
风把我吹入河道
芦苇的褐色嘴唇
可怕的河道还没有彻底走出。
但是我相信我的船完好无损；
即便下沉，也是为了回应
那永恒声音的劝说，
阻止我到你那里的海浪。

## Having a Coke with You

is even more fun than going to San Sebastian, Irún, Hendaye, Biarritz, Bayonne
or being sick to my stomach on the Travesera de Gracia in Barcelona
partly because in your orange shirt you look like a better happier St. Sebastian
partly because of my love for you, partly because of your love for yoghurt
partly because of the fluorescent orange tulips around the birches
partly because of the secrecy our smiles take on before people and statuary
it is hard to believe when I'm with you that there can be anything as still
as solemn as unpleasantly definitive as statuary when right in front of it
in the warm New York 4 o'clock light we are drifting back and forth
between each other like a tree breathing through its spectacles

and the portrait show seems to have no faces in it at all, just paint you suddenly wonder why in the world anyone ever did them

I look
at you and I would rather look at you than all the portraits in the world
except possibly for the *Polish Rider* occasionally and anyway it's in the Frick
which thank heavens you haven't gone to yet so we can go together the first time
and the fact that you move so beautifully more or less takes care of Futurism
just as at home I never think of the *Nude Descending* a Staircase or
at a rehearsal a single drawing of Leonardo or Michelangelo that used to wow me
and what good does all the research of the Impressionists do them
when they never got the right person to stand near the tree when the sun sank
or for that matter Marino Marini when he didn't pick the rider as carefully
as the horse

it seems they were all cheated of some marvelous experience
which is not going to go wasted on me which is why I am telling you about it

## 与你一起喝可乐

比去圣·塞巴斯蒂安①、伊伦②、昂代伊③、比亚里茨④、巴约纳⑤更有趣
或者胜过在巴塞罗那加西利亚大街饱餐一顿
要么是因为穿上橙色衬衫你看起来更像一个快乐的圣·塞巴斯蒂安人
要么是因为我痴情于你，要么是因为你迷恋于酸奶
要么是因为桦树周围鲜亮的橘黄色郁金香
要么是因为我们的微笑在人们和雕像前显得密不可测
很难相信，当我和你在一起的时候还会有这样的安宁
就像雕像一样肃穆而令人厌恶
在纽约四点钟温暖的阳光下我们来回穿梭
像在壮丽的景色中呼吸的一棵树

① 圣·塞巴斯蒂安：San Sebastian，西班牙北部城市。

② 伊伦：Irun，西班牙北部巴斯克地区的一个小镇。

③ 昂代伊：Hendaye，法国比利牛斯-大西洋省的一个市镇。

④ 比亚里茨：Biarritz，法国西南部比利牛斯-大西洋省、比斯开湾沿岸的一个市镇，著名海滩度假胜地。

⑤ 巴约纳：Bayonne，法国西南部一城镇，位于比斯开湾和西班牙边界附近。

肖像展览似乎根本看不到人脸，只有涂料
你突然会觉得世界上怎么会有人这样做

我瞧着
你，与世界上所有的画像相比我更愿意看着你
除了偶尔会看看《波兰人骑士》①反正是在弗里克
谢天谢地，你还没去过那个地方，这样我们可以一起首次去
你走起路来如此优美或多或少体现了未来主义
就像在家里一样，我从来不去想《下楼梯的裸女》②或者
在练习时不去想一幅曾经让我惊叹的列奥纳多③或米开朗基罗④的画
印象派画家的研究又有什么用呢
当太阳落山时，他们找不到合适的人站在树旁
或者是马里诺·马里尼⑤，如果他没有像挑选马一样认真地
去挑选骑手

他们似乎都被一些神奇的经验所蒙蔽
这不会在我身上浪费，这就是我告诉你关于它的原因

① 《波兰人骑士》：*The Polish Rider*，荷兰著名画家伦勃朗·梵·莱茵（Rembrandt HarMenszoon van Rijn，1606—1669）1655年作品，藏于纽约弗立克美术图书馆。

② 《下楼梯的裸女》：*The Nude Descending a Staircase*，法国艺术家马塞尔·杜尚（Marcel Duehamp，1887—1968）于1912年创作的油画，现收藏于美国费城艺术博物馆。

③ 列奥纳多：（Leonardo da Vinci，1452—1519）意大利文艺复兴时期画家。

④ 米开朗基罗：（Micellangelo Buonarroti，1475—1564）意大利文艺复兴时期画家、雕塑家、诗人。

⑤ 马里诺·马里尼：（Marino Marini，1901—1980）意大利雕塑家。

# 约翰·阿什贝利
## (John Ashbery，1927—2017)

约翰·阿什贝利 1927 年 7 月出生于纽约罗彻斯特，童年在安大略湖畔的农场度过。阿什贝利最早梦想成为一名画家，在中学期间阅读了一系列现代诗人的作品之后，对诗歌萌发了浓厚兴趣，开始学习诗歌写作。

在哈佛大学读书期间，阿什贝利与后来成为著名诗人的罗伯特·克里利(Robert Creeley)、罗伯特·布莱(Robert Bly)为同班同学。除此之外，他还结识了肯尼斯·可赫①(Kenneth Koch)、芭芭拉·爱泼斯坦②(Barbara Epstein)、弗兰克·奥哈拉、爱德华·戈里③(Edward Gorey)等文学界朋友。哈佛毕业后，阿什贝利进入哥伦比亚大学学习，1951 年获得文学硕士学位。

20 世纪 50 年代初期，由于获得福布莱特项目资助，阿什贝利去了法国。在法国，他同诗人皮埃尔·马托利④(Pierre Martory)一起生活了 9 年，彼此相互学习、相互鼓励，结下了深厚友谊。后来他将皮埃尔的多部作品翻译成了英文，如《唯一问题》(*Every Question but One*)、《风景在门后》(*The Landscape is behind the Door*)、《风景画家》(*The Landscapist*)等。期间，曾多次担任《艺术与文学》(*Art and Literature*)杂志的编辑。与此同时，阿什贝利还翻译了法国谋杀悬疑小说、出任《纽约国际先驱导报》欧洲版的艺术编辑、担任《国际艺术》(*Art International*)的艺术评论家、《艺术新闻》(*Art News*)巴黎记者等。回到美国后，阿什贝利除了担任《艺术新闻》的编委的工作，还为《纽约》(*New York*)和《新闻周刊》(*Newsweek*)等杂志撰写艺术评论。1976 年到 1980 年期间还担任过《党派评论》(*Partisan Review*)的编辑。

20 世纪 70 年代，阿什贝利曾任教于布鲁克林大学。20 世纪 80 年代初，阿什贝利离开布鲁克林来到巴德学院(Bard College)，担任该校语言文学教授，2008 年退休。2017 年 9 月 3 日阿什贝利在位于纽约哈德森的家中去世，享年 90 岁。

阿什贝利是一位成就斐然的诗人。1983 年他当选美国艺术科学院院士，是纽约州 2001 年到 2003 年桂冠诗人，担任美国诗歌学会主席多年。他的诗歌作品几乎荣获了美国诗坛所有大奖：普利策奖、国家图书奖、耶鲁青年诗人奖(the Yale Younger Poets

---

① 肯尼斯·可赫：(1925—2002)纽约诗派主要诗人之一，剧作家。

② 芭芭拉·爱泼斯坦：(1928—2006)文学编辑。

③ 爱德华·戈里：(1925—2000)作家。

④ 皮埃尔·马托利：(1920—1998)对美国“纽约派”诗人产生重大影响的法国诗人。

Prize)、博林根奖(the Bollingen Prize)、露丝·莉莉诗歌奖(the Ruth Lilly Poetry Award)①等。

阿什贝利是个多产作家，一生笔耕不辍，作品丰富，主要包括诗歌集《图兰朵及其他诗》(*Turandot and Other Poems*，1953)、《几棵树》(*Some Trees*，1956)、《网球场誓约》(*The Tennis Court Oath*，1962)、《河流与山脉》(*Rivers and Mountains*，1966)、《春天双梦》(*The Double Dream of Spring*，1970)、《三首诗》(*Three Poems*，1972)、《凸面镜中的自画像》(*Self-Portrait in a Convex Mirror*，1975)、《游艇上的日子》(*Houseboat Days*，1977)、《众所周知》(*As We Know*，1979)、《影子火车》(*Shadow Train*，1981)、《波浪》(*A Wave*，1984)、《流程图》(*Flow Chart*，1991)、《洛特雷蒙特宾馆》(*Hotel Lautreatmont*，1992)、《星星也在闪耀》(*And the Stars Were Shining*，1994)、《你能听到吗，鸟儿?》(*Can You Hear，Bird?* 1995)、《蓄势待发：早期五本诗集》(*The Morning of Starting Out*，1997)、《奔波中的女孩》(*Girls on the Run*，1999)、《在此签名》(*Your Name Here*，2000)、《中国人的悄悄话》(*Chinese Whispers*，2002)《我要游荡到何方》(*Where Shall I Wander*，2005)、《来自空中的笔记》(*Notes from the Air*，2007)、《世俗国家》(*A Worldly Country*，2007)、《星座图》(*Planisphere*，2009)、《1956—1987年诗歌集》(*Collected Poems 1956—1987*，2010)、《简短问题》(*Quick Question*，2012)、《风道》(*Breezeway*，2015)、《喧闹的鸟儿》(*Commotion of the Birds*，2016)等。除了诗歌外，阿什贝利还创作了一些小说、散文和戏剧，翻译了一些法国著名诗人的作品，如《傻瓜的安乐窝》(*A Nest of Ninnies*，1969)、《三部剧》(*Three Plays*，1978)、《1953—2003年散文选》(*Selected Prose*，2005)、《法国诗歌翻译集》(*Collected French Translations：Poetry*，2014)等。

阿什贝利在诗歌创作初期就特别重视向前辈现代诗人学习，如W.H.奥登、华莱斯·斯蒂文斯，特别是法国超现实主义诗人，因此他的诗歌带有鲜明的先锋派艺术特色。

## Some Trees

These are amazing：each
Joining a neighbor，as though speech
Were a still performance.
Arranging by chance

---

① 露丝·莉莉诗歌奖(The Ruth Lilly Poetry Award)：露丝·莉莉1986年设立的一个诗歌奖项。露丝·莉莉诗歌奖每年向在世的美国诗人颁发10万美元的奖金，以表彰其杰出的终身成就。它是授予美国诗人的最负盛名的奖项之一，也是全美最大的文学奖之一。

To meet as far this morning
From the world as agreeing
With it, you and I
Are suddenly what the trees try

To tell us we are:
That their merely being there
Means something; that soon
We may touch, love, explain.

And glad not to have invented
Such comeliness, we are surrounded:
A silence already filled with noises,
A canvas on which emerges

A chorus of smiles, a winter morning.
Placed in a puzzling light, and moving,
Our days put on such reticence
These accents seem their own defense.

## 几棵树

这些树很神奇：每一棵
都与相邻的一棵连在一起，仿佛言语
是一场寂静的表演。
偶然安排

就像和它商量好要在
今天早上从那个世界来
相见，你和我
突然成了那些树想要

告诉我们的就是：
即它们仅仅在那里
就有某种意义；即不久

我们就会接触、相爱、解释。

而且庆幸自己没有虚构
这种优美，我们周围都是：
业已充满噪音的寂静，
一张画布浮现出

微笑的合唱队，冬天的早晨。
安排在令人恍惚的灯光下，运动，
我们的岁月呈现出这般静寂
这些夸张的动作似乎是为了自卫。

## Meditation of a Parrot

Oh the rocks and the thimble
The oasis and the bed
Oh the jacket and roses.

All sweetly stood up the see to me
Like blue cornflakes in a white bowl.
The girl said, "watch this."

I come from Spain, I said.
I was purchased at a fair.
She said, "none of us know."

"There was a house once
Of dazzling canopies
And halls like a keyboard."

"These the waves tore in pieces."
(His old wound—
And all day: Robin Hood! Robin Hood!)

## 鹦鹉的沉思

啊！岩石、套管、
绿洲、床铺
啊！夹克和玫瑰。

全部诱人地呈现在我面前
犹如一只白色碗里的蓝色玉米片。
女孩说，“瞧这个。”

我来自西班牙，我说。
有人在集市买下了我。
女孩说，“我们都不知道。”

“曾经有一所房子
屋顶令人眼花缭乱
大厅宛如键盘。”

“海浪把它们撕成了碎片。”
（他的旧伤——
而且整日间：绿林好汉！绿林好汉！）

## Chaos

Don't ask me to go there again
The white is too painful
Better to forget it
the sleeping river spoke to the awake land

When they first drew the wires
across the field
slowly air settled
on the pools
The blue mirror came to light

Then someone feared the pools
To be armor enough might not someone
draw down the sky
Light emerged
The swimming motion

At last twilight that will not protect the leaves
Death that will not try to scream
Black beaches
That is why I sent you the black postcard that will never deafen

That is why land urges the well
The white is running in its grooves
The river slides under our dreams
but land flows more silently

## 混乱

别叫我再去那儿
白色太令人伤感
最好把它忘记
沉睡的河流对苏醒的大地说

他们起初在田地
拉上电线
空气慢慢地凝固
在池塘上
蓝色的镜子亮了起来

接着有人担心池塘
成为厚重的盔甲不会有人
把天空拉下
光线出现
四处游动

最终阑珊的光线将无法保护叶子
死亡不会喊叫
漆黑的海滩
这就是我为何要送你永远不会淹没的黑色明信片

这就是为何大地敦促水井
白色在槽沟流淌
河流在我们入梦时悄悄流动
但大地的运动更加无声无息

## People Behaving Badly a Concern

Aggressive panhandling, public urination, verbal threats,
public nudity and violation of the open container law①
followed us down the days, for why
are we here much longer,
or even this long? I ask you
to be civil and not interrupt night's business.

It was fun getting used to you,
who couldn't have been more nicer.
This was as modern as it had ever been.
They were influenced by him: some dirty magazine
on the air tonight. (Amid the chaos, reports of survivors.)

Didn't the flowers' restoration cat fugue keep spilling,
and like that? It wouldn't be the first time, either.
The pro-taffeta get up and laugh,
investigate or communicate. The night you were
going to stay up late, others will kiss,
and he talks about you, and I don't know what.
Come in, anyway,

① Open container law：指禁止在公共场合如街道、广场或行使的车辆上喝酒。

and don't lack for tales of the Assertion.

We're talking civilian unrest.
Yes, well, maybe you should take one.

(Do not bite or chew.)

## 不文明行为需要关注

强行乞讨、当众小便、言语恐吓、
众人面前赤身裸体、公共场所酗酒，
我们业已司空见惯，那么我们
为什么在这儿呆这么久，
或者直到现在？我请你
文明一点，别妨碍夜间工作。

可笑的是你对此已经见怪不怪，
你可真是个大好人。
这里像以前一样摩登。
他们受了他的影响：今晚播送的
某种下流期刊。（在乱七八糟、幸存者报道中插播）

难道不会再播放一些花卉修复的小猫赋格①，
或诸如此类的东西？这也不是第一次了。
喜欢塔夫绸的站起身笑了笑，
了解或沟通。你准备熬夜的
那个晚上，别人要亲吻，
他说到了你，而我不知道说了些什么。
不管怎样，进来吧，
别错过了那些看法的传言。

我们在说市民骚乱。

---

① 小猫赋格：即 *The Cat's Fugue*，《小猫的赋格》，意大利作曲家多梅尼科·斯卡拉蒂(Domenico Scarlatti，1685—1756)的作品。

是的，呃，或许你应该取其一。

(不要咬而要嚼。)

## Album Leave

The other marigolds① and the cloths②
Are crimes invented for history.
What can we achieve, aspiring?
And what, aspiring, can we achieve?

What can the rain that fell
All day on the grounds
And on the bingo tables?
Even though it is cleaning.

The statue turned to a sweeter light,
The nearest patrons are black.
Then there is a storm of receipts: right,
Sand the bowl did not let fall.

The other marigolds are scattered like dust.
Sweet peas in dark gardens
Squirt false melancholy over history.
If a bug fell from so high, would it land?

## 专辑留念

有一些金盏花和布料
是为历史而发明的罪行。
我们可以获取什么，抱负?
什么，抱负，我们能够获得?

---

① Marigolds：由 Mary (the virgin)和 Gold 拼缀而成。
② Cloths：(统称)牧师

雨即使在荡涤尘垢，
那么整日落在大地
落在宾果游戏的台面
它得到了什么呢?

雕像转向更温柔的灯光，
最接近的赞助者是黑人。
于是收益大幅飙升：对，
饭碗没让沙子落下。

一些金盏花犹如灰尘四散。
黑暗花园里的香豌豆①
将虚假的忧伤撒向历史。
如果虫子②从如此高的地方落下，它会着地吗?

## The Hero

Whose face is this
Stiffed against the blue trees

Lifted to the future
Because there is no end?

But that has faded
Like flowers, like the first days

Of good conduct. Visit
The strong man. Pinch him—

There is no end to his
Dislike, the accurate one.

---

① 香豌豆：Sweet peas，也可做亲爱的人儿讲，相当于 darling，my dear 等。
② 虫子：指要人、名士、臆想的怪物等。

## 英雄

这是谁的脸
在绿色树木的映衬下这般僵硬

被抬举到未来
因为没有尽头?

但是像花儿一样
它已经枯萎，像品行良好的

最初的日子。去拜访一下
这位伟人。捏他一下——

无时不讨厌
他，的确如此。

## When the Sun Went Down

To have been loved once by someone—surely
There is a permanent good in that,
Even if we don't know all the circumstances
Or it happened too long ago to make any difference.
Like almost too much sunlight or an abundance of sweet-sticky,
Caramelized things—who can tell you it's wrong?
Which of the others on your team could darken the passive
Melody that runs on, that has been running, since the world began?

Yet, to be strapped to one's mindset, which seems
As enormous as a plain, to have to be told
That its horizons are comically confining,
And all the sorrow wells from there, like the slanting
Plume of waterspout: doesn't it supplant knowledge
Of the different forms of love, reducing them

To a white indifferent prism, a roofless love standing open
To the elements? And some see in this a paradigm of how it rises
Slowly to the indifferent heavens, all that pale glamour?

The refrain is desultory as birdsong; it seeps unrecognizably
Into the familiar structures that lead out from here
To the still familiar peripheries and less sure notions:
It already had its way. In time for evening relaxation.
There are times when music steals a march on us,
Is suddenly perplexingly nearer, flowing in my wrist;
Is the true and dirty words you whisper nightly
As the book closes like a collapsing sheet, a blur
Of all kinds of connotations ripped from the hour and tossed
Like jewels down a well; the answer, also,
To the question that was on my mind but that I've forgotten,
Except in the way certain things, certain nights, come together.

## 日落时分

曾经被人爱过——当然
是一种难以忘怀的美妙之事，
即使我们并非清楚是何缘由
或者是久远之事，都无关紧要。
就像阳光过于充足，或者甜粘、
焦糖味的东西太多——谁能说这有什么不好?
开天辟地伊始世间就流行着一种无源旋律
你的团队中哪一位能将它削弱?

然而，必须指出，一旦类似
平原之大的身心被困，
它的视野滑稽地受到限制，
于是悲伤由此倾泻而出，
如同排水口倾斜的缕流:
难道要取代对爱的不同形式的理解，
把它们压缩成一个冷漠的白色棱镜，

成为一种矗立于世间毫无遮拦的爱?
而且有人从中发现一种样板，它是怎样
一步一步地迈入冷漠的天堂，全部苍白的魅力?

这一迭句杂乱无章像鸟鸣;
它不知不觉地渗入熟悉的结构中
由此延伸到依旧熟悉的外围和不那么确定的观念:
它已经有了自己的方式。晚上正好歇息一下。
音乐有时蹑手蹑脚地向我们逼近，
突然莫名其妙地近在咫尺，流淌在我的手腕;
当书像折叠的床单一样合上时，
你每晚低声细语说的那些真心话
是否已经背离了当时的种种含义而模糊不清，
像宝石一样扔进了井里;
这个问题的答案也一直在我心里，但我已经忘了，
只剩下某些事情、某些夜晚，在一起的情境。

# 肯尼斯·考克
## (Kennith Koch, 1925—2002)

肯尼斯·考克 1925 年生于俄亥俄州的辛辛那提。考克从小对诗歌兴趣浓厚，喜欢英国浪漫主义诗人作品，特别是雪莱和济慈。在哈佛大学学习期间，他结识了后来同为纽约派诗人的奥哈拉和阿什贝利，受他们的影响和帮助，考克开始了诗歌写作。

哈佛毕业后，考克去了哥伦比亚大学攻读博士学位。他后来受聘于哥伦比亚大学英语和比较文学系，教授诗歌欣赏和写作。

考克虽然开始诗歌写作的时间很早，但直到 20 世纪 70 年代才引起了诗坛和评论界的关注。20 世纪 90 年代考克的成就迎来了高峰，各种荣誉接踵而来：博林根诗歌奖(1994)、丽贝卡·约翰逊·博比特国家诗歌奖①(1996)、古根海姆诗歌奖(1996)、福布莱特(1996)、英格拉姆-梅林基金(1996)、当选美国艺术文学院院士(1996)、菲贝塔·卡帕诗歌奖②(2000)等。

考克的主要诗集包括，《诗》(*Poems*, 1953)、《Ko：或者，地球一季》(*Ko: or, A Season on Earth*, 1959)、《永久地》(*Permonently*, 1961)、《谢谢你及其他诗》(*Thank You and Other Poems*, 1962)、《1952—1953 年间的诗》(*Poems from 1952 and 1953*, 1968)、《与女人同床而眠》(*Sleeping with Women*, 1969)、《和平的快乐及其他诗》(*The Pleasures of Peace and Other Poems*, 1969)、《当太阳要继续》(*When the Sun Tries to Go On*, 1969)、《爱的艺术》(*The Art of Love*, 1975)、《复制》(*The Duplications*, 1977)、《来自空中》(*From the Air*, 1979)、《1951 年安娜燃烧之谜》(*The Burning Mystery of Anna in 1951*, 1979)、《白天和夜晚》(*Days and Nights*, 1982)、《1950—1982 诗选》(*Selected Poems 1950—1980*, 1985)、《在边沿》《*On the Edge*, 1986)、《地球上的季节》(*Seasons on Earth*, 1987)、《在伟大的大西洋铁路上：1950—1988 诗选》(*On the Great Atlantic Railway: Selected Poems* 1950—1988, 1994)、《一列火车》(*One Train*, 1994)、《海峡》(*Straits*, 1998)等。

除了诗歌外，考克还创作了一系列戏剧和散文，特别是关于诗歌阅读和写作的作品，对诗歌教学具有重大指导和帮助作用，如《愿望、谎言和梦想：教小孩写诗》(*Wishes, Lies and Dreams: Teaching Children to Write Poetry*, 1970)、《玫瑰，你从哪里变得那么红》(*Rose, Where Did You Get that Red*? 1973)、《我从来没有告诉过任何

---

① 丽贝卡·约翰逊·博比特国家诗歌奖：(the Rebekah Johnson Bobbitt National Poetry Prize)，美国唯一的国家诗歌大奖，设立于 1988 年，每两年评选一次，用来奖励过去两年作品最优秀的诗人。

② 菲贝塔·卡帕诗歌奖：(Ingram-Merril Foundations)，20 世纪 50 年代诗人詹姆斯·梅林(James Merrill, 1926—1955)设立，梅林去世后的第二年取消。

人：在疗养院教写诗》(*I Never Told Anybody：Teaching Poetry Writing in a Nursing Home*，1977)等。

考克晚年身患白血病，2002 年 7 月在纽约去世。

考克的诗歌从一开始就带有很强的反理性、反传统的特点。他不屑于陈旧、索然无味的主题和单一、毫无变化的形式。在他看来，现代美国诗坛仍然无法摆脱艾略特的影响，"《荒原》给这一时代提供了无比精确的资料，仿佛是，艾略特是文学的大独裁者。在诗歌领域没人胆敢视而不见或越雷池一步，而批评家对反讽、歧义和张力则大加赞扬——还有我不愿说的其他事。"(《地球上的季节》1987 年)，所以在他看来，诗歌要发展就必须要有突破和创新。

## You Know All This

The first, violent year
  I could not swim or float;
A dark and balanced fear
  Hung on me like a coat.

The second year it rained,
  The rain was strict and odd;
The fur of fear remained
  But I whistled Scheherazade.

The summer of the third
  I stripped with some dispatch;
Still finding me absurd
  You still struck me like a match:

Flaming, naked, stung,
  I held you for a year,
Persistent as a tongue,
  Infecting you, my dear.

My hands, somnambular,
  Have kept you like a vow;
No matter where you are

We touch each other now.

## 这些你无一不知

第一个，暴力的一年
　我既不会游泳也不会漂浮；
一种黑暗和适度的恐惧
　像外套罩在我身上。

第二年下雨了，
　雨下得犀利且反常；
恐惧的皮毛依然存在
　但我口哨吹起了谢赫拉莎德①。

第三个夏天
　我完成了一件报道
还是觉得滑稽可笑
　你仍然像火柴一样点亮了我：

燃烧、裸露、刺痛，
　我拥抱了你一年，
像舌头一样执着，
　感染你，亲爱的。

我的手，梦游者，
　发誓抓住你不松手；
现在无论你到哪里
　我们都如影相随。

## The Art of Poetry

To write a poem, perfect physical condition
Is desirable but not necessary, Keats wrote

① 谢赫拉莎德：《天方夜谭》中的苏丹新娘。

In poor health, as did D. H. Lawrence. A combination
Of disease and old age is an impediment to writing, but
Neither is, alone, unless there is arteriosclerosis—that is,
Hardening of the arteries—but that we shall count as a disease
Accompanying old age and therefore a negative condition.
Mental health is certainly not a necessity for the
Creation of poetic beauty, but a degree of it
Would seem to be, except in rare cases. Schizophrenic poetry
Tends to be loose, disjointed, uncritical of itself, in some ways
Like what is best in our modern practice of the poetic art
But unlike it in others, in its lack of concern
For intensity and nuance. A few great poems
By poets supposed to be "mad" are of course known to us all,
Such as those of Christopher Smart, but I wonder how crazy they were,
These poets who wrote such contraptions of exigent art?
As for Blake's being "crazy", that seems to me very unlikely.

...

... Just how good a poem should be
Before one releases it, either from one's own work or then into the purview of others,
May be decided by applying the fowllowing rules: ask 1) Is it astonishing?
Am I pleased each time I read it? Does it say something I was unware of
Before I sat down to write it? and 2) Do I stand up from it a better man
Or a wiser, or both? or can the two not be separated? 3) Is it really by me
Or have I stolen it from somewhere else? (This sometimes happens,
Though it is comparatively rare.) 4) Does it reveal something about me
I never want anyone to know? 5) Is it sufficiently "modern"?
(more about this a little later) 6) Is it in my own "voice"?
Along with, of course, the more obvious questions, such as
7) Is there any unwanted awkwardness, cheap effects, asking illegimately for attention,
Show-offness, cuteness, pseudo-profundity, old hat checks,
Unassimilated dream fragments, or other "literary", "kiss-me-I'm-poetical" junk?
Is my poem free of this? 8) Does it move smoothly and swiftly
From excitement to dream and then come flooding reason

With purity and soundness and joy? 9) Is this the kind of poem
I would envy in another if he could write? 10)
Would I be happy to go to Heaven with this pinned on my
Angelic jacket as an entrance show? Oh, would I? And if you can answer to all these Yes
Except for the 4th one, to which the answer should be No,
Then you can release it, at least for the time being.
I would look at it again, though, perhaps in two hours, then after one or two weeks,
And then a month later, at which time you can probably be sure.

...

As for following fashionable literary movements,
It is almost irresistible, and for a while I can see no harm in it,
But the sooner you find your own style the better off you will be.
Then all "movements" fit into it. You have an "exercycle" of your own.
Trying out all kinds of styles and imitating poets you like
And incorporating anything valuable you may find there,
These are sound procedures, and in fact I think even essential
To the perfection of an original style which is yours alone.
An original style may not last more than four years,
Or even three or even two, sometimes on rare occasions one,
And then you must find another. It is conceivable even that a style
For a very exigent poet would be for one week only,
After which it would be exhausted, limping, unable to sustain any wrong or right.
By "exigent" I mean extremely careful, wanting each poem to be a conclusion
Of everything he senses, feels and knows.
The exigent poet has his satisfactions, which are relatively special,
But that is not the only kind of poet you can be. There is a pleasure in being Venus,
In sending love to everyone, in being Zeus,
In sending thunder to everyone, in being Apollo
And everyday sending out light. It is a pleasure to write continually
And well, and that is a special poetic dream
Which you may have or you may not. Not all writers have it.
Browning once wrote a poem every day of one year
And found it "didn't work out well". But who knows?

He went on for a year—something must have been working out.

And why only one poem a day? Why not several? Why not one every hour for eight to ten hours a day?

There seems no reason not to try it if you have the inclination.

...

## 诗歌艺术

要写诗，健康的身体是必要的，
但不是必须的，济慈写诗是
身体状况不好，D. H. 劳伦斯也是。
疾病加上年龄过大是写诗的障碍，
但都不能单独构成障碍，
除非患了动脉硬化——
我们认为这是一种老年病，
因此是一种不利因素。
心理健康当然不一定是创造诗歌之美的
必要条件，然而多数情况下，
一定程度的心理健康似乎
是必要的。精神分裂的诗歌
往往是松散的、脱节的、缺乏自我批判，
在某些方面就像我们现代诗歌艺术实践中的优秀作品，
与其不同的是它不大关注强度和细微差别。
我们一定都熟悉那些被认为是“疯子”的诗人写的
一些著名诗篇，比如克里斯托弗·斯马特①的作品，
但我不知道这些诗人有多疯狂，
写下如此严谨艺术的奇妙作品?
至于布莱克的“疯狂”，我觉得不太可能。

……

① 克里斯托弗·斯马特：(Christopher Smart，1722—1771)英国诗人，主要作品有《羔羊的欢乐》《献给戴维的歌》等。

……一首诗，无论是选自于自己的作品
或者是后来收录进他人的作品，
在什么情况下才能发表，
取决于是否满足以下条件：问 1)是否有惊人之处？
每次读到它是否有愉悦之感？是否说了一些
开始写作时我浑然不知的事情？2)这首诗会使我更加优秀
或者更加智慧，或者兼而有之？或者两者不能分离？
3)的确是我写的
或者是我从其他地方偷来的？(这种情况时有发生，
虽然概率很小。) 4)是否透露了我个人一些一直不想
让别人知道的事情？5)是否足够“时髦”？
(后面再详谈) 6)是用我自己的“声音”吗？
当然还有一些显而易见的问题，比如，
7)有没有不必要的尴尬、廉价的效果、荒谬地谋求关注、
炫耀、卖萌、貌似深奥、陈旧的约束、未曾同化的梦片段、
或者其他“文学的”“吻-我-我-富有诗意”的垃圾？
我的诗里没有这些？8)诗歌过渡是否流畅、果断，
从兴奋到梦想，然后涌向理智，
带着纯洁、健全和欢乐？9)假如这首诗是别人写的
我会羡慕他吗？10)把它用别针别在天使夹克衫上作为进天堂的
出入证我会乐意吗？啊，我会吗？除了第四个问题答案是“否”外，
其他问题你的回答均为“是”的话，
那么你就可以发表了，起码目前如此。
不过我会再看一下，或许两小时后，
或许一周或两周之后，
或许一个月之后，这样就可确保万无一失。

……

至于追赶时尚的文学流派，
这几乎难以抵御，眼下我觉得没有什么害处，
但是越早形成自己的风格越好。
这样将所有“流派”融入其中。你就有了自己的“练习周期”。
尝试各种风格，模仿所喜欢的诗人
吸收能够发现的全部有价值的东西，

这些都是行之有效的方法，实际上我认为
是能使自己独创的风格臻于完美的必要手段。
一种独创的风格延续或许不超过四年，
甚至三年或者两年，有些情况下偶尔还不到一年，
于是就要寻求另一种风格。可以想象对
严谨的诗人说来一种风格只用于一首诗，
用过之后就会筋疲力尽、步履蹒跚、难以继续保持好或者不好。
说到“严谨”我的意思是非常认真，希望每首诗都是
他所感觉、所体验、所认识的东西的终结。
严谨的诗人有自己的满足，比较独特的满足，
但是你不能仅仅局限于成为这样一种诗人。做个维纳斯是种乐趣，
把爱送给每个人，做个宙斯，
给众生送上雷鸣，做个阿波罗
每天撒播光明。持续不断地写作是种乐趣，
这是一种独特的诗的梦想
你或许有或许没有。并非每位作家都有。
勃朗宁曾经有一年每天写一首诗
后来发现“效果不太好”。但谁知道呢?
他坚持了一年——一定是出了什么事。
为什么一天只写一首? 为什么不是几首? 为什么不是每天八小时到十小时每一小时一首?
如果你喜欢不妨可以试试。
……

## You Want a Social Life, with Friends

You want a social life, with friends.
A passionate love life and as well
To work hard every day. What's true
Is of these three you may have two
And two can pay you dividends
But never may have three.

There isn't time enough, my friends—
Though dawn begins, yet midnight ends—

To find the time to have love, work, and friends.
Michelangelo had feeling
For Vittoria and the ceiling
But did he go to parties at day's end?

Homer nightly went to banquets
Wrote all day but had no lockets
Bright with pictures of his girl.
I know one who loves and parties
And has done so since his thirties
But writes hardly anything at all.

## 你渴望社交生活，和朋友在一起

你渴望社交生活，和朋友在一起。
充满激情的爱情生活
还有每天都能够努力工作。
实际上三者中你或许会拥有两个
两个就能让你春风得意，
但永远不会让你占尽三个。

时间不待人，我的朋友——
虽然黎明开启，但午夜结束——
找时间去爱，去工作，去交朋友。
米开朗基罗喜欢
维托丽娅[1]和天花板
但他晚上会去聚会吗?

荷马每晚都去参加宴会
白天整日写作但没有镶着
他的情人照片的盒式吊坠。
我认识一位作家
三十多岁就整日参加派对

---

① 维托丽娅：(Vittoria Colonna，1492—1547)意大利女诗人。

一生几乎一事无成。

## On Beauty

Beauty is something personified
As a beautiful woman, and this personification is satisfying
In that, probably, of all the beautiful thing one sees
A beautiful person is the most inspiring, because, in looking at her,
One is swept by desires, as the sails are swept in the bay, and when the body is excited,
Beauty is more evident, whether one is awake or asleep.
A beautiful person also suggests a way
To be at one with beauty, to be united with it, physically, with more than our eyes,
And strange it is, this tactile experience
Of beauty, and the subject of many other works. The first beauty one sees
That one is conscious of as "beauty", what is that? Some say
"The mother's face—but I do not think
The baby is conscious of anything as "beauty"—perhaps years after
When he looks at Carpaccio's *Saint Ursula*, he thinks of "mother"
Subconsciously, and that is why he finds her "bella—
Poi anche bellissima", as he says in Italian
To the guard or fellow-viewer at his side. The guard smokes a cigarette
Later, on the steps of the palazzo, and he gazes at the blue sky,
And for him that is bellissima. Perhaps the sky reminds him
Of someone's eyes. But why is that, that human reminder,
If that is what accounts for beauty, so enchanting? Like a thigh. The island of Kos
Is extremely lovely, as are many other Greek islands—Lemnos,
Poros, and Charybdis. We could sail among them, happy, fortunate
To be in such places, yet tormented by an inner sense
Of anxiety and guilt, beleaguered by a feeling we had torn
Ourselves from what is really important, simply for this
Devious experiencing of "beauty", which may be nothing but a clumsy substitute
For seeing our mothers again.
...

## 论美

美有时被拟人化
为一位美丽的女性，这种做法令人心旷神怡
在人们见到的所有美的事物中
美丽的女性可能最让人心动，因为，看见她，
就会有欲望的冲动，犹如海湾被卷起的风帆，当身体受到诱惑，
美显而易见，无论你是清醒还是熟睡。
一个美丽的女性也暗示了一种不仅在视角上
而且在肉体上与美相随、与美为伴的方式，
非常奇妙，这一美的
感官体验，许多其他作品的主题。人们第一次见到的美
他所意识到的所谓的“美”，是什么？有人说
“母亲的面孔”——但我认为
婴儿意识不到“美”的事物——或许几年之后
当他看到卡尔帕乔①的《圣·乌苏拉》②时，他下意识地
想起了“母亲”，而这就是为什么他觉得她“美——
真的很美，”他用意大利语对身旁的卫士或观众说。卫士抽着烟卷
后来，在宫殿台阶上，他凝望蔚蓝色的天空，
心里想这就是美。也许天空让他想起了
某人的眼睛。可是，如果这个引起人们回忆的东西就是美，
为什么它会像大腿一样如此令人着迷？和希腊其他众多岛屿——
利姆诺斯、波罗斯、查理迪斯一样，科斯岛
非常美丽。我们在岛屿中间航行，在此感到快乐、幸福，
虽然被内心的焦虑和罪过而纷扰，受困于脱离了
真正重要的东西的感觉，仅仅为了这一“美”的欺骗性体验，一种
为了重见母亲的笨拙替代。
……

---

① 卡尔帕乔：(Vittore Carpaccio，1450—1525)威尼斯画派的叙事体画家，在绘画上深受贝利尼影响。

② 《圣·乌苏拉》：传说中，Saint Ursula（乌苏拉）是 Brittany（布列塔尼）的公主，她嫁给了 Pagan(异教) 王子，使他归信基督教。为纪念乌苏拉，创作了九幅画。

## Paradiso

There is no way not to be excited
When what you have been disillusioned by raises its head
From its arms and seems to want to talk to you again.
You forget home and family
And set off on foot or in your automobile
And go to where you believe this form of reality
May dwell. Not finding it there, you refuse
Any further contact
Until you are back again trying to forget
The only thing that moved you (it seems) and gave what you forever will have
But in the form of a disillusion. Yet often, looking toward the horizon
There—inimical to you? —is that something you have never found
And that, without those who came before you, you could never have imagined.
How could you have thought there was one person who could make you
Happy and that happiness was not the uneven
Phenomenon you have known it to be? Why do you keep believing in this
Reality so dependent on the time allowed it
That it has less to do with your exile from the age you are
Than from everything else life promised that you could do?

## 天堂

一直令你消沉之事从它的
双臂抬起头并且似乎又想和你交谈
这无法不让你激动。
你不顾及家和家人
徒步或驱车前往
那自以为这种现实形式
可能的存留之地。结果一无所获，你
不会再进一步接触
重新回来试图忘记
那唯一感动过你(好像是)和赋予你永远拥有的东西

但是以虚幻的形式。
然而你总是遥望地平线
那里——对你有害？——有你永远找不到的那种东西
还有，如果没有在你之前到来的那些人，你可能永远无法想象。
有人会让你幸福而这种幸福不是你所理解的那种少有情形
你怎么会这样想呢？你为什么一直相信这个
完全依赖于规定时间的现实？
这与你流放的年龄无关
相比生命承诺你能做的一切？

## To My Old Poems

(January 2000)
You had no independence
From me, in, say, nineteen sixty-three
I was already thirty-eight years old
And you were eight years old
I wanted to care of you
Make sure you were in the best books and magazines
Printed on good paper and in type that was clear. A couple of you
Became independent entrepreneurs
And laughed back at me from anthologies
While, with feet painted by ill-fitting shoes, I walked through France
Dying to find something new to go with you. In these years
You became almost my enemies, cruelly, I thought,
Showing me what I could no longer do. At this time
You seemed one and the same as my youth
Not separate from me
As I was then but as I was now.
But you were always separate from me.
You who are made out of words.
One thing you do is not respond
Which is all right, since what kind of poems would you be
if you were capable of responding?
That's not what's meant by an "answerable style."

One wants a poem to be still.
But I'd like to know where you got your music—
From other poems, I know, but from where else?
And if the ability to make you is a gift that comes back—
One of you arriving, or being finished.
Like an ace or a king or a queen
In the hand of my otherwise foolish life. In any case
You're friendlier than you have been for a long while—
Things seem to be all right between us now.

## 写给我早期的诗

(2000 年元月)
你没有摆脱我,
比如在一九六三年
我已经三十八岁
那时你才八岁
我想照顾你
确保你[1]刊登在一流的书籍和期刊上,
印刷纸张上乘,字迹清晰。你们中有几个
成了独立创业者
从选集中回过头来嘲笑我
而我,穿着夹脚的鞋,双脚疼痛地走遍了法国
竭力寻找与你相匹配的新东西。这些年
你几乎成了我的敌人,太残忍,我觉得,
指点我不能再做什么。这个时候
你似乎紧紧跟随着我
我年轻时就这样,
犹如我那时而不是现在。
但是你总是与我不在一起,
文字组成的你。
你做的一件事是拒绝回应
这没有错,如果你能做出回应

---

① 你:在这里指"他的诗"。

那会成为什么样的诗?
那不是常说的“已知的形式”
人们喜欢诗歌一成不变。
但你能说说你的音乐来自哪里——
来自其他诗歌，我知道，但还有别的地方吗?
而假如创造你的才能是一种回归的天赋——
那么你们中的一个出现，或者结束。
就像我原本愚蠢生命手中的
A 牌、K 牌或 Q 牌。不管怎样
与长期以来不同，你对我更友善了——
现在我俩之间好像能够和睦相处。

## You Were Wearing

You were wearing your Edgar Allen Poe printed blouse.

In each divided up square of the blouse was a picture of Edgar Allen Poe.

Your hair was blond and you were cute. You asked me, “Do most boys think most girls are bad?”

I smelled the mould of your seaside resort hotel bedroom on your hair held in place by a John Greenleaf Whittier clip.

“No,” I said, “it's girls who think that boys are bad.” Then we read *Snowbound* together.

And ran around in an attic, so that a little of the blue enamel was scraped off my George Washington, Father of His Country, shoes.

Mother was walking in the living room, her Strauss Waltzes comb in her hair.

We waited for a time and then joined her, only to be served tea in cups painted with pictures of Herman Melville.

As well as with illustrations from his book *Moby Dick* and from his novella, *Benito Cereno*.

Father came in wearing his Dick Tracy necktie: “How about a drink, everyone?”

I said, “Let's go outside a while.” Then we went onto the porch and sat on the Abraham Lincoln swing.

You sat on the eyes, mouth, and beard part, and I sat on the knees.

In the yard across the street was a snowman holding a garbage can lid smashed into a likeness of the mad English king, George the Third.

## 你穿着

你穿着埃德加·爱伦·坡的印花上衣。
上衣每一方格都有一幅埃德加·爱伦·坡的画像。
你头发金黄，楚楚动人。你问我，“男孩一般都认为女孩坏吗?”
你头戴约翰·格林里夫·惠蒂埃①式发夹，秀发整齐，散发出海滨度假酒店客房的霉味。
“不”，我说，“是女孩觉得男孩坏。”然后我们一起读《雪困》②。
并在阁楼上跑来跑去，脚上的国父乔治·华盛顿鞋蹭掉了一小块蓝珐琅。

母亲在客厅来回踱步，头发上插着她那把斯特劳斯·华尔兹梳子。

我们等了一会，然后走了过去，母亲给我们端来了茶，茶杯上绘有赫尔曼·梅尔维尔的画像。

还有他的书《白鲸》和中篇小说《班尼托·西兰诺》里的插图。

父亲走了进来，打着迪克·特蕾西③领带。“诸位，我们喝点怎么样?”他说。

我说，“咱们到外边待会儿。”于是大家来到门廊，坐在画着亚伯拉罕·林肯图像的秋千板上。

你坐在眼睛、嘴巴和鼻子的部分，而我坐在膝盖上。

街对面的院子里有一个雪人，手里拿着一个垃圾桶盖，盖子破烂不堪如同精神失常的英国国王乔治三世。

## Sun Out

Bananas, piers, limericks
I am postures
Over there, I, are
The lakes of delectation
Sea, sea you! Mars and winsome④
buffalo

---

① 约翰·格林里夫·惠蒂埃：(John Greenleaf Whittier，1807—1892))美国诗人。

② 《雪困》：Snowbound，约翰·格林里夫·惠蒂埃1866年出版的长篇叙事诗。

③ 迪克·特蕾西：Dick Tracy，美国连环画，主要讲述便衣侦探特莱西的故事。1990年美国导演沃伦·比蒂拍摄了同名电影，汉译为《至尊神探》。

④ winsome：形容词，意思为“惹人喜爱的”；而此处有意分开来写，就成了“战胜一些”的意思；两种意思都解释得通，是诗人有意的文字游戏。

They thinly raft the plain,
Common do

It ice-floes, hit-and-run drivers,
The mass of wind.
Is that snow
H-ing at the door? And we
Come in the buckle, a
Vanquished distinguished
Secret festival, relieving flights
Of the black brave ocean.

## 日出

香蕉、码头、五行打油诗，
我是摆出姿势
在那边，我，是
令人愉快的湖泊
大海、大海你！火星和战胜
一些(惹人喜爱的)水牛
它们稀稀落落地穿过那平原，
司空见惯

浮冰块、肇事逃逸的司机、
大风。
是雪在
敲打门吗？我们
系着安全带前来，一个
被征服的重要的
神秘节日，险象丛生的
黑色海洋上的救援飞行。